Something Borrowed, Something Black

Something Borrowed, Something Black

A Peter Macklin Novel

Loren D. Estleman

FORGE®

A TOM DOHERTY ASSOCIATES BOOK
NEW YORK

This is a work of fiction. All the characters and events portrayed in this novel are either fictitious or are used fictitiously.

SOMETHING BORROWED, SOMETHING BLACK:
A PETER MACKLIN NOVEL

This book is printed on acid-free paper.

Edited by James Frenkel

Design by Jane Adele Regina

A Forge Book
Published by Tom Doherty Associates, LLC
175 Fifth Avenue
New York, NY 10010

www.tor.com

Forge® is a registered trademark of Tom Doherty Associates, LLC.

Library of Congress Cataloging-in-Publication Data

Estleman, Loren D.
      Something borrowed, something black : a Peter Macklin novel / Loren D. Estleman.—1st ed.
          p. cm.
      "A Tom Doherty Associates book."
      ISBN 0-312-87863-X (acid-free paper)
      1. Macklin, Peter (Fictitious character)—Fiction. 2. Los Angeles (Calif.)—Fiction. 3. San Antonio (Texas)—Fiction. 4. Murder for hire—Fiction. 5. Honeymoons—Fiction. I. Title.

PS3555.S84 S59 2002
813'.54—dc21

2001054752

First Edition: April 2002

Printed in the United States of America

0 9 8 7 6 5 4 3 2 1

In Memoriam

Fred Bean:
A good enough man for any world

Something Borrowed, Something Black

ONE

Johns Davis remembered feeling a chill the first time he entered the mission building of the Alamo, where Mexican troops in Napoleonic shakos and crossed white belts bayoneted and were bayoneted by the defenders of the Republic of Texas. At the time he'd associated the sensation with the presence of the spirits of the honored dead. Now he knew it was the air-conditioning.

He'd made many visits to the crumbling shrine since establishing himself in San Antonio, and familiarity and repetition had worn the gloss off sacred history. Still, he suspected the Daughters of the Texas Republic of cranking down the thermostat at least two degrees annually, so that the mere act of stepping in from the sun-hammered flags of the Plaza was like plunging into a mountain stream. It was sad when the pull of the arcade drove the keepers of the flame to special effects.

It was a weekday, and the tourist season with its gridlock of history buffs, education-bent parents, and ox-faced children in synthetic coonskin caps was over. A couple of dozen whispering visitors loitered in front of glass cases containing flintlock rifles and moth-eaten guidons, obeying signs asking them to avoid touching the parchment-colored walls, sealed though they were by coats of glaze. Davis strolled out the back door, across the courtyard where a docent in a wool suit stood sweating and shuffling three-by-five cards with notes on Travis, Crockett, Bowie, and the names no one bothered to remember, and entered the gift shop.

Here the crowd was bigger, inspecting Alamo keychains and Kachina dolls and the inevitable T-shirts reading, MY PARENTS WENT TO THE ALAMO AND ALL I GOT WAS THIS LOUSY T-SHIRT. Inside the door he pretended to browse among some pennants and rolled posters as he made his way to the back, where a well-built black man with gray in his short hair and the start of a double chin stood examining a box containing a log cabin building kit. He wore a tailored lightweight tan suit and Davis noticed a slightly lighter patch of skin on the third finger of his left hand where he normally wore his Super Bowl ring. Davis found this half-assed attempt at going incognito touching.

"It says ages three and up, " the man said by way of greeting. "You think a three-year-old kid could figure out how to put one of these together?"

"A *retarded* three-year-old kid." Davis smiled. "When I was that age I was carving my own struts from balsa to build a toy plane. They might as well sell 'em already assembled, for all the challenge they offer. You want to put him to work? Give him a coffee table."

"My old man told me he built wood planes. You ain't that old."

Davis didn't argue with him. At sixty-one he was the ideal weight for his height, worked out three times a week at a gym, and tinted his hair a light sandy brown. People who didn't know him when it was black would not guess he'd gone entirely gray. Most of his acquaintances thought he was in his middle forties. Back in his grifting days, he'd posed successfully as a retired NFL player, selling nonexistent shares in well-known computer software corporations, borrowing money on the promise of interest once he'd established his Trans-America Football League, and charging two-thousand-dollar suits and cases of single-malt Scotch to well-placed widows (and some not-quite widows) who enjoyed telling their friends they were sleeping with a professional athlete. He still had the build, and although he greatly preferred his present circumstances, it was comforting to know that if they failed him he could take up where he left off.

He looked around for wood to knock, but found none. Even the logs in the log cabin kit were plastic.

"I got a good relationship with my ex," the man said. "She could shake a lot more out of me if she knew everything I was in. If I give this to my kid and he gets glue and shit in his hair, she might get pissed off enough to take another look."

"So build it with him. Call it a bonding experience, excuse the pun."

"I can't spend that much time with the whiny little son of a bitch." The man returned the box to the shelf. "Why'd you pick this place? River Walk not public enough for you?"

"That's the idea. If you want to attract attention, set up a midnight meet in the park. What you got?"

The black man turned his back on a woman browsing nearby, drew a doubled-over manila envelope from an inside breast pocket, and held it out. Davis didn't take it. Most Americans automatically accept an offered object, but most Americans haven't spent years avoiding summonses and subpoenas. He asked what was in the envelope.

"Medical report on Jackson. He fractured his ulna in a pickup game day before yesterday."

"What's that? That thing in your throat?"

"That's the uvula. The ulna's a bone in your forearm."

"They scratch him?"

"They don't know about it, and he ain't telling 'em. He didn't go to the team doctor. He was on the d.a. list most of last season and he don't want to get traded. He's starting Sunday."

"Who says?"

"The guy that got me the report. You going to question that?"

"I question everything but the pregame show. Any X rays?"

"He risked a burglary beef just getting the report. Anyway, you can fake X rays. This has the doc's signature."

"Yeah, like you can't fake that." Davis took the envelope and tapped the man's chest with the end. "If Jackson snaps a hundred-yard pass Sunday, I'm looking for you, your guy, *and* the doc."

"Yeah, yeah. Just remember me when he fumbles."

Davis slid the envelope inside his blazer. "Get your kid the John Wayne video. It'll keep him busy three hours. Your old lady'll be so grateful she'll take you back."

"Man, that's the last thing I want. I just don't want her to know about the Safeway in Houston." He slid the shrink-wrapped VHS tape of *The Alamo* out of the revolving rack. "Think he'll understand it?"

"What's to understand? It's the Duke."

A small crowd had gathered in the courtyard to hear the lecture. Davis circled around it and cut back through the mission, where he stopped to poke a dollar bill into the donation box, then touched the forbidden wall on his way out the big oak double door.

The air outside was thick and hot and smelled of the river. When he'd first arrived from Chicago, accustomed to the wind shaving off Lake Michigan and the abrupt changes of season, he'd thought he'd never get used to the heat, but he'd acclimated quickly. It had helped that returning East was not an option. He'd slept with the wrong not-quite widow, gotten careless and sold the same bogus shares to two investors who knew each other, made a couple of other miscalculations that had taken the shine off Lincoln Park and the Sears Tower. In the end it had been a good thing. He liked westerns and really was proud of Texas's history, and it was comforting not to have to change his address every few weeks. And no one begrudged a bookie his profit, or at least not seriously enough to do anything more about it than question his parentage. That was okay, because he really was a bastard and a son of a bitch. He had the birth certificate and the ironing-cord scars to prove it.

He'd parked his bottle-green Jaguar on Crockett, down the block from the Menger Hotel, where Teddy Roosevelt had sipped ginger beer in the mahogany-paneled bar and recruited Rough Riders for the war with Spain. He was eager to read the report, which if it was genuine would pay off the place in Galveston, to start. But the only spot he'd been able to find was in the sun, and the air would be too hot inside the car until the climate control got its toe in. He'd go over the material at home with one of Eugenia's margaritas.

He couldn't imagine a more pleasant reading experience. In the four years he'd been running his sports book, he'd never had a tip that looked so much like early retirement. Inside information of that type was the Philosopher's Stone in his business, the Grand Slam, the Royal Flush, the six-figure rare coin that drops out of the ceiling while you're replacing the insulation. It was the stuff of urban legend. His source, second-string player that he was in his prime, flop that he'd been in business and his personal life, maintained extensive contacts throughout the world of professional football and had yet to fail him. Of *course* Davis had given him shit over it; it was the kind of thing that only happened to someone else.

He threw himself into the fabric-covered seat—leather was never the wise man's choice in the Sun Belt—folded and transferred the paper sun-shield from the dash to the bucket on the passenger's side, and started the engine, sliding down the windows to let out the heat. He was reaching for the blower to the air conditioner when he smelled stagnant sweat.

Something whirled over his head and closed around his neck with a jerk. He was yanked back in the seat, his backside and thighs lifted from the cushion. His hands went to his throat, but the thin wire was sunk too deep in flesh. His throat shut down. Blood whooshed in his head. His tongue swelled and his eyes stuck out like fingers.

His right hand swept down, clawed air, found the shift lever on the steering column, and flung the indicator into drive. He jammed his heel down on the accelerator. The car shot ahead into a loading zone, where the right front tire struck the curb, forcing the wheels left. Davis got his fingers around the bottom of the steering wheel and spun it in the direction of least resistance. The Jaguar swept out into Crockett, crossed the center line, and sideswiped a delivery van, whose driver swerved and sent the van into a spin that ended when it slammed head-on into a low-slung Chevy Nomad filled with Mexican youths in the opposite lane. The Chevy's horn honked; a polite noise and belated.

The man behind Davis's seat (it was always a man when a garrote was involved) lost his balance when the Jaguar struck the van, regained it as the car careered into the left lane, and leaned back with an animal grunt. Davis lost contact with the seat. Only his shoulder blades pressed against the top of the headrest. His foot came away from the accelerator. He made gurgling noises and felt froth on his chin. The scenery stopped spinning across the windshield and separated into black-and-white checks. Tiny vessels burst in his eyes, making light popping sounds like bubble wrap. His palm struck the steering wheel with a thump. He cuffed it like a flywheel. The Jaguar leaned into a wailing U-turn in the middle of the broad street. The stainless-steel grille of a medium-size truck whirled past, a line of pecan trees planted along the sidewalk, clusters of pedestrians. He saw a round Hispanic face, a flushed, shining, touristy face, the faces of a woman and the baby she was holding, a white-haired old man wearing huge glasses like Harry Carey's. He could have picked them all out of a lineup.

It all stopped with a wallop. The windshield turned white and disintegrated.

Davis woke up thinking he was home in bed. The ceiling looked strange. A minute went past before he realized he was looking at the headliner of the Jaguar. He was sprawled across both front seats with his back bent over the console. His head ached and his throat felt like rusted iron.

Memory slammed back in and his hands went to his neck. The thin wire, some kind of nylon fishline, was still tight, but he got a finger under it and pulled and it came away along with a ragged patch of skin. He was aware of faces outside all the windows and the shrill of a siren getting louder.

He hauled himself sitting, bits of broken glass streaming off him. In a sudden panic he slapped his chest. He felt the stiffness of the envelope still in his inside pocket and relaxed. Through the space where the windshield used to be, he recognized the sandstone wall and part of the brass plaque that identified the Menger. The Jaguar had jumped the sidewalk and rammed the hotel to the right of the entrance.

He climbed up onto his knees, disregarding the crunching glass, and peered into the backseat. He could tell by the position of the man's head where he lay on the floor between the seats that his neck was broken. His sphincter had released, filling the car with reek. The face was twisted toward him. It was a youngish, pale sort of face, almost eyebrowless, and unknown to him. He'd expected nothing else. They always sent strangers.

TWO

Peter said, "I'm back."

And almost before he had the door shut behind him she was all over him, kissing and grappling, healthy muscles working under smooth naked skin. Laurie was two-thirds his size but twenty years younger and nearly as strong. She was the only grandchild of an Ohio farmer, had milked cows, pulled weeds, and wrestled the steering wheel of an aged and disgruntled tractor for a dozen summers before joining her first health club. Laughing and growling, she had him half undressed before he appeared to remember he was still holding the copy of the *Los Angeles Times* he'd gone out to get. He let it drop to the floor to free his hands.

From that point on the advantage was his. Peter was forty-four and looked it, with gathers at the corners of his slightly grim mouth, and did not appear particularly fit. But he carried her effortlessly to the bed and threw her down on it and was on top of her on the first bounce, dragging down the thin straps of her camisole and inserting a corded thigh between hers to press himself against her. His ferocity frightened her a little, as it had the first time, but it made her ravenous too, and proud. She was the woman who had discovered this savage thing, buried so deep beneath the ordinary exterior, and the knowledge filled her with proprietary satisfaction, as if she'd found Tut's tomb, or better yet, the Loch Ness Monster. She tore at the buttons of his shirt and raked her nails across his hard chest with its sparse covering of hair. Between them they managed to push his trousers and shorts down to his knees and then he was inside her with his violence and heat. The penetration made her cry out.

Afterward, he lay on his back with the sheet up to his waist, reading the paper while she ordered room service and then dressed. Peter was in the shower when the waiter came, a young Hispanic, polite and handsome in an overpolished sort of way, like the bullfighter in *The Sun Also Rises* with Tyrone Power. Laurie sent him off with a generous tip on top of the guaranteed fifteen percent gratuity, then set out the breakfast things, humming softly the theme from the old movie, which was playing all week on AMC. Splurging thrilled her. Before Peter she'd had to budget everything, even an occasional Saturday night out. There was much to be said for marrying a man who'd made enough from his own business to retire young. There would be no arguments over money, for one thing, and he wouldn't be working late when she wanted to prepare a candlelit dinner for two followed by an evening of lovemaking.

Or so she guessed. She actually knew very little about her husband of twenty-four—no, twenty-*five* hours. She wasn't even sure if he ate breakfast, usually, or what he liked. But he'd been so absorbed in his newspaper, sighing contentedly as his heartbeat returned to normal, and she hadn't wanted to disturb him by asking.

The shower stopped running. Moments later she heard a *clink* and knew he was getting ready to shave. A man of regular habits, her husband, good hygiene, and consideration for others. She had yet to catch him leaving the toilet seat up. *What a stiff,* she could hear her girlfriend Cindy saying. Cindy liked bad boys: perennial five-o'clock shadow, parking tickets in the glove compartment, two years' payments left on the Corvette. It didn't matter that such men used her like toilet paper and left the moment they smelled commitment. It did to Laurie, which was why the next twenty years with Peter stretched before her as smooth and comfortable as sunshine on blacktop.

He came out with a towel wrapped around his waist and smiled when he saw the breakfast cart. He had a child's appreciation of the basics, like good food and a full night's sleep, and although he limited his indulgence in both, he took no pains to conceal his pleasure from her. She felt trusted.

She stopped pouring coffee to admire him. He was a good-looking man, in an average way. Even his thinning temples became him. His good physical condition was more apparent without clothes—no bulging biceps or six-pack abs, but no spare tire, either, and she knew from intimate experience that he seldom winded—and unlike some lovers she'd had, he didn't flex or strike poses to present himself to advantage.

She realized belatedly that he'd transferred his smile from the cart to her. "Would you mind leaving me the towel?" he asked. "I might spill hot coffee in my lap."

She blushed and looked down quickly. "I got scrambled *and* fried. I can take them either way, but I wasn't sure about you. I hope you like pancakes."

"I like just about everything, except beets and cooked carrots." He moved the upright chair over from the writing desk in the corner and held it for her.

Eating, she took care to notice how he doctored his coffee and whether he tasted his eggs before he sprinkled them with salt and pepper. He used very little syrup, just enough to moisten the pancake on top of the stack, and no butter. "Do you avoid fats?" she asked.

"It depends on my plans for the day. I don't like to load myself down if I'm going to be moving around. You said you wanted to see where they filmed the original *Ten Commandments*. The concierge told me that's clear up in the hills." He bit off a corner of dry toast. "You know there's nothing left to see."

"I know. It will be easier for me to imagine."

"You must be the only member of your generation who cares about anything made before *Star Wars*."

"My father made me watch old movies with him on cable. After a while I got to prefer them. That was just about the time he left." She drank orange juice.

"Some might say you married me to take his place."

His eyes smiled, so she contented herself with flicking drops at him from her water glass. "Next time I'll marry a kid."

"I'd better be dead. One divorce was enough."

She knew he'd been married before, that there was a son who was nearly her age, but he never seemed to want to talk about it. She wondered if his first wife had bothered to notice the little things, the way she was trying to do. She was a child of divorce herself, and knew they were the things that mattered. They built and built and eventually exploded if left unaddressed.

"Did you tell Roger we were getting married?" she asked.

"I don't know where he is right now. I got a postcard a month ago. He was in Amsterdam."

"What's he doing there?"

"Finding himself, I suppose. Smoking weed and probably worse with his new Dutch friends. Anyway, he's probably not there now. He's hitchhiking across Europe. He thinks he invented the idea."

"Don't you get along?"

"We've got a great relationship. Him in his hemisphere, me in mine." He stuffed his mouth with pancake, and she knew that was the end of that line of conversation.

She didn't press him. There seemed to be a diplomacy to these first days, areas best not wandered into. She wondered if it was normal, and supposed for the sake of her peace of mind that it was. She knew so little about Peter, yet he knew so much about her. Laurie was a chatterer, mercilessly mining her background for incidents with which to fill awkward silences. He knew she was twenty-one, that she'd grown up in a suburb of Dayton, spending her summers and then her life after age thirteen on the farm following her parents' breakup, and that she'd left home at eighteen to attend nursing classes at Ohio State, interning as a receptionist in a family practice center in Toledo. There she'd met Peter, who came in to have a suspicious mole removed, returned twice more for examinations, and came back a third time to ask the pretty blonde receptionist to dinner. She'd liked his looks, his quiet manner, and—professional prejudice—the way he paid attention to his health and acted upon the messages his body sent him. She could not care about a man who did not care about himself. They were married six weeks later.

Her mother, still embittered over her own marriage, had not approved. She and Peter were contemporaries, but her antipathy went beyond that. She seemed to suspect him of something, and he seemed to realize that and resent it. Not that they ever discussed their differences: Their stiff politeness toward each other reminded Laurie of the tension at home when she was small, and which she escaped by watching Jimmy Stewart or Merle Oberon emoting in some Hollywood Anytown. Mother had been especially hostile toward Laurie's decision not to keep her maiden name. But Laurie believed in total commitment, and anyway she had never liked having to spell the German surname for people and correct their pronunciation. It pleased her independent spirit, in these slavishly post-feminist times, to have personal stationery printed reading *Mrs. Peter Macklin.*

After breakfast, she sat on the edge of the bed and watched him dress. She was pleased to see him dispense with a tie in deference to California Casual, drawing a navy blazer with plain buttons on over an open-neck shirt and gray trousers. He dressed unobtrusively and always in good taste, but she decided she would do something about those white shirts and uninspired solid ties. Just because she was moving into a furnished life didn't mean she couldn't change the wallpaper.

"Let's forget about the hills," she said. "I want to drive up the coast."

"What about *The Ten Commandments?*"

"Let's break them. I want to see the ocean. The closest I've ever seen to one is Lake Huron."

"We'll have to rent a car. I'm pretty sure the tour bus doesn't go up the coast."

"I'll call the concierge while you take off that blue bag and change into a polo shirt." She lifted the telephone receiver.

"When did I lose control over my life?"

"I believe it was when you said, 'With this ring.' Concierge, please," she said into the mouthpiece.

While she was waiting, Peter said, "We can have lunch in Santa Barbara. Five years ago there was a great little seafood place built on a pier. Maybe it's still operating."

"What were you doing here five years ago?"

"Sales trip. California goes through camera equipment like Detroit goes through tires."

"I always thought the head of a company had salesmen to do that."

"I didn't say I ran Microsoft. *I* was the salesman." He drew a blue knitted polo out of the top drawer of the bureau and pulled it on. Over his undershirt. *Baby steps,* Laurie told herself.

"Where's that concierge?" she asked. "I have to pee."

"Go ahead. I'll man the fort." He held out his hand for the receiver.

"My hero. Get a convertible." She went into the bathroom as he sat on the bed and reached for the second section of the *Times*.

While freshening up, she got an idea. She stripped down to her black bra and panties, squirted perfume under her chin, and tried a couple of poses before the full-length mirror on the door. She was a healthy girl, smoothly muscular, and looked after her tan. At age eighteen she'd been runner-up for Miss Toledo. If she'd won she'd have gone on to the state competition in Columbus, and if she'd won there, she'd have represented Ohio at the big show in Atlantic City. Drop-dead gorgeous, she'd been called, more times than she could count. Only not quite dead enough to take the crown.

On impulse she unhooked the bra and let it drop to the floor. Nice and perky and surreptitiously brown. Five years anyway before gravity took over.

She walked out of the bathroom on the balls of her feet to accentuate the line of her legs, swaying her hips like Marilyn Monroe. "Of course, if there's something you'd *rather* do with the top down . . ." She stopped with one hip cocked and rested a hand on it like Mae West.

Peter was still on the telephone, the newspaper crumpled on the carpet by the bed. He made a noise with his tongue against his teeth and banged down the receiver. The report made her jump.

"I've been on hold five minutes," he said. "I'll go down and talk to the concierge face-to-face. If he hasn't skipped to Mexico."

He got up and went out. He'd never once looked at her.

Alone and half-naked in the room, she realized she was still on tiptoe and lowered her heels to the floor. She felt as if she were deflating.

She worried a cuticle. Had she come on too strong? No, Peter was no prude, nor was he one of those neanderthals who always had to be in control. He hadn't minded her taking the initiative before. Maybe she'd worn him out. If so, it was the first time the age difference had asserted itself. He'd looked energetic enough striding out.

More likely he was preoccupied. He was that way sometimes: here with her one moment, sweet, attentive, and then a hundred miles away the next. Lost in his head. Maybe he was still thinking about Roger. Sometime, something had happened between father and son, something he didn't yet trust Laurie enough to tell her about.

So many things to learn.

She picked up the wrecked newspaper and laid it on the breakfast cart. DETROIT leapt out at her from a headline on the front page of the second section. She wondered if he'd read the article and that was what had distracted him. Detroit was his home, headquarters to the chain of camera stores he'd owned. Coming on it unexpectedly in a hotel room in Los Angeles, he might have been reminded of old concerns. The headline itself—L.A. POLICE QUESTION DETROIT CRIME BOSS—was so remote as to mean nothing.

THREE

"Who got it?"

"Childs."

"Christ. Just this morning I prayed to the Holy Virgin he'd forget to wear his vest next time a cooker gets hit."

"He left Narco. Anyway, you're not supposed to do that."

"Who the fuck cares? I'm not a Catholic."

Detective Lieutenant Christie Childs overheard this exchange on his way to the cooler. The doors in the morgue were soundproofed, but they were always being left open a crack, and voices traveled along the subterranean corridor as clearly as across water.

He decided not to mention it as he entered the room where the two attendants were standing next to the gurney. Since the beginning of the year he'd resolved to let such remarks slide off him. Slight and black, one half-inch inside the regulation height for male officers in the San Antonio Police Department, he wore his suits snug and corrected his vision with gold-rimmed glasses that made him look like Herbie Hancock. He was thirty-three but could pass for seventeen, a dubious advantage that had stuck him on the Liquor License Bureau for five years, scamming bars whose personnel sold alcohol to minors without asking to see ID. Fellow officers called him the Child Detective, not always behind his back. At such times he gave thanks for his surname.

Given his race, "Boy Detective" might have resulted in a number of violent episodes.

The look on the attendants' faces, when he strode in so abruptly on the end of their conversation, gave him grim satisfaction. Letting them wonder how much he'd heard and what he might do about it was better than chewing them out. The high road was worth the trip when it got improved results.

" 'Morning, Lieutenant," said Anderson, the taller of the pair and the one who had prayed to the Virgin Mary. He was flushed and balding and his face was dimpled all over with acne scars, an overripe orange.

"Yeah. This the Johnny Doe from Crockett?"

Anderson nodded. "You never saw a neck snapped so clean. His head broke the front seat when he hit it."

The corpse stretched naked on the gurney belonged to a man in his late twenties or early thirties, thin black hair plastered to his scalp, with a hole in his left earlobe from which a tiny gold hoop had been removed when the body was stripped. Ribs showed clearly beneath the blue-gray skin. The man appeared to have only one testicle.

"Just like Hitler," Anderson said, following Childs's gaze. "Maybe it's why he became a button. Some kid teased him in gym class and he brained him with his locker." His chuckle was hollow in the room full of sheet-covered corpses. He was still waiting for the lieutenant to lower the boom.

"What makes him a button?" Childs asked.

"Well, the garrote." This was the other attendant, a man smaller than Childs, with an elaborate handlebar moustache and a lump of snuff pushing out his lower lip. "You don't just walk around with one of them in your pocket if you don't know how to use it."

"If he knew how to use it, maybe he wouldn't be here. We'd be looking at the other guy." Childs took hold of the wrist near him and turned it. The skin felt rubbery. "What do you think he used on his fingers?" There were raised welts on the tips, white as grubs.

"Acid, according to the M.E.," said Anderson. "Sulfuric or hydrochloric. That had to hurt."

"Stupid. Prints grow back."

"They were starting to already," said the man with the handlebars.

The lieutenant stroked one of the mutilated tips with his thumb, feeling the scar tissue. He let go and rubbed the ink residue off his thumb onto the sheet. Forensics had finished with the body. "Thoughtful of him to give us a head start. The FBI keeps a separate file on doctored prints in its database."

Anderson chuckled again, with more confidence this time. "It'll only help if he was printed since the acid."

"No tan. That makes him an out-of-stater or a vampire. We'll rule out New Mexico and Arizona, skip California for now. Non-Southwesterner with a record, a pierced ear, and a touching nostalgia for a murder weapon that went out with Luca Brasi. I'm betting we find a match." Childs looked up. "Or does your Holy Virgin frown on gambling?"

The attendant's face turned a paler shade of red. "Sorry, Lieutenant."

"Sorry, Lieutenant," echoed the other.

Childs said, "Mm-hm," and went out. In the corridor he smiled thinly. Sometimes the low road had its points.

He thought of his office in Homicide as a sanctuary from rednecks.

Home was no oasis. His wife, who unlike him was a native of Texas and a do-it-yourselfer, had textured the living room walls to resemble adobe, hung shadow-catchers and George Catlin prints, and scattered Comanche rugs throughout the house until it looked like all the others in the neighborhood, decorated with the same merchandise from the same shops in the Rivercenter Mall. Even the plates Childs ate from had cloven hoofprints imbedded in them, reminding him unappetizingly of a cow pie. He never felt more like a Milwaukeean than when he was communicating with his fellow officers, tall, windblown

Marlboro men all, who drove rust-ravaged pickups and wore Wranglers on weekends with Skoal cans making identical miniature crop-circles in the hip pockets, and he scarcely felt less like an outsider while trying to unwind with a glass of tawny port in the cowhide-covered chair in his den.

Only at work, when his door was closed and he settled behind his glass-topped desk to read reports and place calls, did he experience some relief from the tensions that (if the truth be told) held him together, like the ocean's stresses preserving the outlines of a sunken galleon centuries after parasites had eaten away the tenons. He was not a galleon. He could resist becoming a cowboy only so long without support. He'd had the buff-colored walls repainted a soothing forest-green, put up his academy class picture and black-and-white art photos of Lake Michigan in brushed-steel frames, and dressed the desk in a chrome-cornered pad and matching pen-and-pencil set from the Sharper Image catalogue. The picture frame on the desk, bound in tan imitation buckskin with visible stitching, was an exception, but the wedding shot mounted in it was the only one he had in which his wife wasn't wearing a bandanna blouse, or barbecuing ribs. She'd given it to him to celebrate his promotion to an office.

He called the medical examiner, who'd been absent when he'd visited the morgue. Cause of death—compound fracture of the second cervical vertebra—was no surprise, and the M.E. agreed with Childs that the deceased had been new to the Sun Belt, although his reasons were more scientific and based on bloodwork and the condition of the liver. He learned that the man had dined on steak and eggs, a local staple, two to four hours before death, and that he had cocaine in his system and had been abusing it for some time, from the perforations in his septum.

"Modern-day berserker," the M.E. said, his El Paso drawl making the distinctly non-Texas reference sound more absurd than it was. (Why were these people so ashamed of any knowledge not connected to the Lone Star State?) "Some of these hitters prefer to pump themselves up before the job."

"Where's he from?"

"Great Lakes. That's a guess, but I'd ring in with it on *Jeopardy*."

Childs waited. He knew if he kept quiet at such times he would be spared asking unnecessary questions. He also knew it was exactly this refusal to play the regional game that made him unpopular.

The M.E. was no exception. He cleared his throat and went on in a less folksy tone. "He had enough mercury in his liver to rise with the temperature. They eat a lot of freshwater fish back there. The contamination level's high from all the industrial waste."

Home sprang to mind. "Milwaukee?"

"Or Chicago, or Detroit, or Toledo, or Cleveland. Green Bay and Buffalo, if you want to bracket it, and go inland a couple of hundred miles. Put Michigan in the center and draw a circle about as wide as the distance from Houston to Amarillo."

"I *know* it's a big state, Doctor. I drove a U-Haul here from Wisconsin. Thanks," he added, belatedly and to no avail, he was sure. He was getting to have fewer friends in town than Santa Anna.

He broke the connection, dialed the extension for Sergeant Murillo, and told him what the M.E. had said. Murillo knew what buttons to push at the Houston office of the FBI.

The information was encouraging enough to make him leave the office and brave enemy territory. He found Officers Benteen and Gonzales leaning against the wall on either side of the one-way glass outside Interview Room A, where Davis, the owner of the Jaguar in which the John Doe was killed, was finishing his formal statement in the presence of a suitcase tape recorder and Detective Sill. The uniformed officers, who had been first on the crash scene, straightened at Childs's approach. Benteen, fucking cowboy, wore his department piece low on his hip with pearl grips on the handle and was always chewing a toothpick. His partner was chunky, with black hair growing back from a straight line just above his eyes. It was Gonzales who had spotted the garrote after Davis threw it out the car window, and picked it up before anyone in the crowd could make away with it. The man belonged on the plainclothes squad but would probably never get there as long as he was stuck with Benteen.

"Anything?" Childs asked.

"Not a damn thing, L.T." Benteen sucked his toothpick. "He don't know nothing, he don't see nothing. Just like that Kraut sergeant on that old TV show. Just another Chicago hood."

He started to say more, but Childs shushed him. Sill was holding up the loop of fishline. The lieutenant leaned into the scratchy speaker.

"You said you cut your neck in the accident," the detective said. "The only thing in the car that could make that sort of wound was this. You're saying it was never around your neck?"

"Why would it be? I'm telling you, I smacked up the car when I saw the guy in the rearview mirror. He was probably getting set to jump the wires when I came back and surprised him. Jags top the list for car thieves. They boost one, then they go to Disney World."

"See that stain? A DNA test will tell us if it's your blood."

"I might've bled on it after I was cut. Maybe the guy's a fisherman, it fell out of his pocket. Why would anyone want to strangle me? I'm a retired investment counselor."

"Yeah? What's the IPO on Dallas Monday night?"

Childs smiled at that. Sill was a big man with a well-trimmed moustache and had been told one too many times he looked and sounded like Ben Johnson, but he had a deadpan like a wall, against which a thousand alibis had dashed themselves to pieces.

Johns Davis fingered the white bandage at his throat. It resembled a clerical collar. "I'm the victim here. If you want me to say on tape I ever placed a bet for a third party, you'd better let me call my lawyer."

"Come on, Davis. We don't do Vice any favors. You lucked out yesterday. Odds are you'll run out of Jags long before whoever it is you pissed off runs out of buttons."

"He wanted the car."

"Six-to-five Sill hangs a material-witness tag on him," Benteen said.

Gonzales grunted. "Better not place it with Davis. You're into him for a yard already."

"Shut up, asshole. He's kidding, Lieutenant."

Childs turned away, losing interest, and almost bumped into Sergeant Murillo. Murillo and Officer Gonzales might have been twins, except the plainclothesman was more fat than chunky, with a double chin and less intelligent eyes. What he lacked in personal initiative he made up for in unquestioning obedience. People liked him: other cops, citizens, even some of his collars. Childs liked him, God alone knew why. The man wasn't a conversationalist.

Without greeting, the sergeant held up a computer printout with an FBI heading, identifying the John Doe. It ran several pages.

FOUR

When Peter returned, ten minutes after he went out, he was as he had been before, tender and playful. Laurie was so relieved she almost forgot to attack him again. She'd drawn on a new silk wrapper she'd bought for the honeymoon, but it vanished so quickly she wondered later why she'd bothered with the expense.

This tussle was briefer, less heated, but just as satisfying, and left them still energized. The concierge called while they were freshening up to tell them their car was waiting in front of the hotel entrance. Twenty minutes later they were seated in an apple-green Camaro convertible, fighting their way through Valley traffic and out of the smog, where they could put the top down and be like Cary Grant and Deborah Kerr.

Peter was an accomplished driver. He caught all the green lights with ease, reacted instantly (and without cursing, which was even more impressive) when a Jeep Wrangler with children in the backseat cut across three lanes of traffic suddenly, forcing him to relinquish the lane to avoid a collision. He drove a steady five miles above the limit, slowing down gently when he spotted police cruisers, a hundred yards before Laurie noticed them herself with her young eyes, and changed lanes with almost unconscious smoothness, always choosing the one that was moving more consistently. She put all this down to the experience of numerous sales trips.

"Didn't you bring a camera?" she asked then. "You sold them all those years. You'd think you'd have a good one."

"I got out of the picture-taking habit. There wasn't much worth preserving those last few years, and then I was alone. Anyway I look like a gargoyle on film. Except for my driver's license I haven't had my picture taken in ten years."

"Well, I want one of us together. Next drugstore we see, let's buy one of those disposable Kodaks. We'll get someone to snap us with the ocean at our backs."

"I'd rather just drive."

She looked at him briefly, but said nothing. He'd sounded casual, but something in his tone invited no discussion.

The morning was overcast, their lunch in Santa Barbara disappointing. The restaurant Peter remembered had changed hands and slipped downhill. Laurie's steamed clams were soggy and tasted of the can, with the ocean almost close enough to touch, its waves rolling jeeringly toward them outside the windows and presumably loaded with the fresh article. Peter expressed his opinion that the place had been bought by the Combination. "The Organization, I guess they call it here."

"The Mafia, you mean? How can you tell?" Gangster films fascinated her. She looked around, saw no fat Italians in silk suits with their napkins stuck under their chins.

"Just a guess. Every time they try to make an honest dollar they screw it up. Just like the government."

He was smiling. The moodiness he'd shown twice that morning seemed to have passed. He cupped his hand over hers where it rested on the table, and they spoke again of where they would live after he sold his house in suburban Detroit. They'd agreed the place needed more work than they cared to put into it. Although she would not have brought it up, Laurie was relieved that she would not have to spend the rest of her life in the place that had witnessed the deterioration of her husband's first marriage. California was discussed, and Florida; sunny places were the inevitable alternative among Midwesterners.

"Do we have to decide right away?" she asked. "Can't we just travel, and see what suits us?"

"Should we be Gypsies? I can't play the violin or pick pockets."

"Better not try. To pick pockets, I mean. You're too law-abiding. You couldn't help looking guilty."

They started back. In Montecito, exploring a little shop, Laurie found a small framed oil painting of a ruddy-faced man with a blue bandanna tied around his head. It made her think of a Gypsy, although Peter thought it was more likely a self-portrait of an overage hippie from Berkeley. She bought it anyway. "To remind you not to pick pockets."

The sun came out when they were back on the road. They stopped often to get out and look at the ocean from railed promontories set aside by the Highway Department. She saw her first sea lion belly-flopping its way onto a sunny rock, and kissed Peter long and passionately before a heart-wrenching orange-and-purple sunset. Laurie, a former recording secretary for her high-school environmental action group, knew that auto and factory emissions were the cause of the vivid colors, but she was too drunk on the feral beauty of the Pacific to care. She was on her honeymoon in a fairy-tale place with a man who, she was amused and delighted to learn, would change lanes to avoid running over a fat seagull dozing on the asphalt.

She beamed at him. He looked grumpy. "Wouldn't want the animal rightists on our backs," he said.

"Yeah, yeah." She placed a hand on his thigh and leaned over to peck his cheek. Settling back, she brushed his crotch as if on purpose, and smiled to herself at the instantaneous reaction. They were the same age below the belt.

"Oh, Mr. Macklin."

The couple, approaching the elevators with their arms around each other's waist, sprang apart as if caught in an illicit act. The baby-faced clerk behind the desk was holding up an envelope. They went back.

Peter tore loose the flap, removed a scrap of hotel stationery, and read the handwritten message quickly. Laurie was watching his face. It didn't change, a troubling sign. He glanced toward the pink light of the bar, then stuffed paper and envelope into his pants pocket and kissed her. It was a parting smack.

"Is she pretty?" She made it sound teasing. A small cold fist had closed in her stomach.

He smoothed her hair. She'd cut it short recently, and he'd approved, quite against the prevailing male preference. "It's a he," he said, "and he isn't even handsome. We used to do business. I'm afraid I have to be polite."

"Why? You're retired."

"He's one of the ones who made that possible. It won't take long, promise."

"It better not. That waiter who brought breakfast was pretty cute."

He smiled, but she could tell his attention was elsewhere. He kissed her again and left. It was the third time that day he'd gone away from her before actually leaving.

She resisted the temptation to look inside the bar. She didn't want to be one of those wives. Her mother had always been checking on her father, and although he'd given her ample reason, Laurie had always wondered if it wasn't her mother's jealousy that had driven him to fulfill her worst fears. Anyway, she was certain there was no other woman in the present picture.

Riding in the elevator, she asked herself why she found so little comfort in that.

He found Carlo Maggiore where he expected, alone in a horseshoe-shaped booth big enough to seat six. It was in a corner, with a view of the entrance. In the right mood, if the booth was occupied when he came in, Maggiore might pick up the party's bill and send a couple of bottles of good wine or twelve-year-old Scotch to the new table. He was also capable, like the Midwestern crimelord he was, of relocating them physically to the street. Since the man was rising to smile and offer his hand, no heavy lifters in sight, Macklin suspected there was a gathering of happy drinkers somewhere on the premises.

"Put on a few," Maggiore said, lowering his hand unshaken. Ignoring it had been a gesture of caution on Macklin's part, not distaste. He never surrendered the use of his right hand in such company. "Marry a good cook, I always say. Looks don't last."

"You look different, too." Macklin weighed the same as he had for years, and knew the other was aware of it. The crime boss, however, had trimmed down. He looked younger, too, almost Macklin's age, and had probably had some help with that. His sandy hair appeared thicker, his forehead as smooth as a blister. He'd acquired an even tan in place of his Detroit pallor and done something about the congenital hump on his left shoulder. It seemed to be a combination of good tailoring and expensive surgery.

"Well, you might as well wipe your ass with your money if you don't spend it. What you drinking?"

"Water."

"Glenlivet it is." He snapped his fingers, summoning a waitress in a green jerkin; the bar's theme was *The Adventures of Robin Hood*, starring Errol Flynn. Posters and production stills covered the walls. "Two more of the same." He sat down.

Macklin sat on the end of the booth, allowing himself the second-best perspective. He could see most of the room and part of the entrance. When the drinks came he let his stand untasted.

Maggiore stirred his twice, then sipped, leaving in the swizzle and holding it out of the way with his thumb, just like a Mack Avenue thug too lazy to take the spoon out of his coffee. "Why L.A.? Fixing to live out here?"

"Just a vacation. I heard you'd settled in."

"Can't seem to stay out of the papers. It's better than Detroit, though. I don't just mean the weather. I can always count on some movie star getting caught with his dick out on Sunset and booting me to a back section. I saw your wife. Nice snatch."

Macklin gave him nothing, which was what he felt. Plainly this irritated the other, who when he was a boy would have been the kind that fed Drano to dogs. He sat back. "I'm not mad at you, if that's what you're afraid of. You tried to kill me, but that was personal. This is business."

"I'm retired."

"Me too. Well, semi-. Them new government laws raised the bar too high. These days I'm in the entertainment industry."

"Drugs or unions?"

"Some other things, too, but I won't bore you. It's out-of-town work I'm talking about. When I found out you were around I couldn't believe I didn't think of you before."

"Who fucked up?"

Maggiore showed a set of worked-over teeth. "You didn't forget how things work. I admit you weren't my first choice. Not because I didn't think you could handle it. Because of the other thing."

"You mean my trying to kill you."

"I had kind of a block over it, I'll say that. But it's like they say here, you'll never work in this town again—until we need you. The money's good. Fifty large."

"I'm okay for money."

"I can see you think it's too hot. It isn't. I'm talking lower-middle talent. No one anybody'd miss."

"Then use one of your regulars. They're on salary."

"That was my first idea. He fucked up, like you said. Now I need to upgrade."

"I'm still retired."

Maggiore looked at his watch, a thin one with a blue face held on with an asymmetrical band. "I've got another incentive."

"I wondered when you'd get around to it."

"I invited another old friend. He's a little late."

"Another fuckup?"

"Hey, it's California. Place has a permanent case of jet lag. The kind of talent I need's scarce out here. This one can't tell time, but he knows how to keep count. Well, you know him. Here he is now."

Macklin spotted him at the same time, coming in from the lobby with that loping gait you seldom saw in the city, even a noncity city like Los Angeles. *Of all the gin mills in all the towns in all the world . . .* He changed his mind and took a drink.

———

In the room, Laurie took her impulse purchase out of its sack and leaned it against the wall atop the low bureau facing the bed. The man in the bandanna reminded her of Peter. Not because of what he'd said about their becoming Gypsies or because the ruddy face bore any resemblance, but because of what the eyes were doing. Although the man was smiling, they were turning inward, and appeared mildly saddened by what they saw. She could not tell if the man was in mourning or simply trying to remember what the sensation was like. Finally she decided she was trying to get too much out of what was really an amateurish painting, and turned away.

She selected one of the nightgowns she'd bought for the honeymoon, dusty-pink and weighing only a few ounces, with a transparency that had made her face burn when she'd looked at herself in the full-length mirror in the store dressing room. It was long enough to drag behind her—cutesy short baby-dolls nauseated her, and anyway her thighs were not her favorite feature—and when she stopped walking, the hem drifted forward and floated to rest around her bare feet. The man who would not react to such a garment was either seriously injured or dead.

The room, like the hotel itself with its glossy black-and-white photos of glamorous old-time stars in the lobby, was done in classic Hollywood motif: white-on-white drapes and carpet and a sleigh bed with a headboard upholstered in white satin. Carole Lombard would have felt at home in it. Laurie spent some time arranging the pillows and propped herself into a sitting position atop the slick spread. When Peter unlocked the door she would gather in her legs and stretch her arms languidly out to the sides, resting them along the tops of the pillows. It was the pose that felt the least ridiculous among those she'd rehearsed.

She noted the time on the digital alarm clock on the nightstand. Twenty minutes seemed enough for Peter to have a drink with a former business acquaintance and make his way up to the room. She fixed herself more comfortably, picked up the remote, and switched on the TV. Nick and Nora Charles were greeting the usual suspects on AMC, but for once Laurie had no patience with the leisurely pace of the 1930s film. She switched to Nick

At Nite and fell asleep thirty minutes into an *I Dream of Jeannie* marathon.

"Laurie, wake up."

She smelled Peter's scent before she was awake enough to open her eyes. He avoided colognes and aftershave, but his particular musk was a pleasant combination of warm skin, the slightly woodsy soap he preferred, and a gingery-leathery something she suspected he'd been born with, that reminded her of the interior of a well-kept automobile. She was so glad he was there, rescuing her from a dream in which some tart in an *Arabian Nights* costume was trying to steal him away from her (while William Powell and Myrna Loy looked on) that she forgot she was mad at him. With her eyes still shut she snaked her arms around his neck and lifted her face to be kissed. He obliged. His lips tasted faintly of scotch. She unwound one of her arms and groped for the buttons on his shirt.

He closed a hand over hers, stopping her. "Darling, I'm so sorry," he said. "I have to go out again. I only stopped in to tell you."

Her eyes sprang open. There was light in the room, but she knew without looking it was still dark outside. The TV was still on. She recognized Major Healy's irritating babble. Jeannie was working her magic yet.

She drew back against the pillows to see Peter clearly. His expression was gentle and loving and regretful, but his eyes were remote. He was in that other place.

"It's a stupid legal thing," he said before she could ask the question. "A snag over the sale of my business. I sold it to a firm here in L.A., and there's a state tax thing involved. I have to fly up to Sacramento and file a deposition. It has to be in person."

She looked at the clock. It was almost eleven. He followed her gaze.

"I booked a midnight flight. I'll be back by midmorning. We'll meet in the hotel restaurant at noon." He paused. "I'll make it up to you. I'll bring a shovel and dig up every last plaster prop from *The Ten Commandments* while you watch."

"You'll be exhausted."

"I'll sleep on the plane. I didn't expect to get much rest on this trip anyway."

He smiled then, and he looked so much like a little boy who'd been caught hiding the pieces from a lamp he'd knocked over that she couldn't think of a single harsh word.

"Why does it have to be tomorrow morning?"

"Tomorrow's the deadline. If I miss it the state of California will slap a lien on the assets. The new owners will turn around and sue me. They can't win, but I'd be five years proving it. The lawyers have been trying to reach me in Michigan and only found out today I'm here in town. Best thing to do is to make it go away."

"I'll ride with you to the airport." She started to get up.

"Uh-uh. You'll need your sleep. Especially if you plan to wear that nightgown tomorrow."

Smiling dopily, she assumed a semblance of the vamp pose. "Why waste it tonight? You've got an hour."

"Of which thirty minutes belong to the freeway between here and LAX. I'll just change my shirt. I smell like a rank tiger."

"You smell wonderful."

She watched him pull off his polo shirt on his way into the bathroom, ached at the sight of his naked back with the odd arrowhead-shaped scar beneath his right shoulder blade, where he said he'd had a cyst removed. She'd told him he'd had a butcher for a surgeon. She heard water splashing, then he came out and put on the white shirt she'd talked him out of wearing that morning. By then she was under the covers. She'd felt cold suddenly in the thin gown.

"Now you look like a little girl," he said. "I feel like a pedophile."

She was suddenly angry. "I'm not your little girl. I'm your wife."

"That's what the man said." He looked at her with no expression. There was nothing in his eyes now, not even distance. He was leaning down to kiss her again when she sat up, snatched hold of his collar in both hands, pulled his face against hers, and bit his lower lip hard. She tasted salt and iron on her tongue.

He broke contact, put a hand to his lips, and looked at the blood on his fingers. "Think you can hold off eating me alive till I get back?"

She was still holding his shirt. She pulled herself close and whispered in his ear. He actually colored.

She held her wicked grin until he'd let himself out. Then she cried. After ten minutes she decided to stop behaving like a child bride and called room service.

FIVE

Johns Davis felt terrific.

He knew he should be worried, and that he would be when the euphoria of survival wore off and he began to dwell on the fact that an attempt had been made on his life—an *attempt* on his *life*—and would probably be followed by another. At the same time he knew that whoever had given the order would hold off until the police began to lose interest. He was safer now than he'd ever been or would ever be again. But that wasn't the reason he felt so good.

Once, working to close a deal on fictional software-company stock over dinner in Morton's steak house in Chicago, he'd gotten a piece of medium-rare Black Angus rib-eye caught in his windpipe. At first it was annoying, and he hoped to get it loose without embarrassing himself. One second later, he hoped he wouldn't die. His companion across the table had just begun to notice his predicament when Davis managed to cough, projecting the bit of gristle into the napkin he was holding against his mouth. He took in a sweet lungful of air in a wheeze, and after apologizing for the disruption resumed his meal a minute or two later. From that point on he took smaller bites and chewed each thoroughly before swallowing. Although he failed to make the sale—not because of the incident, but because the potential buyer's assets were tied up elsewhere—Davis had spent the rest

of the day in wonderous consideration of the details that surrounded him and a new appreciation for pleasures he'd taken for
granted, such as the musty-iodine taste of Glenlivet, the smell
of freshly laundered sheets, the damp on his skin from the wind
off the lake when he met someone at Soldiers Field. Being alive
was the single greatest invention since the Swiss bank.

In time, he'd grown accustomed to not having choked to death
in Morton's, and apart from taking more care with his knife and
fork and refusing to speak with his mouth full, he might never
have gone through the experience. Today was the first time he'd
thought about it in years. Leaving police headquarters, enjoying
the air-conditioned chill inside the cab after the heat on the sidewalk, he wondered if there might be a way to market such joie
de vivre without actually having to strangle the customer.

He'd spent four hours with the police, much of it sitting alone
in a stiff chair in Lieutenant Christie Childs's office, whose cool
colors and shiny surfaces had given him the disorienting sensation of having been suddenly transported back East, and at the
square table in the interrogation room (*interview* room, they
called it these days), waiting to give his statement. Cops were
the same all over, leaving you alone for long uncertain periods
to wonder what they knew and how much they were finding out
while your imagination simmered. He knew the protocol. He'd
been brought in for questioning downstairs when the mayor was
running for reelection on an anti-vice platform, and he'd done a
ninety-day bit in the Cook County Jail when he mixed up his
appointments and pitched a ten percent interest in the Trans-
America Football League to a storm-door manufacturer who
turned out to have taken a seven-figure loss when the World
League went belly-up eight years earlier. That was stupid, but
not half as stupid as cops thinking the same tired strategy that
worked on teenage burglars was just as effective with seasoned
pros. He didn't have to be able to see through the two-way mirror to know they were just sitting around taking telephone calls
and discussing Shania Twain's ass. Letting him get ripe.

He hoped they'd withhold the garrote angle from the press.
In his business, word of mouth was his friend, publicity and

notoriety were not. His coded Rolodex was filled with the telephone numbers of oil executives and corporate attorneys who enjoyed impressing acquaintances with the confidence that they had their very own bookie, reveling in this brush with the underworld, but let them switch on A.M. *San Antonio* and learn that the mob had indeed targeted him as one of its own and they would change those numbers in such volume Southwestern Bell would have to introduce yet another area code to handle the demand. It was an irony of his sphere of illegal endeavor that he had to remain as respectable as a deacon or a presidential candidate.

Bohdan Schevchenko.

That was the name on the sheet Lieutenant Childs had read aloud from when that cop Sill, the cowboy cocksucker, had finished taking Davis's statement. Davis had wanted to say *Gesundheit*, but he knew it was the wrong audience. Schevchenko was the character with the broken neck in the back of the Jag, immigrant from the Ukraine when the Iron Curtain rusted through, with suspected ties to the Russian Mafia, until yesterday under INS investigation for possible deportment. He had aliases, of course: Billy Bod, B.S., Shemp, Taras Bulba—Sean O'Reilly, which made even Sill snort. He'd been arrested four times in Detroit: once for assault with intent to commit great bodily harm less than murder, thing involving some poor fucker with sixteen shattered ribs and a pelvis broken in eleven places (Schevchenko was still wearing his steel-toed boots when they brought him in); three for homicide. Walked when witnesses and the bag-of-bones failed to pick him out of the lineup. Owned three convenience stores, what they called party stores back there, in Detroit and suburbs. This ten years after he washed ashore with a couple of hundred rubles in his pocket, good for two meals at McDonald's if he didn't order the big shake. Land of opportunity.

Riding down St. Mary's, watching tourists descend the steps to the Riverwalk, Johns Davis felt his euphoria fading. The fact that the police would be watching him, paranoid about the greasy old Sicilian Boys Club moving in on the birthplace of the Texas Republic (as if they hadn't had tenure since Joe Bananas broke from Brooklyn in the sixties), was an annoyance, nothing more. He'd have to be careful whom he met with outside the office, not accept any bets over the telephone from anyone whose voice he didn't recognize. His line had been tapped before, with or without a court order, and if they'd wanted to take him down they had plenty enough already. They wouldn't do that, because it would create a vacuum, and Vice would be another eighteen months finding out who'd inherited the book and whether he was the sort of fellow they could live with the way they did with Davis. It was the anonymity of his clients he had to protect, which meant taking measures that would affect the efficiency of his operation and probably cost him some customers. He'd make up for all that after the cops lost interest.

Someone had tried to kill him. That was more than annoying. Whenever he turned his head, the bandage around his neck reminded him just how close the noose had come to severing his windpipe. It still hurt to swallow. He'd had his life threatened in the past: Someone he'd stung when he was on the grift, or some unskilled help he'd hired wanted a partnership and came on like the Black Hand. Bellyachers. They never followed through. Sometimes even now, a CEO or a lawyer who thought he was Chris Darden got pissed over a bad call or an incomplete pass and accused Davis of fixing the game. A lot of bookies might have taken offense and sent someone to hurl the ass-wipe down an air shaft. Davis always shrugged it off. Sore losers forgot their threats the next time a fumble was recovered in their favor.

You took the lemons with the honey. A number of Davis's colleagues dipped into capital and bought personal protection, ex-cop bodyguards to start their cars, heat-sensitive alarms for when they stayed home to jerk off in front of the Playboy Channel. Not Davis. If you were going to lock yourself up, why not let the law do it for you? Let them stand the bill, and use what you saved to arrange for the little comforts.

Safety was a mythical concept. As a wise man once said—he thought it was Al Capone, or maybe Huey Long—bodyguards always shoot second.

It had him vexed. He'd have plenty of time to be scared later, when the grace period ran out. Even in the midst of desperation and panic during the act, he'd kept asking himself *why*. *Who* wasn't important, and now that he could think without fear of immediate death or self-incrimination, he could guess the answer to that one. He'd directed the driver to his home. Now he leaned forward and gave him an address on Flores.

The number belonged to the Hotel Brazil, a white frame Spanish Colonial mansion with functional black shutters and potted palms on the balconies. Davis paid the driver and walked around to the back, where a kind of greenhouse had been built onto the original structure, enclosing a dining room and bar in heat-reflecting glass. More palms and ferns with fronds as big as windmill sails grew out of spaces left among the terra-cotta tiles on the floor. Near the roof, yellow canaries and green para-keets—live birds, living out their spans indoors—made a chir-ruping racket and occasionally dive-bombed the help. The waiters and busboys, trained under fire, went on smoothing the table linens and setting out the silver without flinching. Couple of bills to the health inspector per visit to look the other way on that, Davis thought. No telling how many silk dresses and bowls of French onion soup were spoiled by the splatter from above.

A Chicano waiter opened the door to inform him the dining room would open at four o'clock. Davis was pretty sure he used eyeliner.

"Please tell Señor Rivera that Johns Davis would like a moment of his time."

"John Davis."

"Johns," he corrected. "With an *s*."

The waiter tipped his head forward—nice touch, not a lot of Mexicans could manage it without caricature—and closed the door politely in his face. Two minutes later he returned and opened it wide. "Señor Rivera is in his booth."

He threaded his way among the tables packed too closely together, looking at the floor to avoid slipping on birdshit and above to avoid avian collision. The place had begun to attract cigar-smoking young professionals from downtown, and Rivera had added tables without regard to the fire ordinances as they applied to building capacity: There was another couple of bills a week, with maybe a standing reservation for the fire marshal and a young lady of his choosing. A row of *Casablanca* fans suspended from the center girder stirred the aroma of good Corona-Coronas and Tennessee sour mash.

Spanish Rivera was seated in a horseshoe-shaped booth at the end of the bar, sorting cash-register receipts from one pile onto another on the table. In between he paused to enter amounts into an electronic calculator that made a pleasant little prerecorded noise identical to the *chunkety-chunk* of an old-fashioned mechanical adding machine. He was a brown-skinned septuagenarian with thick black glossy hair that may or may not have been his original color but was almost certainly a wig, toreador-style sideburns, and a moustache that looked like a caterpillar. Thirty or so pounds ago he may have looked like Gilbert Roland. He wore a white linen suit, French cuffs with platinum links, and a big silver-and-turquoise ring on the third finger of his left hand. His real name was Vincente Syracusa. He'd come to America with his mother in 1928 after his father was executed by Mussolini along with all the other mafiosi in his village in Sicily.

"You look like a priest today, my friend," he greeted, without looking up from his receipts. "Have you renounced Satan and women since we spoke last time?"

"Well, Satan, I guess, though I can't say if he's given up on me. Women seem to have. I was in an accident yesterday. That's what I came to talk to you about."

"I heard you smashed up your expensive foreign car. You should buy American. Give a little something back to the country that's been so good to you. I myself have been driving the same Ford Lincoln Continental for fifteen years. One hundred and eleven thousand miles. If it stops working tomorrow it owes me nothing. Then I will go out and buy another Ford Lincoln Continental."

"Ford owns Jaguar now. Anyway, I didn't come here to talk about the car. It's the man who was in the backseat."

"I heard about this, too. A slipshod attempt. It's a new century, and the garrote is so—Turkish. Even children in high school know enough to use firearms."

"I'm kind of glad he didn't. I was rooting for myself." Davis smiled, but the old man was scowling at his figures. "The man's name was Bohdan Schevchenko. I was wondering if you'd heard of him."

"A communist? I dislike communists. They are almost as bad as fascists."

"I don't know how he voted. He was a hitter from Detroit. If there's a contract out on me I thought you might know something about it."

Spanish Rivera looked up for the first time. He had black eyes, something Davis had only read about in books. They belonged to a conquistador, and had probably been the reason Vincent Syracusa had decided to pass himself off as some kind of South American nobility. They seemed to swallow whatever light shone into them.

"I'm not asking you if you signed off on it," Davis added hastily. "In Chicago, whenever someone in New York or Vegas wanted to send in a stone killer, they had to clear it through the Outfit, the local family. If Detroit did this by the numbers, I figure they'd come to you and ask permission. I'm not asking you to intervene. I'd just like to know where I stand. I mean, if I've pissed someone off, I need to know who so I can find out what it was and make things right."

Rivera's eyes moved, and Davis realized the room was silent. The rustle of linens and clinking of silver and stemware had ceased. The waiters were eavesdropping. Caught in the act, they left their stations and drifted on out the back door into the kitchen.

"The order may not have come from Detroit," Rivera said when they were alone. "The city is a clearinghouse for assassins."

"I thought of that. If it's someone local behind it, bringing in someone from outside would be one way to avoid drawing fire. I mean, if it was an illegal operation."

" 'Unsanctioned activity' is a better term." Rivera rested the hand wearing the heavy ring on his calculator. "My granddaughter attends computer-science classes at the University of Texas. Whenever she makes an error, or the computer malfunctions, a message informs her that the program has performed an illegal operation and will shut down. An entire generation is being taught to think of an illegal operation as a minor mistake that is easily corrected. Do you have children?"

"None I know of." Davis smiled again, got nothing back.

"Just as well. One worries. You are a good man, my friend, a man of trust. When you came to San Antonio and asked my permission to do business, I will be honest, there were those who said you would try to steal from me, you were not *paisan*, lying and cheating was your stock in trade. I decided to give you a chance. I have never had to wait even a day to receive my commission, and the accounting has always been acceptable, within the margin of variability. If for any reason someone of my association has taken it upon himself to bring you harm, he will answer for it."

"Would you have any idea who it might be?"

"That may be a question I should be asking you. If, through oversight or distraction, you have failed to acquit yourself as scrupulously with someone else as you have with me, that person will be the one with whom I must deal."

"When I lose, I pay off right away. I never chisel the odds."

"Then the burden is upon me. I accept it."

Davis thought about that until a screeching birdfight among the palms broke his concentration. "Thank you, Señor Rivera."

"My friends call me Vincent."

Davis thanked him again and said good-bye, although he didn't call him Vincent. It had not seemed an invitation the way he'd said it, any more than Rivera's pledge of faith had satisfied him that the proprietor of the Hotel Brazil had had nothing to do with the attempt on his life. Those old *capi* were past masters at the art of appearing to answer a question without giving up any information.

The old man was not called "Spanish" because of the surname he'd assumed or his resemblance to a half-forgotten Hispanic movie actor. In the suite of rooms on the top floor of the hotel where he directed all criminal activities in greater San Antonio, he kept shelves and shelves of books on the history of the Spanish Inquisition, the largest such collection in private hands. From them he had drawn inspiration for the many colorful ways in which he'd had his enemies put to death in the days when he was establishing his authority. It was said his big silver ring was made from fillings pried out of their teeth before they died.

SIX

In the morning, Laurie Macklin dialed room service, then broke the connection before anyone picked up. She was suddenly sick of the room. She put on slacks, a light top, tied her hair up in a scarf so she wouldn't have to fuss with it, and went downstairs. When the waiter at the reservation desk told her the restaurant was full and the wait was twenty minutes, she put on a pair of sunglasses with tortoiseshell rims she'd bought for the honeymoon and walked up Sunset.

It was a beautiful day, sunny and relatively smog-free, with only a light-yellow haze fuzzing the HOLLYWOOD sign in the hills. She walked up a gentle grade, admiring the Spanish Modern houses with their red tile roofs still holding out against the creep of skyscrapers, and marveling at the fact that she had the broad sidewalk to herself. In Dayton on a day like that, the street would be busy with pedestrians even on a workday. Automobile traffic, of course, was steady, spiderlike Porsches sharing the pavement with pickups plastered with mud and held together with chickenwire. Beverly Hills and East L.A. were only minutes apart by freeway, like New York Street and Dodge City bunted up next to each other on the Universal back lot. No wonder there had been riots; but she saw no signs of the destruction now. Not like Detroit, where they were still clearing away the debris from 1967.

She had a cinnamon roll and a cup of espresso at a counter operated by a solidly built young Mexican with a grinning skull tattooed on his wrist, encircled by a red-eyed serpent. She hadn't noticed the tattoo, which she interpreted as a gang insignia, until after she'd ordered, and with a flutter she'd wondered if the place was safe. But it was spotlessly clean, the griddle wiped and the stainless-steel sinks gleaming (no mysteries there, unlike the situation in an upscale restaurant where the food was prepared behind closed doors), and as she stirred cream into her cup, seated comfortably on an upholstered stool while a Spanish-language station played salsa on the radio behind the counter, she decided she was probably not in danger of being raped or taken hostage. She tipped the young man a dollar. He showed her a set of capped teeth and said, *"Muchisimas gracias, señora."* She wondered if he was an out-of-work actor.

In a china shop six blocks from the hotel she handled a cookie jar shaped like James Dean in his red Windbreaker, then remembered there would be someone else living in the house from now on and that their tastes might not be similar. Happily surrendering her independence, she put it down. She bought a soup tureen with a Mexican sunrise enameled on the lid, a present for her mother, and arranged with the clerk—a tall young woman with her hair streaked black-and-white up the middle like a badger and lips painted black—to ship it east.

The journey out had lifted her spirits. Outside the entrance to the hotel she gave an undernourished boy in filthy tennis shoes five dollars for a map to the stars' homes and told him to keep the change.

She felt sticky, so she showered, slipped into a sleeveless blue dress that had a startling effect on her eyes, fixed her hair carefully, and put on the pearl necklace Peter had given her for a wedding present. She'd tanned visibly just in the time she'd been out, and the pearls shone against her skin. A touch of perfume behind each ear and her husband would think twice before leaving her alone again in the big bad city.

A bald, brown-faced waiter seated her in the restaurant a few minutes before noon. She explained that she was waiting for someone, ordered iced tea, and unfolded the map to the stars homes. She'd bought it on impulse, pitying the wretched boy, but she was seriously considering punishing Peter for his neglect by forcing him to accompany her on a bus tour. He preferred to drive himself. Airplanes and taxis irritated him. On the trip out he'd amused her by paying close attention to the flight attendant as she demonstrated safety procedures and pointed out the emergency exits. When Laurie had teased him about it, he'd smiled sheepishly and said he guessed he was an incurable neurotic. It was as close as she'd come to catching him in an untruth. He was the least neurotic person she'd ever known, and was in fact almost frighteningly calm under circumstances that would have unhinged a cardinal. At LAX their bags had been practically the last to emerge on the carousel, and all he'd said was, "Well, I was beginning to wonder." Then he'd spent the entire ride in the cab on the way to the hotel looking out the windshield and back window as if he were the one doing the driving.

The map was cheap and shoddy, garishly colored, and most of the points of interest were connected with actors and directors who were dead or in retirement elsewhere. The fabulous mansions, those still standing, would have been partitioned off for apartments long since, or used by Arab oil sheikhs and rap stars enjoying their three weeks in the spotlight. But it did provide a layout that helped her establish her bearings in the confusing sprawl of freeways, parks, suburbs inside suburbs, and crooked streets and boulevards named for saints she'd never known existed.

"Miz Macklin?"

She looked up, expecting a waiter. She'd been surprised the first time she'd called downstairs to be greeted by name, and had wondered if the entire staff was subjected to a daily briefing on the names of guests checking in and out. But the man standing in front of her table was no waiter.

He was tall, absurdly so, with most of his height in his long legs, like a straw that had been split more than halfway up its length. They were encased in stiff new blue jeans that would crinkle behind the knees when he walked, held up by a wide brown tooled-leather belt with a square brass buckle. The heels of his cowboy boots—some kind of lizard, dyed bright red, with glossy black wingtips—added three inches he didn't need, and he nearly brushed a hanging light fixture with the crown of his cream-colored Stetson when he swept it off his head. He wore a calico shirt with pearl snaps. His Adam's apple stuck out through the open collar, an almost obscene protruberance. It cried out for a kerchief to conceal it.

She hesitated. He had straw-colored hair, pale blue eyes, and a long rectangular jaw that slid sideways when he smiled, like a cow chewing. He could have been thirty or forty-five.

"Yes?" She folded her map.

"Pleasure to make your acquaintance, ma'am. I'm Roy Skeets. It's *Le*roy, actually, but you don't have to bother with that. Folks generally call me Abilene."

"You mean as in Abilene, Texas?"

"That or Kansas, whichever you like. See, they named the one in Texas after the one in Kansas. Kansas had money and no beef, and Texas had beef and no money, so I guess some Texan thought it wouldn't hurt to grease the pan. Like naming your kid after a rich uncle. But there I go, talking your ear off first thing. Promised myself I wouldn't." He unsnapped the flap on a shirt pocket and took out a square of folded paper.

She stared at it. She'd suspected a pickup: someone who'd seen *Midnight Cowboy* a time too many but hadn't watched long enough to learn the Gary Cooper routine was a bust. Maybe he was a bit player moonlighting as a messenger, and hadn't time to change out of his costume between jobs. She took the paper and unfolded it. She recognized Peter's handwriting.

Darling,

I'm stuck in Sacramento overnight. This will introduce Abilene, an old friend, who is flying to L.A. to keep you company until I can get away.

I'm so sorry. I'll make it up to you.

Love,
Peter

She kept her head tipped back awkwardly as she refolded the note and opened her handbag and slipped it inside. She was afraid that if she tilted forward, the tears would spill from sheer gravity. "Would you excuse me just a minute, Mr. Abilene?" She kept her voice even.

"Sure thing, ma'am. But it's just Abilene. There's no mister about it."

She went to the ladies' room. A woman stood at one of the sinks, inspecting her teeth in the mirror. Laurie locked herself in a stall, sat on the toilet lid, and dug her nails into her palms to keep from sobbing aloud.

She was angry at herself, not Peter. She'd married a stranger. She'd denied herself the comfort of her faith in him, believing that by the time the test came she'd know all she needed to face it. It had never occurred to her the test would come so soon. Was there a woman in Sacramento, some old girl-in-the-port from sales trips past? Was he even *in* Sacramento? For all she knew, he'd taken another room in that very hotel, where the two of them were in bed right now, laughing at the stupid Ohio farm-girl pining alone for her husband.

Not the same hotel, she thought. As little as she knew Peter, she knew he would never be so incautious. Or so stupid. And any way she looked at it, she couldn't figure out where Abilene fit in. The ridiculous cowboy was out of place anywhere outside a Roy Rogers film.

By the time she heard the door closing behind the woman, she had attained control. Peter could do his explaining when he got back. How well he did it, or how poorly, would tell her just as much about the man she'd hooked up with.

She left the stall, washed her face, and took time reapplying her makeup, making sure no trace of swelling or redness re-mained. When she returned, Abilene was seated in the other chair at her table, smoking a cigarette. When he saw her, he crushed the butt out in a saucer and stood. His Stetson rocked gently on the table where he'd placed it on its crown. The man's awkwardness made her smile. It was as if he never spent time with women.

"It seems I've been stood up for lunch, Abilene," she said. "Did you eat on the plane?"

"Plane?" Did he hesitate? "Oh, no, ma'am. Pretzels only. I'll chow down with you on one condition." His long jaw slid sideways.

"What's that?"

"I get the check. A man never lets a woman pay for his grub, and a gentleman never lets her pay for hers. My Uncle Bud taught me that."

"I guess your Uncle Bud never read Gloria Steinem."

"Ma'am, Uncle Bud never read a stop sign. That's how he died." He pulled her chair out and held it for her. Then he sat back down.

Their waiter arrived. Laurie ordered a Cobb salad and another iced tea. Abilene asked for a steak sandwich, baked potato, and a beer, selecting Miller when the waiter informed him the bar didn't stock Dos Equis. Abilene spent some time explaining how well done he wanted his steak.

"I thought westerners preferred their beef bloody," Laurie said when they were alone.

"Not this one. I was an orderly in a hospital one whole summer. I mopped up enough blood to last me. Where you want to go after lunch? I know all the spots the chamber of commerce don't. I been out here ten years and I got a good car."

"You don't live in Sacramento?"

This time he didn't hesitate. "No, I just go up there with Mr. Major when he wants company. It's dull as a spoon. There's dust on the fire trucks."

"Is Mr. Major an associate of Peter's?"

"Yes, ma'am. They go clear back to Detroit, before Mr. Major came out here."

"Does Mr. Major sell cameras?"

"He sells everything. So where you want to go first? Chinese Theater, I bet. Try on Marilyn Monroe's footprints for size."

"You're sweet to offer, but I'm comfortable alone. I'll just wait for Peter, and you can go on about your business."

"Beg pardon, ma'am, but you're my business. L.A.'s a tricky place till you get used to it, and even then it's got tricks left. A lot of the bad neighborhoods look just like the good. You don't know which is which till you're in it. You get hurt, I might as well go back home. There won't be no work for me out here."

"Where is home, Texas or Kansas? I can't place your accent, and I've seen every western ever made."

"Arkansas. Little nothing town called Blytheville. You never heard of it. I ain't been back in twenty-five years."

He was older than she'd thought. There were hairline fissures around his eyes. The irises were nearly as pale as the whites. "And where were you in between Blytheville and Los Angeles?"

"You call it. Chicago, Vegas, Miami, Atlantic City. Wherever there was doing to be done."

The waiter brought their drinks. Abilene stopped him as he was pouring his beer from the bottle into a tall glass. "Not down the side, hoss. I like some cloud."

The waiter stopped tilting the glass and allowed a head of foam to build up. When the waiter left, Laurie said, "I thought everything was all settled with the sale of Peter's business. What can you tell me about this tax problem?"

"Not a thing, ma'am. I'm just one of the little injuns." He grinned his sideways grin. "Know who said that? Richard Boone in *Big Jake*. He was talking to John Wayne."

"Do you like westerns?"

"I never had the choice. Every time one came to the theater in town, Uncle Bud snatched me up and we went and seen it." He swallowed beer and licked the foam off his long upper lip. "I was in a Clint Eastwood picture one time. They cut me out."

"Are you an actor?"

"No, I was part of a crowd. Mr. Major had an investment."

"Was it a western?"

"It was one of them damn monkey pictures. I wouldn't of went to see it if I wasn't in it. I took a girl. Well, I wasn't in it anyway, so I didn't get laid that night. Begging your pardon, ma'am."

"I don't think you want my pardon at all, Abilene. I think you're one of those men who says what he wants to and to hell with what anyone else thinks."

"It's a failing. It sure is."

Laurie put down her glass and picked up the map to the stars' homes. "Do you know where Harrison Ford lives?"

"I stopped keeping up with that stuff when they quit making westerns. I can show you where Joel McCrea used to live, and Randolph Scott."

"That's going back."

"Older's better, and black-and-white's best."

"Did your Uncle Bud say that?"

"No, ma'am, he sure didn't. I just this minute thought of it."

Their meals came. She waited impatiently while the waiter set everything out and determined that nothing else was needed. When he was gone—she didn't know if it was anger at Peter that made her say it, or delight at the absurdity of her companion—she leaned forward and said, "Abilene, I think this is the beginning of a beautiful friendship."

He let his jaw slide. She laughed at him.

SEVEN

The Goliad Rod and Gun Club was a tradition nearly as old as the Alamo, and even though the original building had burned down and its replacement abandoned forty years ago in favor of larger quarters on eleven rolling acres outside San Antonio, the man who entered either place for the first time felt the same compulsion to remove his hat. This had to do in some measure with the huge painting that hung in the club's entrance hall depicting the massacre by firing squad of four hundred seventeen Republic of Texas patriots by General Santa Anna's men at Goliad in 1836, a work commissioned by the charter members. Mostly it had to do with the club's reputation as the last of the great Texas whorehouses.

It was not to be compared with the Chicken Ranch outside Dallas, any more than the two cities resembled each other. Here the overpowering Victoriana was absent, the women were by custom restricted to the upper floors, and the broad double-entendres and elbow-nudging that prevailed in the downstairs parlor of the more famous establishment would have encountered only well-bred silence at Goliad. The club was not a front. The business that was transacted upstairs was regarded as a logical extension of the sporting interests that dominated the spacious ground level, where working men of a particular class signed out firearms for target practice on the back range and changed clothes in the locker room to improve their casting skills in one of the two man-made lakes that were kept stocked with catfish, trout, and large-mouth bass. The leather slingback chairs and sofa where the members drank good liquor and discussed business and politics might have been found in any executive lounge, and the well-appointed bedrooms were indistinguishable from those of the hotels in the Convention Center. Even the graft paid to the local authorities was maintained at a discreet level, subject to the normal rate of inflation. For the most part the police and sheriff's department and the Texas Rangers allowed the club to remain open because its personnel didn't hesitate to report incidents and because they knew where to look whenever an outsider of questionable reputation was seen in the area. But only for the most part.

Austine Holland, the woman who managed Goliad for its corporate owners, was widely believed to have been the reason the club was not shut down in 1992, when the son-in-law of a Texas Supreme Court justice died of a cocaine overdose in one of its bedrooms. Rousted from his bed by a telephone call from his hysterical daughter, the justice placed a call to the home of the director of the Department of Public Safety in Austin, who promised to begin an investigation that very evening. Ninety minutes later, Public Safety officers dispatched by the department's chief of detectives visited the justice and explained that there would be no investigation and that the news agencies had already been notified of the death of his daughter's husband of an apparent heart attack suffered at home. A furious second call to the director confirmed the decision. Should the justice wish to protest, he was advised that undercover officers were prepared to swear that his daughter was observed in the company of her husband on a number of occasions when cocaine was obtained from a well-known dealer in Hemisfair Park. At a press conference the next day, a visibly aged justice announced that he had been granted a leave of absence in order to accompany his daughter on a visit to the state of Washington, where at her late husband's request his ashes would be scattered from an observation platform on Mt. Rainier, after which the pair would leave for a "healing trip" to Scotland.

Neither the reporters who covered the event nor the San Antonians who followed it were taken in. Those who were only partially in the know assumed that Austine Holland kept extensive files in a safe place on clients with ties to the state government. She did, of course, but that was not the reason for the swift action in the matter of the justice's son-in-law. Only a few were aware the Holland woman was a paid informant who kept the authorities apprised of organized-crime activities throughout central and south Texas.

Lieutenant Christie Childs had never met the woman, although her code name—*Cassiopeia* locally, but he understood she had a different designation for each law-enforcement agency she dealt with, and that she alone knew them all—had come across his desk in reports, played like a trump card by the author, who knew that no further authentication was necessary. Popular fiction to the contrary, organized crime rarely fell within Homicide's jurisdiction. Those yahoos in Fraud and Vice considered her their personal property. They wouldn't appreciate the fuck from back East paying her a visit. He looked forward to seeing her for that reason, if for no other. He'd met more than his fair share of whores in Milwaukee when he was in uniform, and didn't buy into the romance of the soiled dove. They were walking petri dishes of communicable disease, needle-pierced and pimple-faced, with hearts made of solid shit. Even the high-priced ones didn't have much in common with Miss Kitty. They could just afford a better grade of heroin.

A woman who'd been to school to burr the edge off her Panhandle accent took his name over the telephone, placed him on hold for five minutes, then informed him that Mrs. Holland would see him at two P.M. That irritated him. He couldn't expect a snitch to be seen walking into police headquarters for an appointment, but he had anticipated speaking to her directly and hammering out a place to meet on neutral ground. Being told to present himself at her office after lunch made him feel as if he'd been granted an audience. Nevertheless he agreed. If the Bohdan Shevchenko business broke right, there could be an inspectorship in it, and possibly an opening in Dallas or some other real city where Casual Friday did not mean faded Levi's and a bolo tie.

The entrance to the club, a faux marble lintel supported on thick columns, made him think he was attending an exhibit at a museum of modern art. Glass-and-chromium doors mounted on pneumatic closers sucked him into the air-conditioned presence of *The Massacre at Goliad*, where a bubble-blonde receptionist behind a window found his name in a book and asked him to wait while she lifted a telephone receiver. He wondered who else's name was in the book, or if there were different books for different kinds of visitors. That made him wonder how many visitors left their real names. Waiting, he glowered at the romantic painting of the martyrs of the Republic nobly accepting their fate at the hands of the Mexican rifle squad; as if they hadn't scattered for cover like any other band of seasoned irregulars the moment the weapons were raised. Texas worshiped her dead like no other culture since Imperial China.

"Lieutenant Childs? I'm Jeanine Ryder, Mrs. Holland's secretary. Will you come with me, please?"

The woman who had entered through an interior arch was as tall as he, dressed in a tailored ash-rose suit and rubber heels that made no noise at all on the black-and-white tiles. She was black, with hair cropped close to her skull, which was well shaped. Her smile was professional and friendly. He recognized the worked-over accent from the telephone. She pumped his hand once. She had a firm grip.

"Is there a *Mr.* Holland?" he asked as he accompanied her through the arch.

"Not since before I came to work for her. I understand he went missing in Vietnam."

They crossed through the carpeted lounge, deserted at that hour of the day, and climbed a broad staircase with a mission-style oak banister. Framed prints of what looked like lithographs from *Harper's Weekly* hung on the staircase wall: Pony Express riders, Indian depredations, Civil War battlefields with smoke scudding across cannons and lines of infantry. He was annoyed, while following her down a hallway lined with numbered doors like a hotel's, to realize that his ears were burning, like some teenage boy's during his first visit to a brothel.

Without knocking, she led him into a corner suite, with tall windows in two walls looking out on one of the lakes and the golf course next door. It looked like an ordinary hospitality suite, with a small bar with a mirrored wall behind it, club chairs, a love seat, and a large, glass-topped desk with a telephone and fax machine. The woman who was sitting behind it stood and reached across to shake his hand.

"Thank you for coming, Lieutenant," Austine Holland said. "I tried to move an appointment so I could see you in town, but the gentleman had already left."

She wasn't what he'd expected. She was a plump, comfortable-looking sixty, with straight gray hair to her shoulders cut into bangs just above her eyes and no makeup. She wore a long, heavy, cable-knit blue sweater—on a ninety-degree day in the shade—over a navy dress with fat white leaves printed on it and a string of beads the size of crabapples around her neck, white and obviously made of cheap soapstone. There were nets of wrinkles at the corners of her eyes and her dentures were very white, even against her pale skin. She had calluses on her hand.

"Thanks for your time, Mrs. Holland."

"These are ready to go, Jeanine. I ran out of stamps." She handed a brick of sealed No. 10 envelopes to her secretary.

"I bought you a roll just last week. Why don't you send e-mail, like everyone else?"

"Why don't I just pee in the snow? The effect lasts just as long. Some of us still like to mess with rag paper and ink. Run along now and lick stamps like a good girl."

The black woman left.

"Have a seat, Lieutenant. Can I get you a drink, or are you one of those Joe Friday types, all duty and no fun?"

"It's a little early for me, thanks." He sat in one of the club chairs. "I'm investigating something that happened in town the day before yesterday. I thought you might know something about it."

"The attempted strangling. What a fucked-up business. Excuse my French. I'm an El Paso girl. My father sold groceries near the bridge. He called it a supermarket because it had two cash registers. The stockboys were wetbacks and by the end of the first week they were fluent in all the four-letter words."

She had the broadest accent he'd heard since he came west. "I see this informant business works both ways," he said. "No one outside the department's supposed to know it was a strangling attempt."

"Don't be too hard on your officers. San Antonio's a small town, and I run the barbershop. Did you bring me anything?" She sat down and pulled her chin into her neck. She looked like an albino frog.

He took a long fold of paper from his inside breast pocket and pulled it across the desk. "I had the department computer whiz run this off from what we got from Detroit and Washington. From a taxpayer's standpoint we can thank this bookie Davis for saving us the cost of deportation."

The sheet contained the arrest information on Schevchenko and a photo obtained by fax from Immigration and Naturalization. She studied it for thirty seconds, then put it down. "We didn't meet, but that doesn't mean he wasn't here. I'll circulate it among my young ladies."

"I'd appreciate that, but it isn't precisely why I'm here. I'm not doing the door-to-door."

"I know that, Lieutenant."

"I need to find out why Davis was targeted, and if it was a mob contract."

"Are you coordinating your investigation with the FBI?"

"It's too early to say."

"You mean you *won't* say. Have you been to see Spanish Rivera?"

"I wanted to talk to you first."

"But you're not talking to me. Even a slot machine requires you to put something in the slot."

"I thought you were more or less on permanent retainer."

"I'm not talking about money. If San Antonio is attracting federal attention, a number of people need to know it. I don't know how you did things in Milwaukee, but out here, information is not a perpetual-motion machine. It feeds on facts in order to produce facts."

He laughed, a short bark, surprised and bitter. Who the hell had told her he was from Milwaukee? "I'm not your snitch. You've got things backwards."

She pushed the sheet his direction. "Thanks again for coming, Lieutenant."

"Ma'am, are you refusing to cooperate with an officer of the law?"

"The officer of the law is refusing to cooperate with me. Do you think you and I and four thousand police are the only ones who know about our arrangement? If I didn't give the people I answer to something in return for what they give me, they'd have cut out my cunt and dumped me off the Riverwalk ten years ago. That's the standard prescription for a woman in my line. Sicilians are poets. If you want to feed a killer the needle in Huntsville badly enough, it means Mr. Rivera knows when the DEA is targeting south Texas so he won't lose his investment in a carload of heroin coming in from Turkey by way of Matamoros. I'm a broker, Lieutenant, not a communist. There has to be an equal exchange of goods or services in order for the system to operate. If there isn't, I'm the one who gets operated on. I don't use my cunt much these days, but I'd sort of like to hold on to it for old times' sake."

She smiled as she spoke, displaying the whole of her dentures. She looked not at all like a complacent frog.

"I'll discuss it with the chief." Childs couldn't think of another answer.

"When you do, please ask him how his grandson is. He was trying to walk last I heard." She picked up the sheet. "I'll ask some questions. For now, though, you might want to tell INS that Bohdan Shevchenko is probably another alias. Whoever forged his papers combined the names of two heroes from Ukrainian history. They might appreciate the information, and you'll see I'm right."

EIGHT

It was a good day, although—it went without saying, so of course she said it often, but only to herself—it would have been better with Peter.

Abilene, who really did know his way around Hollywood, took her to Mann's (formerly Grauman's) Chinese Theater, where she mastered the urge to try out Jean Harlow's footprints like the prototypical tourist but bought a poster in the gift shop that showed James Dean standing in the boat crossing the Delaware while John Wayne rowed and Humphrey Bogart draped his trench coat over Marilyn Monroe's shoulders. She goggled at the pagoda facade and neon dragons that represented isolationist America's idea of what the Orient was like and was truly surprised by the information, supplied by her escort, that the theater was one of three originally built by Sid Grauman, each more exotic than its predecessor. Sadly, the Egyptian had been gutted and the Spanish was no more. "That Jew took a bath in the Crash," Abilene said.

"How do you know so much?"

He grinned his slanchwise grin. "Mr. Major says I'm a sponge. That's why he promoted me. Said I was wasted in the field."

"Were you a salesman?"

"Closed my share. Toss your poster in the back. We still got

Tom Mix's house and the canyon in Malibu where they shot westerns before sound."

He drove a new black Jeep Grand Cherokee, waxed to a lacquer shine, with a chromed custom exhaust system that gleamed like his boots. Except when he was shifting he drove one-handed, his left elbow resting on the sill of his open window. That arm was burned a dark cherry-red up to the point where he folded back his shirtcuff.

They'd discussed having dinner at a place on Highway 1, a barbecue joint where he said the stars still went sometimes when they didn't want to be seen, but the trip to Malibu had exhausted her. She pleaded a headache and he took her back to the hotel. The night man who looked like one of the Beach Boys checked and told her there were no messages.

"Are you sure? I'm expecting my husband tomorrow, but I don't know what time."

"I'm sorry, Mrs. Macklin. I'll buzz you if anything comes in."

At the elevators she shook Abilene's hand. "Thank you. I'm afraid I took your whole day."

"Seemed like five minutes with a cold beer. How about Tijuana tomorrow? Show you where Will Rogers went to get laid. It's a fudge factory now, but I hear if you know a guy you can buy good weed. That's just a rumor. I never mess with that shit. Beg your pardon, ma'am."

"Thank you, but I'm sure Peter will be back in the morning." The headache was suddenly no longer just an excuse. She'd had enough yee-haw to last her a long time.

"I'll call you at nine. Just in case he ain't."

He was still standing there wearing his lopsided grin when the doors slid shut.

On her floor she rummaged through her handbag and failed to find her key card. She supposed she'd left it in the room. Feeling drained, she returned to the lobby, where the Beach Boy smiled and gave her a replacement. On her way back to the elevators she stopped and turned. Abilene was stretched out in a figured armchair with his boots propped up on a glass coffee table. He lifted his Stetson off the bridge of his nose to look at her, then resettled it.

She hovered a moment, undecided, then turned again and boarded the elevator. The hat covering Abilene's face might as well have been a wall between them.

In the room she double-locked the door and put on the chain. The two suits and one of the sportcoats Peter had brought on the trip hung in the closet. She smelled his faint scent when she leaned in to hang up her dress. It tore at her heart and comforted her at the same time. *A man may leave his wife, but not his clothes.* It made her laugh and so she didn't cry. He would be back tomorrow.

She put on the simple cotton shift she'd decided to pack at the last minute, having heard that the nights were cool in southern California. She'd smiled at her foolishness when she'd taken it out the day they checked in. She'd forgotten she had someone who would keep her warm. But after the strange scene in the lobby she felt less uneasy wearing it than she would have in any of the other flimsy and frivolous things she'd brought.

In bed she thought. Did Abilene imagine he was protecting her? Did he take his charge to look after her so literally? It seemed so old-fashioned, so much in keeping with his ludicrous clothes and *beg your pardon, ma'am*'s, that she could not accept it as an explanation. Most likely he lived too far away to bother going home if he planned to check on her in the morning as he'd said.

There had been no recognition in his expression. That was the part that chilled her, even more than learning that he'd staked himself out in the lobby like some kind of loyal dog. Even a tired dog would have thumped its tail once. It was as if she had ceased to exist for him as a social creature the moment after they'd said good night.

Was she being stalked? Such things happened all the time, to celebrities and ordinary women. But the stalkers, the ones she'd seen being arraigned on television, all ran to a sinister type. They didn't inspire derision, like the cowboy downstairs. Stalkers tried to blend into their surroundings. Abilene stood out like—well, like the Chinese Theater. No, he was just doing what he thought was expected of him by Peter and that Mr. Major. Whoever he was.

Even so, she wished Peter had left a number where she could reach him. She needed to hear his quiet chuckle when she confided her anxiety, the sound not carrying far enough to reach strange ears. That, and the way he steered her into doorways so that no one would see him kissing her in public, made her feel safe in their private world. She had thought she would punish him for deserting her, but she knew now she would be incapable of keeping that resolution when she saw him. She would run to him, in the lobby or on the street, and he would just have to put up with her making a spectacle of them both.

The telephone woke her. She hadn't realized she'd slept. Blades of light glittered at the edges of the heavy curtains that covered the window. The digital clock read 8:59. She couldn't believe she'd been unconscious so long.

"Peter?"

" 'Morning, Miz Macklin. No smog today. This is the day they shoot the postcards."

"Oh, hello, Abilene. I thought it was Peter."

"I guess I don't need to ask if he got back. What do you say we strap on the nosebag downstairs and get us an early start on Tijuana?"

"That's sweet, but my head is pounding. I'm not used to the dirty air. I'd just like to stay in the room today. Anyway, I don't want to be out when Peter comes back."

"Why don't I bring you up some aspirin? These hotel folk'll sock you ten bucks for a teeny bottle and charge a tip on top of it."

"No, I just need rest."

The pause that followed begged her to fill it. *Did you spend the whole night in the lobby?* She gripped the receiver hard, as if to hold back the question.

"I'll call you later," he said then. "Them walls get close after a spell."

She had breakfast sent up, but she left most of it, and all but a sip of coffee. Her nerves were frayed enough without the caffeine. She went around the TV dial twice but found nothing that held her attention more than a few seconds. Abilene had been right about the walls. She showered, dried her hair, and put on pleated comfortable slacks, a light top, and flats for walking. She didn't bother with makeup. She wondered if he was still downstairs. She thought about calling and asking a clerk, but she was afraid that if Abilene was there the clerk would ask him to leave. She didn't know if it was the prospect of insulting him that made her afraid or if it was Abilene himself. In any case she didn't want anyone thinking she was a hysterical woman.

On her way down she realized she should have called down to arrange for a cab. She didn't want to ask at the desk and have to wait. Even if Abilene had left she didn't know when he might come back to call up to the room. Once outside the hotel she would take a chance on flagging down a taxi.

The chairs in the lobby were empty. A line of people was waiting to register. She started for the door—and withdrew behind a column just as Abilene looked up from a display of neckties behind the glass wall of the gift shop. From that position he had a clear view of the main entrance on Sunset.

Her heart clattered. Was he her protector, or her prison guard? She was afraid, then angry. She wanted to march up to him and tell him to tell his Mr. Major she was a big girl who could take care of herself. In the next moment she knew she wouldn't do that. She hated scenes. Her parents had made scenes.

A carpeted hallway next to the elevators led to sunlight, perpendicular to the main lobby. She turned that way and followed it to a side door opening onto a one-way street. Just before she pushed through, she glanced back. No one was following.

She walked toward Sunset. There would be cabs there. It was not like New York, where they lined up in front of the hotels. Presumably everyone in L.A. had a car unless there was something wrong with them, in which case they could make an appointment to be picked up.

At Sunset she turned away from the hotel, where Abilene might have seen her walking past. Twice she spotted cabs in traffic and waved, but both times the cars cruised past. They had passengers. She kept glancing back as long as the hotel was in sight, but saw only the doorman in his white Prussian uniform in conversation with the bell captain, the latter leaning against his baggage cart.

After ten minutes a canary-yellow Capri with its ON DUTY sign lit up, swung into the curb in front of an unmarked apartment building and let out a woman in her fifties carrying a sack of groceries. She left the rear door open. Laurie stepped toward it. A long arm stretched past her and swung it shut with a bang.

"Cabs are for poor people in this town," Abilene said. "It's how they stay poor. How's your head?"

He towered over her in a red-and-white yoke shirt, crisp black jeans with copper rivets, and black boots that glistened like eels. Only the Stetson and the crooked grin were the same. He must have had a change of clothes in the Jeep and cleaned up and shaved in the men's room in the lobby. He'd drenched himself in Aqua-Velva.

"Oh—much better." Her cheeks felt hot, and she knew they were red. She was sure he could hear her heart beating. "I thought I'd go shopping."

"I parked my crate behind the hotel. Where you want to go?"

"Really, I'd rather walk."

"Run's the word. I had to high-step it to catch up. You in a hurry? No one's in a hurry out here. Even the earthquakes take their time."

She met his pale gaze. "Please don't be offended. I'd rather be alone."

"No good."

Her heart speeded up. She hadn't thought that was possible. "What do you mean, 'No good'? I want to be alone, I said."

"No good means *no good*. Something was to happen to you, I'd never hear the end of it from Mr. Major. This town ain't as friendly as it looks. There's gangs and druggies. White slavers, I ain't shitting. Snatch you off Sepulveda in broad daylight Monday and Saturday they're bidding on you in Beirut. I could tell you stories you won't hear from the chamber of commerce."

"I'm a nurse in training, Abilene. I've visited neighborhoods in Toledo at night that make the worst in Los Angeles seem like Disneyland. I just want a day to myself."

"I'll keep my trap shut. You won't even know I'm around."

His hand closed on her arm.

Laurie looked around. The cab had left. There wasn't a pedestrian in sight and the traffic on the street continued past as if the cars were drawn by invisible cables with nothing living inside them. The city itself was like some great self-propelled machine, going about its business without need or regard for the people who crawled over its surface. She knew he'd told her the truth about white slavers. She could be abducted there on the street as easily as if she were cornered in an uninhabited desert.

He pulled gently, and she went with him. All the way to where his black Jeep stood against the curb behind the hotel she thought, *Kidnapped, I'm being kidnapped.* But she said nothing. She went with Abilene.

"There's a store in Tijuana I know you'll like," he said as he started the engine. "They got Louis Vuitton bags hanging like lanterns from the ceiling. Louis hisself wouldn't know 'em from the genuine article."

She was only half listening. She had to concentrate. She had a plan. It was probably unnecessary and she would feel silly later—she wasn't really being *kidnapped*, for God's sake—but she knew now there was no talking to Abilene. She could not picture Peter tolerating him for long as a companion. It had probably been a business thing: He'd wanted to sell out, Mr. Major had been thinking of buying, Abilene was a valued employee. You couldn't expect to close a deal by insulting a man's taste in help. Well, she'd had enough of the fellow, and she wasn't hoping to sell anything. When he stopped for the light at Western, she hit the door handle and pushed.

A hand shot out and grasped her wrist. It wasn't the polite

hold of before. His fingers were strung with wire. Pain shot up to her elbow when she tried to twist free. She yelped.

He held on. He was watching the light and a braid of muscle stood out along his jaw. When the light changed, he popped the clutch and they bolted forward. Rubber chirped, Laurie fell back in her seat. The momentum swung the door shut. Still holding her with one hand, Abilene leaned into a hard right turn from the inside lane, gunned the engine, and was well up Western before the line of drivers he'd cut off had time to react. Their horns sounded querulous and far away. He turned right again into the parking lot of a concrete-and-glass convenience store, circled behind the building, and braked inches short of the cinderblock wall. Gasoline whumped around inside the tank.

He let go of her wrist then. A brown Dumpster filled the window on her side, preventing the door from opening.

She turned to glare at him. "Just what—"

His fist was a blur. A blue light snapped inside her skull. Her mouth stung and her head hurt where she'd bonked it against the window. She tasted salt and iron. Her vision swam. When it cleared, Abilene's face was two inches from hers. He was gripping her upper arms, cutting off her circulation. She smelled Aqua-Velva and something sickening-sweet on his breath, nauseating: chewing tobacco. His eyes were so pale the pupils looked like pinpricks in ovals of white plastic.

"This ain't the farm, Heidi," he said. "Mr. Major wants you kicking. He didn't say you had to keep your teeth."

NINE

At the last minute he decided not to use the ID that had been arranged for him.

There hadn't been time to research the driver's-license format in his home state, so they'd used a blank passport. The paper wasn't quite right—the quality of the bond was flimsier than government stock and there was something wrong with the eagle in the watermark—but airline employees were less experienced with passports than were customs officials and he'd been confident the flaws would pass unnoticed. The problem was the photograph.

It was ten years out of date. The hair was significantly darker, he'd been wearing it longer then, and his face had filled out a little since it was taken. Old photos in themselves didn't arouse suspicion, but the print was recent, and too glossy. Someone might wonder why, if he'd gone to the trouble of striking off a fresh print, he didn't just pose for a new picture. There were any number of reasonable excuses he might use, but the bare fact that it would cause a busy clerk to give him and it a second look increased the risk factor.

He considered scuffing it up, but resisted the temptation. Artificial aging was an art, and any attempt to streamline the process just called attention to itself. Had he been in charge of the operation, as had always been the case in the old days, he'd have postponed it until it could be done properly, and scrubbed it entirely if the time factor did not allow for the adjustment. If they wanted to cowboy the job, they might as well give it to that Arkansas shitkicker in L.A.

The whole business screamed hurry-up. All his instincts were against it. If you needed a man dead without complications you either planned the thing through or caught him in an alley and bashed in his head with a jack handle. Anything in between was suicide, especially in Texas, where they executed murderers on a conveyor belt, rolling them in one end on gurneys and out the other in coffins. The jack handle was out: not because he wasn't that kind of killer—there was a kind of poetic simplicity in blunt-end weapons, and he had no use for the dainty fellows who crouched behind telescopic sights and never got a drop of blood on their shirts—but because he didn't know the alleys in San Antonio.

There was, now that he thought about it, a third alternative: playing it by ear. That mean scouting as he went, making no plans that could not be changed on site, and in fact changing any plan on principle that had stood long enough to grow stale. He didn't recommend it to beginners, even if he could picture himself sharing hard-won secrets that might one day be used against him. It had to do with knowing what to expect and not expecting too much, while leaving space to react to those events that could not be predicted. It was the same as playing cowboy if you did it out of ignorance, but if you knew the percentages it could actually prove superior to overthinking the operation.

The drawback in his case was he was rusty. He hadn't held a weapon in nearly two years, much less employed one with homicidal intent. His reflexes had slowed, for one thing, and for another, the people whose business it was to prevent him from practicing his craft with impunity had in the meantime acquired a chestful of shiny new tools. He'd congratulated himself on getting out when he had. Now he had to face the fact that if he'd stayed active and kept abreast of the changes as they took place, he'd be in a much better position than he was. He was a manual typewriter racing against a roomful of computer keyboards. The smart thing was to walk away.

That wasn't going to happen, so he didn't dwell on it. It was out of his hands, and had been since he'd been spotted in California by whoever had spotted him. Nothing in that. He'd known men in the work who'd gotten so hung up thinking about the nickel's worth of gas they'd failed to put in the tank, the jammed automatic that could as easily have been a reliable revolver, the major artery missed by a thousandth of an inch, separating a living witness from a dead man; kicking themselves over the dead past until they had no energy left to deal with the present. And in the bargain threw away their future. He'd been dealt a stinker of a hand and he couldn't fold, so he had to do what he could to turn it into a straight flush.

All this came to him in the time it took to use the urinal in the airport men's room and wash and dry his hands. On his way out the door, he folded the false passport inside the damp brown paper towel and poked it through the hatch into the bullet-shaped trash can. He would use his own ID and if it came to checking who'd flown in within forty-eight hours of the killing—well, it wasn't against the law to take an unexplained flight. In any case he felt safer under his own name than under the one the sons of bitches had picked.

He used a pay telephone in the terminal to book the flight, not bothering to cancel the reservation that had been made for him under the other name. That would slow down any attempts to double-check him from the L.A. end: no-shows weren't reported until after a plane left the ground, and even then were usually tied up in the system for hours. By the time they thought to ask for him under his own name, he'd be burrowed in and halfway home. He'd learned to depend upon the infallible inconvenience of air transportation.

He bought a personal-pan pizza in a sterile and soulless cafeteria, ate two slices, and dumped the rest along with the box and his napkin. In the old days he'd skipped eating entirely twenty-four hours before a job, so that his blood would carry oxygen to his brain instead of lagging in his digestive system, but since retiring he'd grown accustomed to regular meals. He didn't want a growling stomach attracting attention. Then he picked up his suitcase, a cheap one made of brown vinyl he'd bought on his way to the airport, along with the jacket and some toilet items he'd stuffed inside just so the X-ray machine would have something to photograph, and joined the line at the ticket counter.

A female clerk in her late fifties, wearing a hairstyle and makeup better suited to a woman twenty years younger, looked at his driver's license and told him she'd found a seat on the aisle. "These midweek flights never fill up as fast as they hope upstairs," she said.

"I was counting on that."

"San Antonio's a nice town. Business or pleasure?"

"Business, I'm afraid. No time to visit the Alamo."

"That's too bad. It's worth it. Well, you're all set. Gate E-11, boarding in ten minutes." She handed him his ticket and boarding pass. "Have a pleasant flight, Mr. Macklin."

TEN

ow's the lip?" Abilene asked.

She touched it with a fingertip. It was puffing. She'd bitten it when he hit her and it was still bleeding inside her mouth. She hadn't experienced that iodiney taste since she'd fallen off her bike when she was ten. She lowered her hand and stared at him without answering, letting the lip speak for her. She hoped he'd think her defiant. Instinct told her it would be a mistake to let him sense fear.

He let his jaw slide sideways. "It ain't bad. You look like Melanie Griffith. You ought to look into that collagen thing when it goes down."

"Who are you?"

"Roy Skeets, though I don't answer to it. We been through that. What you want to know is what I do, and I told you that too. I work for Mr. Major."

"Who is Mr. Major?"

"Charles Major." He waited. "Shit, I keep forgetting you ain't from Detroit. Here."

They were still parked behind the convenience store, with the Dumpster blocking Laurie's door. He slid a folded newspaper from its perch atop the sun visor and spread it on her lap. It was a copy of the *Los Angeles Times* with yesterday's date. The only photo on the page showed a short, middle-aged man standing slightly hunched between two younger men carrying briefcases. CARLO MAGGIORE, REPUTED FORMER DETROIT MOBSTER, ARRIVES AT CITY HALL FOR QUESTIONING, read the caption.

"Questioning for what?"

"This and that. Mostly that. L.A.'s an open city, they don't like it when folks from connected towns come here to settle. That's why the guinea name. He ain't used it in years."

"You work for a gangster?"

"Don't scrape me off your shoe, little nursie. So does your husband."

"My husband is retired from the retail camera business."

The grin slid another notch. "He sold cameras, all right, but just indirectly. And only to police photographers. You could say he helped create the demand. Pete's a wet worker. He kills to live."

"Why are you lying?" she said after a moment. "Did you force Peter to write that note? Where is he? Did you kill him?"

"Well, he ain't in Sacramento, and he ain't dead. Which if he was one or the other amounts to the same thing. He ain't in L.A. neither. If he was, Mr. Major couldn't be. That would wreck the whole point of hiring a kill."

"Don't you mean a hit?" She tried to look contemptuous. It made her lip hurt.

"Nobody's called it that since they stopped using phones to set it up. It gets done on the street now, in crowds and noisy restaurants, where everybody's jabbering and any kid with a scanner and a tape recorder can't listen in. A kill's a kill: not a contract or a hit or a whack job. You're married to a killer, not a mechanic. It's less confusing. Time was, when you told someone to take care of a guy, he'd put a bullet in him, when what you really wanted was to get him looked after. You can appreciate what a mess it was."

"Why do you keep saying that about Peter? He couldn't even run over a seagull."

He pushed back his Stetson with a knuckle. There was a band of creamy skin across the top of his forehead where the hat shielded it from the sun. "If I show you, you promise not to try and jump the fence again? I'd hate to bust that cute little nose, smear it all over your face like a squashed chili pepper."

"You can't show me what isn't true."

He said nothing. She could see her reflection in his dead pale eyes.

"I won't try anything." She could hardly hear her own voice.

He lifted his hand. She shrank back against the door. His grin hardened. He grasped the shifting cane and jerked the transmission into reverse. "There's Kleenexes in the glove compartment. We don't want you bleeding all over the police station."

The building looked familiar, as if she'd seen it in a vivid dream: a narrow tower jutting vertically like the finger of Justice from between a pair of horizontal wings. It wasn't until they'd parked around the corner and begun climbing the steps to the front door that she recognized it. It was Los Angeles City Hall. She'd seen it in fifty movies and in every episode of *Dragnet* on cable, embossed on the gold Zulu shield of Joe Friday's badge 714. Eighteen stories of identical windows with neoclassical marble arches at the base. A number of Hollywood gangsters had defied the law inside only to be shot down by vigilantes on these very steps.

"We're really going into the police station?" she asked Abilene halfway up.

"Think I'll melt?"

They passed through a metal detector into a big echoing room that reminded her of a hotel lobby at checkout time. Men and women in street clothes, officers in uniform, lawyerly types carrying briefcases, and apparent bums in grubby sweatshirts and jeans worn through at the knees trafficked about, jabbering like first-nighters at the theater. At the high front counter sat a short-haired female officer, scribbling on a sheet attached to a clipboard. Laurie's companion waited until the woman looked up.

"Sergeant Thurtell," he said. "Tell him it's Abilene."

"Just Abilene?"

"I bet I'm the only one dropped by today."

The officer used the telephone on the counter, then hung up and handed them each a visitor's pass with a clip attached, instructing them to hang the boldly printed tags on the outside of their clothes. "Sixth floor. Room six-fourteen." She resumed writing.

"Dyke says 'What,' " Abilene said softly.

She looked up again. "What?"

"Thanks, Officer. You have a nice day."

They shared an elevator with two big patrolmen strung all over with weapons and two-way radios. The officers smelled of clean sweat and chewing gum. Abilene, watching the numbers, paid them no attention. When the two men in uniform got off on the third floor, he said, "Let's be careful out there."

One of the officers looked back just as the doors closed.

Six-fourteen was a large, brightly lit room, nearly paved with desks made of laminated panels with woodgrain printed on them. Each desk had its own computer console. A young man rose from behind one to shake Abilene's hand and put on his suitcoat before wishing Laurie good morning. He had frank eyes in a babyfat face and she knew the moment when he saw her split and swollen lip, but his smile didn't change.

"Thought you'd be up in Mendocino," he told Abilene. "Tri-Star's shooting a sure-enough western, big budget. Matthew McConaughey and some fresh slice off the runway. Lots of security work."

"I can't watch these Hollywood boys ride. Anyway, I don't moonlight no more. How's the lion hunting?"

"I gave it up. Orange County sheriffs caught my neighbor using a laser scope at night, confiscated the rifle *and* his car. I figure they can go on eating all the cats and poodles they can keep down. What I got for the pelt wouldn't cover what I owe on the SKJ."

"Bitch." Abilene clearly wasn't listening. "Jake, I need a look at the FBI file on Peter Macklin." He spelled the last name and added Peter's date of birth, which Laurie hadn't known. She took comfort from the fact he hadn't lied about his age.

"I don't know. Brass changed the rules. An officer has to log on with his badge number."

"Who's got the watch?"

The young detective—the nameplate on his desk read SGT. J. THURTELL—made a face. "Captain Birxey."

Abilene grinned.

Thurtell stared. "You're shitting."

"I never shit a shitter."

"Hold on." Thurtell sat down and rattled the keys on his board. After five minutes he grunted, sat back, and swung the monitor around on its lazy Susan for his visitors to view.

The first thing Laurie saw were side-by-side photographs in front and profile of a man's face. Immediately she felt relieved. The man was years younger than Peter, and the sullen expression he wore was not in her husband's repertoire. There was a strong family resemblance. A mistake had been made, and she was so ashamed of herself for the doubts she had begun to feel that she instantly forgave Peter for keeping the secret of a black-sheep brother or first cousin. Then the raw data began to appear.

"Do Jake's superiors know you're paying him for information?"

It was the first thing she'd said since before they left city hall. She'd felt faint staring at the bright computer screen, reading the endlessly scrolling list of arrests, court appearances, and sur-veillance reports in which Peter's name appeared, and the effort of forming words would have sapped the strength she needed to remain standing. She'd kept silent while Abilene thanked the sergeant and all the way out to where he'd parked the Jeep. Abilene was quiet too, for once, rolling down the window on his side to let out the heat and poking tobacco inside his bottom lip from a flat can and waiting for her to say something. Now he made an animal sound in his throat, spat out the window, and wiped the back of a hand across his mouth.

"I don't pay nobody for nothing," he said. "It's like the army."

"You mean he belongs to Maggiore."

"Major. He had it changed in court. Mr. Major don't even

know Jake's name. But Jake knows his, and if he don't, his watch captain does."

"Captain Birxey. Major owns him."

"Funny thing about captains. They come cheaper than lieutenants. It's like that right up to detective commander."

"He owns the police."

"Nobody's that rich."

"Does he own Peter?"

"There was a difference of opinion about that. When Mr. Major left Detroit, Macklin came with him, and made a space for him. Then Macklin went back. He thought he had his pink slip, and maybe he did. But he shouldn't have picked L.A. for his honeymoon, not if he wanted to stay retired. He was seen, and Mr. Major ain't one to let a handy tool lay."

"Who is Peter supposed to kill?"

"Nobody you ever heard of, so why ask? All you got to do is have fun in the sun for a few days till the ball and chain gets back."

"How do you know he'll come back?"

"He left, didn't he?"

She hated looking at his crooked jaw, the way he showed his lower teeth with the black stains between them. "Am I the reason he's doing this?"

"He didn't want to do it at all. If you want to know, he was rude about it, called Mr. Major a hunchback son of a bitch, and Mr. Major don't like folks talking about his hump. That was when he told me to come keep you company. Your husband got real reasonable after that."

"Are you supposed to do something to me if Peter doesn't go through with it?"

"That didn't come up."

"Did it have to?"

He looked at her. His tongue bulged out his bottom lip as he pushed the tobacco around. He shook his head. "I don't see it. You're a pretty little bit, but the studios turn away prettier every damn day, and Macklin's supposed to be a hard old nail. Maybe that's what retirement does to you. Or maybe he wasn't so hard to begin with. You hear a lot of stuff from the field and most of it's horseshit."

"If things don't work out and Maggiore expects you to kill me, why didn't he just have you kill this person instead of going to all this trouble to get Peter to do it?"

He reached above the visor and groped underneath the folded newspaper. "I'm no killer, nursie. Not the professional kind. But if hubby fucks up, or runs, or forgets the play, I can fix you so he won't *want* to come back."

He was even faster than before. His hand streaked down and around and the point of a narrow blade stung the flesh below her right eye. She didn't move. If she blinked or flinched, the skin would break.

"The name's Mr. Major," Abilene said. "Show some respect if you don't want to have to read them hospital thermometers in Braille from now on."

She wet her lips. "Mr. Major."

He withdrew the knife, folding it against his thigh, and slipped it into one of the arrow pockets on his shirt. Then he switched on the ignition. The air conditioner cut in with a whoosh of hot, fishy-smelling air, then cooled down. "There's a cigar bar in Culver City," he said, rolling up his window. "California's got a law against smoking in bars and just about everyplace else, but this one ain't open to the public. If you know somebody you can get a look at Demi Moore sucking on a panatella any Friday night. I can get you in, but you got to promise not to ask for autographs." He shifted into first and eased out into Civic Center traffic.

ELEVEN

For a little over two and one-half hours Monday night, Johns Davis actually forgot he was under a sentence of death.

The event was football on ABC-TV. The Rams were 10-point favorites going in, and if Davis's source could be trusted, their starting quarterback was playing hurt. Davis had laid off short in order to take cautious advantage of the information.

The experience was nearly as harrowing as the fear of losing his life. Certainly it was less pleasant than it would have been had he not been let in on any secrets. On the one hand he stood to drop fifty thousand dollars if Tampa Bay failed to cover the spread. On the other, he feared he'd been too conservative and would not clean up as spectacularly in the event his source was right as he would have if he'd taken a leap of faith. He had just enough of the gambling bug (a rarer condition among professional bookmakers than is commonly supposed) to consider losing no more disastrous than not winning enough.

During the first half, not winning enough didn't appear to be the problem. Jackson completed two passes and ran thirty yards to a touchdown, and didn't seem to be favoring his right arm during the victory dance that followed. But in the third quarter, whatever he'd injected to deaden the pain from the fractured ulna must have worn off. He threw an incomplete, was intercepted twice, and when a Buccaneers tackle took him off his feet two minutes into the fourth quarter, he rolled around on the ground cradling his forearm against his chest and had to be helped to his feet and off the field. A second-string quarterback was substituted, but a turnover in Tampa Bay's favor in the last ten seconds put them three points ahead at the gun. That covered the spread, and Davis was two hundred thousand to the good, give or take an upset among the layoff bets he'd placed.

He poured himself a glass of Glenlivet to celebrate, but the euphoria lasted only as long as the drink. He couldn't help remembering the tip had come his way moments before some psychotic Ukrainian son of a bitch had slung a length of fishline around his throat. Again, as he had over and over for days, he tried to think what he'd done or said recently to set himself up for the cemetery. The haystack containing that needle wasn't large—in San Antonio, Spanish Rivera was the one man a fellow in his line was well advised to keep happy—but he drew a blank just the same.

Davis was no naïf. The word of even a mafioso of the old school carried no more weight than foil, and despite Rivera's protestations of faith, he had not achieved his age and rank by confessing to a man's face that he was plotting against him. His own innocence of transgression meant nothing. A mistake had been made, or Rivera had reasons of his own for creating a vacancy where Davis stood. It might have been something as pedestrian as a relative or some other favorite the old man wanted to move into the bookmaker's place, and he was too polite or embarrassed by the situation to ask Davis to step aside. More than a few gang murders had been arranged out of respect for the victim, whom the men behind the assassinations wished not to insult. The possibility that the insult might have been preferred by the parties involved seemed not to have entered consideration. Organized crime was a Bizarro World. Davis had stopped trying to work out its line of reasoning years ago, for fear he might end up thinking the same way.

An even greater paradox lay in the fact that the same people who were capable of these convoluted thought processes expected everyone else to behave logically. It explained why so many top hoods landed in prison on some dumb charge like possession of a blackjack, because they expected the cops who patted them down to assume they were smart enough to hire someone else to carry their weapons for them. Applying this same theory to Johns Davis in the wake of the botched garroting, they would expect him to react one of two ways, while his own instinct was to confound them by doing the opposite. Flight, to begin with, was a forgone conclusion; he would stay put. He firmly believed no new move would be made against him until after the flurry caused by the first died down, and was determined not to cut short his grace period by forcing an action. Nor was he about to relocate to territory unfamiliar to him and well-known to whatever local talent might be recruited to finish the job. The obvious alternative was to hire protection; for reasons already stated, and for one other, he would go it alone. Apart from being almost exclusively reactive, bodyguards had a long history of being turned. A string of Roman emperors and an even greater number of modern heads of state, crime bosses, shylocks, D.A.s, and bent police chiefs could testify to that if they weren't busy composting consecrated soil. The effect was to increase the firepower in the opposite camp, and at one's own expense. It was like hiring one's own hit.

He got up from his chair. He felt lonely and restless with Eugenia gone. He'd sent his housekeeper to visit her family in Nogales, partly for her protection, but mostly so if he heard a footstep in the house he'd know it wasn't friendly. He spread the slats in the blind covering his living-room window and looked out at the lighted street. A plain panel truck and two cars were parked against the curb. He couldn't see inside them, but he recognized his neighbor's Corvette. The truck was probably police surveillance, but it could also have been hired by whoever had found him inconvenient.

There was a time when cops drove Chryslers, the FBI Chevies, and the mob Fords, preferably Lincolns, and one knew where one stood depending upon which make was spending the most time in his orbit. Then the Germans and Japs had moved in, and then fuel shortages and high gasoline prices led to aerodynamic design, until a Caddy looked like a VW. Prestige meant shit if no one recognized it. So every local bureau, substation, and mob family made its own selection according to its budget. A power window humming down on the driver's side of a sleek gray Town Car could as easily expose a badge as a gun, and for that matter the twerp behind the wheel of a poky four-banger Cavalier could be an off-duty Stationary Traffic patrollie looking for a promotion to Al Ca-fucking-pone. It was a world of knock-offs and you couldn't tell the thugs from the bulls without a program.

The strange car might contain a killer, or more likely a spotter, who would turn over his notes on Davis's movements to Schev-chenko's successor, or it might contain a cop. Same with the panel truck. There was a cop in one of them for certain, but it didn't make Davis feel any less at risk. In 1936, Abe "Kid Twist" Reles, a syndicate enforcer who'd agreed to turn state's evidence against Lucky Luciano, sailed to his death out a skyscraper win-dow while under twenty-four-hour police guard, and the evi-dence of more recent events had done nothing to restore Davis's faith in the Thin Blue Line. The statistics involving police offi-cers moonlighting as contract killers were not encouraging.

He knew he was being watched, and that the only ones doing the watching who cared about his life were those who were de-termined to end it. At this point he'd lived with the knowledge long enough for the novelty to have begun to wear off. In fact the only part of the whole business that retained its bright blue edge was *why*.

The spotter's name was Edison. "Like the guy that invented the lightbulb," he said, in an empty tone that told Macklin he wasn't listening to himself. "No relation, my old man told me. If he was, I wouldn't be living in this shithole."

Macklin looked around. They were standing in the living room of a house in the bucolic-sounding San Antonio suburb of Meadowwood Acres. It was a double-wide trailer that had shed its wheels a long time ago, long enough anyway for trees and shrubs to grow close in and cast a cooling shade. He said the place looked pretty good to him.

"The *house* is okay, if you don't mind no room service and the neighbor's riding mower at seven ayem every Saturday it don't rain, and it never rains. It's Texas I'm talking about. I don't even like westerns. I came out here because my wife missed her family. Two years later she files for divorce and I'm lucky to keep the house. Soon as I can afford to relocate, I'm heading east, stopping every five hundred miles or so and buying something in three stores till three clerks in a row don't say, 'Y'all come back.' I'm stopping there and taking a room forty stories up." He studied Macklin. He had frank brown eyes in a long thin face that wasn't as young as it looked, although he wore his sandy hair in an extreme cut as if to pass for a man still in his twenties. He wore a short-sleeve madras shirt with the tail out over olive-drab cargo pants and scuffed black combat boots. "You're the new wet guy, huh? What's the capital of Texas?"

"San Saba. Whoever came up with that one needs a crash course in geography."

"Well, that was the idea. The Russky couldn't figure it out and I couldn't explain it to him. I'm glad they sent an American this time. They say they gave up that commie shit, but who left except the commies? I did all the sharing I plan to do in the settlement."

Macklin said nothing. The man was less brash than he tried to appear. It may have been part of the youth act, but he suspected Edison preferred being underestimated. He wouldn't be a spotter for long. That was okay, because people who dead-ended there became resentful and lazy and their reports couldn't be trusted.

Not that he trusted spotters in general. He did his own surveillance when he could, and when he'd worked full-time he had insisted upon it. Being handed a fat manila envelope and acting upon the information it contained, when he was the one taking all the risks, was like breaking into a strange room in the dark and finding his way through it based upon someone else's description of the placement of the furniture. It wouldn't be the spotter who barked his shins against a coffee table or fell over an unreported sleeping dog. But it was a hurry-up job and there was no time to start over from scratch.

That was why, when he'd called Edison's number, he'd held out for meeting him in his house rather than some neutral place. A man's living arrangements said a lot about who he was. What Macklin saw when he walked in—a large overstuffed sofa, worn but comfortable-looking, a fabric-covered armchair and a recliner upholstered in tough green Naugahyde, unremarkable pictures on the walls, a little dust, a little bachelor clutter—reassured him somewhat. A lot of sleek low European furniture, rustic cowboy decor, or a python in a glass cage, anything on that order would have told him he was working with a narcissist who was more caught up in his lifestyle than his livelihood. Liking or not didn't figure into the equation. He wasn't there to enjoy the company, just to collect information and decide whether the party who supplied it could be trusted not to leave anything out or embellish what he had. Edison's house was no showplace. Apart from the creature comforts of a portable CD player, a few books and magazines, and a nineteen-inch color TV, it was obviously intended for shelter only. He could decamp in fifteen minutes for the next city, the next job, leaving nothing behind that couldn't be replaced elsewhere. He was either a pro or had hung around pros long enough to know how to look like one, which often amounted to the same thing.

Macklin declined the offer of a drink, approving silently when his host poured himself a diet cola from a plastic two-liter bottle with a generic label in his refrigerator, and the pair sat down in the living room. Edison waited for Macklin to ask each question, then consulted a steno pad covered with an illegible scrawl or some personal code before answering. He added no information beyond what had been requested, proving that he was no showoff while testing his guest's ability to quiz him on the necessary details. He was as cautious as Macklin, with good reason. When an arranged killing blew up, it was often the spotter who took the fall, having exposed himself to more witnesses over a longer period of time, while the shooter was in and out and on his way home or to the next assignment before the first squeal went out. A clumsy interview set the stage for a clumsy hit, and he was best forewarned so he could begin packing immediately. Edison showed no such inclination. No, he wouldn't be spotting much longer. He was ready to move up to the next level, unless he was one of those who preferred not to shed blood while having no reservations about making it possible for someone else to do so. He was a man to talk shop with, share war stories, if Macklin were the type who did that. He wasn't.

He went through the photos Edison handed him, head and body shots taken from several angles with a long lens. He looked at each twice and handed them back. He'd know the face next time he saw it. That would be the last time.

Johns Davis had been in San Antonio eight years. He'd spent seed money he'd brought with him to establish the contacts he needed to run a respectable sports book, which through swift settlement of losses on his part, and short-term hiring among the local strong-arm talent to collect winnings from reluctant customers, had become the place to go in central and south Texas when one wished to place a bet on anything from NBA basketball to curling matches in Edinburgh. He'd done everything according to the rules, beginning with asking Spanish Rivera's permission to operate in his territory in return for a slice off the top, and winning the old Sicilian's confidence with a nearly one-hundred-percent collection record without a single fatality; although orthopedic surgeons in Austin, San Antonio, and Corpus Christi had learned to brace for a spate of compound fractures during the weeks following March Madness and the Super Bowl. When Davis's closest competitor decided to sell his sports book and retire, Rivera brokered the deal, negotiating a price that would maintain his Frank Lloyd Wright house in Galveston the rest of his life, but that would not put Davis so far into the hole he couldn't make it up during the next World Series. The fact that the first illegal gambling operation of its size to fall into non-Italian hands should do so almost without note was yet another sign that great changes had come to pass in the American underworld.

Johns Davis, Macklin learned, was sixty-one years old, a short-con artist who had graduated to the long con in his native Chicago, essentially applying the principles of the simple pigeon drop to the greater profits (and equally greater risks) of stock-market fraud. He'd played a little college ball at Loyola and knew enough about the sport to have passed himself off as a former NFL player and shorn a number of widows of their late husbands' life insurance as well as a couple of big-time speculators who ought to have known better. He had balls and some brains and no known serious health problems, so there would be no making it look like a heart attack or that he'd blacked out while driving along 410. That was no problem, since Macklin had been instructed to make it an open job, meaning the world should know it was murder.

Why this was so, or for that matter why Davis had to die, was not a question he felt compelled to ask. Edison wouldn't know, and if he asked Macklin, his stock would go down in Macklin's estimation. Curiosity was the first casualty of the work. If you knew why and didn't agree with the reason, your subconscious might force you to fuck up the job. Even more certainly, the more you knew, the greater threat you posed to the man who'd given you the assignment in the first place. No one in the Organization blamed the shooter in an unnecessary killing, but if the order might earn general disapproval, the man who issued it was at risk as long as there was someone out there who knew his motives. Macklin's very first killing, twenty years ago, involved a hitter who knew more than was considered safe. Ignorance—or the appearance of it—was the next-best defense against second-guesses.

Of course, the *best* defense was a working weapon. It was to the spotter's credit that he addressed the issue at the very moment Macklin's thoughts turned toward it.

"Carrying yet?"

Macklin said he wasn't.

"Didn't think so, but don't get sore at me for asking. There's an oilman waiting his turn at the needle in Huntsville because the horse's-ass he hired liked the Glock he used in Dallas and checked it through to Amarillo instead of chucking it into the Trinity River right after the mark went down. ATF matched it to a casing he left at the scene and he made a deal for a life sentence. A thing like that can shake your faith in the Pope."

"I never use automatics." Macklin offered no more information.

Edison nodded, understanding, and drank the rest of his cola. "I had the place swept this morning when I heard you were coming. Nobody's listening but the fucking rattlesnakes. Everything you've been told about guns and Texas is straight, but that doesn't mean you want to deal one from a barber or a lady cab driver. When you buy a piece that way you buy its history, too, and if you get picked up with it on you the difference is between a year mandatory for CCW and the needle for someone else's hit. You know about Goliad?"

"The whorehouse?"

"That's like saying, 'The Chicken McNugget place?' when somebody mentions McDonald's. They make as much money legitimately as they do upstairs. You can't go wrong in San Antonio if you put 'gun' or 'Davy Crockett' in the name of your business. You want to talk to Red Cotton there. Austine Holland runs the place, but if it's guns she'll just turn you over to Red, unless there's something about your look she doesn't like. Then you might as well go stand in the middle of U.S. 35 and wait for a tractor-trailer rig to run over you, because you won't be doing business in Texas."

"Until they need me."

"Except you could starve to death waiting for them to admit it. You left the United States when you came here."

"Bullshit. Everyone has to eat and piss, even people in Texas."

"Try telling them that. All you'll get is a speech."

"Do they know what you think of them?"

"They'd be suspicious if they didn't. They're worse than the French when it comes to outsiders going native. They don't thank me for my opinion, but they let me alone."

Macklin was irritated, and he was irritated at himself for becoming irritated. One year out of the loop and he'd turned into a citizen. He changed the subject. "Every cockshop madam I ever knew was a snitch."

"Well, sure. It's a whorehouse. But the Holland woman knows when to use the slow mail. You'll be back in Detroit before anyone acts on the information. I understand this one has to be done quick."

"Who said I'm from Detroit?"

"Don't sweat it. They didn't even tell me your name. Someone pointed you out to me in Toronto ten or eleven years ago. It was a big meet. You were with old man Boniface. I'd heard about you, so I took a good look."

"Not good enough. I'm not from Detroit and I've never been to Toronto."

Edison's face went flat. "My mistake."

Now he was more irritated than ever. He seemed destined to go through life having to kill people he'd started to like.

TWELVE

Leroy Skeets—who had spent much of the first half of his life persuading people to call him Abilene, a town he had never visited except through the magic of cinema—truly did not fear death. He'd been dead, and had found the experience itself not as troublesome as losing his keys.

"Roy, I'm going to kill you," his father had told him the year he turned fifteen. "I'm telling you that on account of I want you to know what's happening. Ain't nobody going to come stop it like in them cowboy pictures you like." Then he'd strangled him to death.

Abilene had fought as hard as he'd ever fought anyone, smashing the old man's nose and gouging his eyes, but Dan Skeets was six foot two and two hundred forty pounds and had served nine years in Little Rock for beating a man to death in a hardware store parking lot. His thumbs crushed Abilene's Adam's apple as if it were a beer can and his big red face with blood gushing out the nostrils shrank to pinpoints and went out like the picture on a TV tube. The boy was in a coma two weeks. When he woke up, a doctor told him the paramedics had jump-started his heart with paddles from no pulse at all, which was nothing new, but Abilene was the first person in the state of Arkansas to come back after he'd been declared brain-dead. That had happened at the hospital, after his mother had agreed to remove him from life support.

So he'd been dead twice. There had been no bright lights, no floating outside himself and looking down from the ceiling, none of that bullshit you heard about that made death sound like going on a ride at Six Flags, but on the other hand there had been no pain, either, just a kind of warm blackness, like drifting off under a thick quilt after a day spent in the raw cold.

He'd been found by his Uncle Bud, who'd stopped by to visit and got suspicious when he found the front door standing open and no sign of life inside. His mother had gone to Wal-Mart before the fight and his father had packed his things and some pawnable items in his army duffel and hitched a ride out of town, having made certain of Abilene before he left. Alerted by the state police in Arkansas, Missouri troopers traced him to a truck scale near Cape Girardeau, but could not determine whether he climbed aboard a rig there or took off on foot. He might have been abducted by aliens for all anyone heard of him after that. Abilene hoped that was true and that the little silver fuckers were still probing the son of a bitch.

Death didn't scare him one little bit, but he would never forget the pain and terror just before, or the weeks of recovery from three separate surgeries to repair his damaged larynx and vocal cords. He still suffered frequently from severe sore throats and lost his voice for days every time he caught cold. Knowing what he did about fear and pain was the chief asset he brought to his work. Too many times in the past, some *capo* had lost his head and had a snitch killed before finding out how much information he'd passed on and to whom, or some clumsy wet worker forgot himself during an interrogation, sticking an icepick too far into the brain or misjudging the strength of the subject's heart. Such cases required delicacy and a certain understanding of just how much a human being can stand. Abilene had that understanding, having been there and beyond. " 'A man has to know his limitations,' " he'd told Mr. Major, the first time they met. "Know who said that? Clint Eastwood. Well, I know mine, and I ain't so high on myself I think they're any bit less than anybody else's." Major had hired him based on that statement.

He'd never killed a man, but as he'd confided to certain people (victims and employers, mostly), he'd made one or two wish they had, and not just at the moment Abilene was working. Some men were more stubborn than others, and the more mule-headed they were, the higher their threshold of pain, the more likely the results were to be life-affecting. Cowards got off easiest. The sight of his knife alone was enough to bring some of them around. Depending upon the seriousness of their transgression, after they'd given up what was wanted they were let loose minus a finger or an ear as a warning to others, or turned over to someone else for quick extinction. Either fate was preferable to crippling. And so he had the reverse view of strength and courage from most of the rest of the human race—having them meant more work for him and a definite lowering of the quality of life for the afflicted party. Such virtues were like conscience, something invented by cops and ministers to make their jobs easier and Abilene's tougher. He himself had never known a twinge of guilt or a moment when protecting someone other than himself, sacrificing his life or his convenience for the benefit of another, seemed a reasonable course of action. All possibility that he ever would had been throttled out of him at age fifteen.

If pressed, he would concede that he enjoyed his work, but the enjoyment was in the satisfaction of a thing done well, not the act itself. He was no sadist, not a pervert who whacked himself off at the sight of hemorrhaging or the memory of a bubbling shriek. The head jobs you read about every day who skinned their victims, cooked their entrails in their brainpans and humped their ice-cold assholes, were individuals he would glady work on for free. That would be the only scenario in which his entertainment would come from the suffering. Abilene contributed. It was the sick shits that gave crime a bad name.

Women were easy. They weren't less courageous than men—some of them had shown themselves to be surprisingly obstinate and resilient—but they cared about their looks. The beauties, particularly, looked upon hamstringing and a simple broken nose as one and the same thing. Often a short rap to the mouth, like the one he'd given the Macklin woman, worked like a dose of salts. There was nothing better than a taste of one's own blood and a glimpse at a life of nights with one's teeth in a jar to put a girl wise. He considered women practical creatures, in the main unburdened with silly notions of stoicism and valor. And on occasion, when time was not at issue and the woman was easy on the eyes, Abilene could get himself a little bonus. Laurie Macklin was cute quail, there was no reason for hurry, and there was a hotel room all paid for and going to waste.

After he saw her back to the room, still in shock over what she'd learned about her bridegroom at the police station, he went back down to the lobby. There he waited for the clerk to finish checking out a fat bastard in an Armani knockoff who insisted he'd watched one less movie than appeared on his bill. Finally the clerk agreed to subtract the charge and the fat fuck hoisted his Samsonite and left.

"Which one he miss, *Big-City Titties* or *My Fair Anus*?" Abilene asked.

The clerk was a good-looking surfer boy and knew it, bleached his eyebrows to match his hair. He looked at Abilene without expression. "I wouldn't know, sir. Movie titles don't show up on the bill."

"Sure. What do they think, robots look up the tapes and stick 'em in? Like Lardass there would stretch out in his jammies and watch four movies in one night with Brad Pitt and Gwyneth Paltrow."

"Three, he said."

"Don't worry, you'll make it up on the next fatty from Chicago."

"Can I help you, sir?"

"Let's find out. I want the room next to twelve-oh-six. One with a connecting door."

"Twelve-oh-eight." The clerk tapped some keys. "I'm afraid that one's reserved. The party's expected by six o'clock."

"That's good. You won't have to move him."

"I can let you have twelve-eleven. Smoking, just down the hall."

"Nope. Twelve-oh-eight. If it's got a connecting."

"It has, but it's taken. I'm sorry, sir."

"Don't be. There's no need to be. This ain't a sorry day for you." The mirror finish on the veined marble behind the registration desk told him there was no one waiting behind him. He took his wallet, tan leather with stitching, *Abilene* tooled on one side, out of his hip pocket and counted bills onto the desk. It took awhile to stack ten of them one on top of another, but that was the idea. He'd tried using hundreds once, but although they did the trick he'd been disappointed by how quickly he'd come to five. Ten fifties added up to the same amount, but they seemed to go on and on and he enjoyed watching the eyes of clerks and receptionists, doormen and hostesses—people who in New York and L.A. made that much in a day, face it, it wouldn't change their lives as much as a good pair of Nikes—get wider and wider until a rap on the back of the head would pop them out like contact lenses. The great thing about the plastic economy was the increasing wizardry of cash. Ten crisp fifty-dollar bills, the new ones with Grant's big knobby face looking bigger and knobbier, had a larger effect than ten thousand dollars printed out on a cashier's check. It meant five hundred bucks Uncle Sam and the prick in the office in back didn't know about. It was like flipping off the president.

The clerk impressed him with his reserve. He picked up the bills and drummed the edges even on the shelf under the counter and slipped them into the inside breast pocket of his blazer, unhurriedly and without breaking a sweat. He tapped the keys again, asked Abilene how he would be paying, accepted the corporate card drawn on the account of Mr. Major's holding company in Burbank, and gave him his key card in its little folder. He explained that room service was available until midnight and that a complimentary breakfast was served between six and eleven A.M.

"Eat it yourself, Frankie. I'm ordering raw oysters in the morning."

THIRTEEN

The gun room and indoor firing range at the Goliad Rod and Gun Club were in the basement, which didn't look or feel like any basement Macklin had ever spent time in.

The bright Texas sun filtered in through vertical blinds over glass doorwalls on the walk-in end and through heat-treated slanted windows like solar panels. The sky looked wavy through the glass, and Macklin supposed the windows were extra thick or multiple-paned, possibly both, to deaden the noise of reports from inside. A silent ventilation system exchanged oxygen for stale air constantly, and humidifiers built into the walls kept the harsh Southwestern climate at bay. The long aisles of varnished wood separating the shooting stands from the targets might have belonged to any aboveground bowling alley in Miami or San Francisco, except for the western touches: What looked like an original Remington bronze of a six-hitch stagecoach clattering down a hill stood four feet high on a pedestal at the foot of the staircase that led down from the club rooms, and the carpet was an industrial-strength variation on a traditional Navajo design. The color scheme was sand and burnt-sienna.

The range, unoccupied in favor of the outdoor facility on a moderate day in the high eighties, was equipped with standard police-type silhouettes, with the occasional whimsical addition. There was a cartoon burglar in a black mask and striped jersey, a hippie flashing the peace sign, and a caricature bearing a slight resemblance to a former U.S. attorney general. The cabinet member had acquired a stitched facial scar and a Nazi uniform, possibly a precaution in the event of a lawsuit. Macklin assumed the Ayatollahs, Saddams, and bin Ladens came out on more public occasions. The targets were suspended from wires and pulleys, enabling the shooters to select the range and inspect the results. The score from the motion picture *Giant* floated softly out of wall-mounted speakers on a cushion of spent gunpowder.

The door to the gun room had no handle. He pressed a button set into the frame, but no sound issued from within, which meant the door had baffles and probably a steel core. Although there was a speaker grid next to the button, no one challenged him through it. Instead a flat buzzer sounded on his side and the lock clunked open. The receptionist he'd spoken to upstairs must have passed Edison's name downstairs through an intercom. Macklin stepped inside and let the door drift shut behind him. It made a little sucking noise easing into its airtight frame.

The room was a vault, but again unlike any in his previous experience. A tenth as large as the indoor range and windowless, it was paneled in real walnut, with a suspended ceiling that shed light through frosted panels from invisible fixtures above. The carpet was green pile and felt spongy beneath his feet. There were ventilators here as well, but they whispered steadily, as if wheezing from a greater effort. There was no other way for air to circulate, and without them whoever was inside would suffocate in minutes if he had no way to get out. The room, Macklin was sure, was a steel box, self-contained and set by cranes directly on the concrete slab that supported the basement before the rest of the building was constructed. In Texas, there was only one commodity that was considered precious enough to warrant such secure storage, and the racks and glass cases that lined the walls gleamed with it. He recognized a Mannlicher elephant gun among the more common Winchesters, Mausers, and venerable Krag repeaters, and saw a number of rifles he couldn't identify, with large bores and black composition stocks, although he suspected he'd have read about them if he'd been keeping up with new developments as he had in the past. Some were fitted with laser sights, an innovation he despised, both because branding a man with a floating red dot and thus warning him he was about to become a victim went against logic and because it eliminated the element of skill, which was the only thing he found worthy of respect in the character of the long-distance sniper. There were shotguns of every make as well, sporting models with hunting scenes engraved on the buttstocks and ambush guns with pistol grips only and barrels too short to be legal in any state, and scores of handguns. These included the homely Colt revolver whose design had not changed dramatically since frontier days and the Glock and Sig-Sauer semiautomatics that had flooded the American market about the same time the Detroit automobile industry went down on its knees before West Berlin and Tokyo. There was roughly two million dollars' worth of ordnance in sight, and probably a good deal more socked away behind hidden panels.

Three walls featured small built-in drawers to waist height, like the ones that contained screws and bolts in hardware stores. Each was labeled with the caliber of the cartridges it contained. The room itself was no larger than an ordinary living room, but it appeared to be a Home Depot of modern weaponry.

"We're a full-service gun club," said the man who shared the room with Macklin. "Which in Texas means we could arm a small revolution. Not *too* small. Which is why I have to ask if your interest is the overthrow of the Republic of the United States of America."

Red Cotton—if he was the man Edison had told him to ask for at Goliad—was a smallish man in his late sixties, with a belt of white hair stretched across his scalp from one ear to the other. He wore gold-rimmed glasses and a leather apron over a plain white shirt with the sleeves rolled to the elbows. Whatever else he wore was hidden behind a workbench with a battered zinc top, to which was bolted a vise with the frame and barrel of a Smith & Wesson Russian revolver—possibly a reproduction— clamped inside it. The barrel had been engraved with an oak- leaf design to within two inches of the muzzle. The man was holding an electric engraving tool. There was a sharp odor of scorched metal, and the last wisp of what had probably been a lot of blue smoke was coiling into a square vent in the ceiling above his head.

What if it is? Macklin thought of asking, but did not. The man looked as if he had even less sense of humor than he. His bald dome and old-fashioned glasses made him resemble a Swiss watchmaker, or what Macklin imagined a Swiss watchmaker would look like in a world of French headwaiters, Italian barbers, and Irish cops. He certainly didn't look like a man named Red.

"I'm not interested in overthrowing anything," Macklin said.

"Didn't think so, but I had to ask. Last year I held two members of the Lone Star Militia here with that Mannlicher for an hour and a half until the Rangers showed up. They were asking about MAC-10s by the case, and things I don't carry, tear-gas canisters and fragmentary grenades. They said in their statements they wanted to hit the Cattleman's Bank in Houston and finance an insurrection. My father died on Iwo Jima. I served three weeks in the marines before they discharged me because of asthma. I pay my taxes and I don't do business with treasonous scum."

"How'd they get this far?" Macklin wasn't curious, but the man seemed to want to make conversation. It probably had to do with spending all day locked in a room with nothing to talk to but recoil springs and hollow-points.

"One of them used someone's name, like you. I'm Red Cotton. I never had red hair, they just started calling me that to tick me off because I hate communists. Only I don't mind it. It has dash, which is more than I can say for my real name. I won't ask yours and don't tell me. If I sell you a weapon I don't care what you do with it as long as you don't use it on an American soldier in uniform or the governor of Texas or the president of the United States. Senators and congressmen are okay, if they're crooked. If you shoot them for their ideology, you'd better not come back here." He tilted his head a fraction of an inch in the direction of the elephant gun.

"I don't even vote."

"Now, you were better off not telling me that. Travis didn't die at the Alamo so you could sit on your dead ass and let a bunch of wetbacks decide who sits in the White House."

"He wasn't doing it for the United States."

"Patrick Henry, then. The point's the same."

"I mean I can't vote. I've got a felony conviction on my record."

"That's different. What's your preference?"

"Thirty-eight revolver. Smith and Wesson, if you've got it. Charter Arms and Dan Wesson are okay, too."

"Buy-American man. Not an automatic?"

"I don't use automatics."

"Smart. No loose shell casings."

Macklin said nothing.

"What about a magnum?" Cotton asked. "Three-fifty-seven's the same caliber but it's got more muscle."

"Too much. I like a bullet to stay where I put it, not pass on through."

"If it's stopping you want, you'd do better with a forty-four or-five. I've got one of the new fifties. I don't know what your budget is."

"Too big a kick. Have you got what I want or not?"

Cotton crouched behind the workbench. There was a sliding sound, and Macklin stepped back instinctively, but the other man merely stood and rested a pull-out tray on top of the bench.

It was lined with gray felt and blue steel. Among the half-dozen handguns nestled in molded depressions were a Smith & Wesson Chief's Special with a two-inch barrel and two other Smiths, a Model 15 Combat Masterpiece and a Model 28, called the Highway Patrolman, with four- and six-inch barrels, respectively. Macklin ignored the snubnose Chief, hesitated over the long-barreled Highway Patrolman, then grasped the Combat Masterpiece by its walnut handle. He swung out the cylinder, confirmed the chambers were empty, snapped it back into the frame with a twist of his wrist, and rotated it with his free palm while holding the hammer back with his thumb. It turned freely, without wobbling. The hammer was a little stiff, affecting the trigger pull, but he distrusted hair triggers. The gun balanced well.

"It hasn't been test-fired," Cotton said. "The hammer'll loosen up after it's been fired around a couple of times. It's straight from the factory, a virgin piece. That'll cost you. I've got another one all broke in; you'll save a couple of hundred, but it was used once, to make a point. Someone put a slug in a ceiling."

"Not interested, unless he took it with him. What about the serial number?" He ran his thumb over the embossed digits.

"On file at the factory, nowhere else. It's unregistered. That's the part that costs."

"What about the six-inch?"

"It's registered to a dealer in Oklahoma City. He died. Natural causes. Trail ends there."

Macklin put down the four-inch and hefted the Highway Patrolman. It was barrel-heavy, but that steadied the aim. The hammer worked smoothly. "I'll try them both."

"Go ahead. I reserved the range for the next hour. No one'll interrupt you."

"No one better."

Cotton laid the Combat Masterpiece on the counter and replaced the drawer. He came up with a box of .38 cartridges, but before handing it to Macklin he removed a harness from a peg behind the counter, climbed into it, took a P-38 from the underarm clip, jacked a shell into the chamber, and returned it to the clip. He did all this without flourish and without looking at Macklin. Then he pushed the box across the counter.

When Macklin was loaded, they went out into the range, where Cotton stood back while Macklin took his place at one of the stands and ran one of the silhouette targets to forty feet. He never risked a working shot at that range except in an emergency, but it would tell him how well the guns were sighted. He ignored the earphones resting on the stand until he'd fired a bullet from each revolver. Some guns were louder than others, and he didn't want to flinch when it counted because he was unprepared for the volume. Then he put on the earphones and emptied both weapons, pausing from time to time to check his marksmanship and to compare the guns' performances.

He removed the earphones. "They're both a little off."

"I can adjust them. Be a minute."

"I adjusted myself already. I'll take the four-inch."

"A lot of people prefer the six."

"I'm one. But it takes all day to haul out."

"Harder to conceal, too."

Macklin said nothing to that. "How much?"

"Thousand. It's a virgin piece, like I said. Throw in a box of cartridges."

"All I'll need is six in the cylinder."

"You might want to keep one empty under the hammer."

"That's an old wives' tale."

"Old wives whose husbands shot their dicks off by mistake."

"I'll dress it in the opposite direction." Macklin peeled ten one-hundred-dollar bills off the roll he'd been carrying since he left Detroit. From old habit he never used travelers' checks or ATMs, drawing out what he needed at home, with a cushion for emergencies. If he ran out he could pawn his luggage.

"Glad to see you don't haggle."

"Would it get me anywhere?"

"Out that door, without what you came for. I hate skinflints more than traitors." Cotton recounted the bills and put them in an apron pocket. "I'll clean it." He picked up both guns from the stand and turned toward the gun room.

"I'll watch," said Macklin, following.

FOURTEEN

At three P.M., Housekeeping rang to ask Mrs. Macklin if they could make up the room. She told them not to worry about it. After she hung up, she realized she should have asked for clean towels, but she didn't feel like talking to anyone so she didn't call back.

She'd had the DO NOT DISTURB sign out since last night, and had asked the operator to hold any calls except from Mr. Macklin. That was habit. She was nearly as terrified to hear from Peter as she was to speak to Abilene.

Culver City the day before had been a nightmare. Not the place itself. It seemed a pleasant-enough area made up of pretty little houses on steep hills with steps leading up to them for what seemed like hundreds of feet. They would be forty-thousand-dollar cottages back home, but Abilene said they went for a quarter-million and were never on the market for long. They went past the Warner Brothers studios, rows of hangarlike buildings she'd seen many times in aerial shots in documentaries about Hollywood. ("*Maverick*, my favorite when I was little," he'd said, pointing out one of the soundstages. "They did all the interiors there. The western town's still standing on the backlot. Hang a sign on the train station saying 'Tombstone' or 'Dodge City' or 'Purgatory,' one of them made-up names, bingo, you're in a different town. You seen all them buildings a hundred times if you watch westerns.") She'd barely looked. He'd insisted on getting out and showing her the steps where Laurel and Hardy kept losing the piano. It looked like all the other flights of steps cut into the hills, and she declined his invitation to climb them.

Nothing distinguished the place from every other he'd driven her through, and she couldn't tell when they'd left Los Angeles and were in Burbank or wherever. She was afraid to say that, afraid not to feign interest, afraid of him, afraid of Peter, afraid, afraid, afraid. Cheerful Spanish Modern houses with white-washed stucco walls and red tile roofs frightened her now the way the long dark hallway on the second floor of her grand-father's farmhouse had frightened her when she was ten and couldn't get *The Shining* out of her head. She didn't know what she might do or say that might make him hit her or stick her with that ugly knife.

Back in the room at the end of that long day, she'd been afraid he'd come to her door. She was no innocent, not like the young women in old movies who didn't know what some men were capable of. She'd been no virgin when she met Peter, and she was pretty sure she'd been raped on a date once, although she'd had too much to drink at the time and knew she would have no satisfactory answer if asked if she'd encouraged the act, and so she hadn't reported it. The way Abilene looked at her sometimes was the same way the boy had looked at her before he'd taken her home and she'd been foolish enough to say her grandparents were out. If Mr. Major hadn't told Abilene not to hit her or threaten her, he probably hadn't told him not to fuck her, either, and even if he had, she had no reason to expect him to obey.

Well, he hadn't come to her door. But she knew if she went out, he'd be there in the hallway waiting, or down in the lobby the way he had been the first night. She'd slept with the door double-locked and the chair that belonged to the little writing desk propped under the knob, and when she woke up she'd turned on the TV for company. It had been on all day. The programs were undiverting: infomercials, weather reports, some-one else's horror in the Middle East, a dumb comedy with Rock Hudson and Doris Day. The Turner channel was playing *Murder,*

Incorporated. She couldn't take more than a minute of that. Gangster films used to be her favorite, but she knew she would never watch one again.

Peter was a gangster. Worse than that, he was a hired murderer like that other Peter in the movie, Peter Falk. Not the cuddly cop on *Columbo.* A rat who knifed people on crowded subways and threatened witnesses with death if they went to the police to tell what they'd seen. Peter—her Peter—would do the same to her.

No. She didn't believe that. When she didn't, at the time she didn't, she was thinking of the look on his face close up when they made love. At the moment of release, there was a vulnerability she knew no one else ever saw. That other Mrs. Macklin would have seen it, but if she'd known what it meant, she'd forgotten, or they would still be married. But there had been no such look or promise of it on the face in the picture she'd seen at police headquarters. That was the face she feared, the one she saw when she thought of him out there now, preparing to murder someone.

This time, though, there was a difference. He wasn't killing for money or to protect himself, but to keep her safe. And so the two faces kept superimposing themselves upon each other, changing from evil to tender and back to evil, like one of those holographic images on a ticket to a sold-out rock concert, depending upon the angle you held it.

She could call the police and the whole thing would end that day. *The whole thing* including her life with Peter, because he would certainly go to prison with Abilene and Major and whoever else was involved. Or she could keep the police out of it and preserve her relationship with a killer. Or if something went wrong on Peter's end, he might be killed himself. She did not know how long he'd been inactive, and supposed one got sluggish and careless in that as in everything else, from lack of practice. When she thought of that, pictured Peter sprawled in a pool of his own blood on some street in some unknown city, staring at the sky without blinking, it was the Peter who'd swerved to miss an inattentive seagull on the Coast Highway she thought of, and not the sullen criminal in the photograph.

That image, of Peter's eyes sightless in a head haloed with blood, was on her mind when the knock came. It startled her as if she'd been dozing and dreaming, and she was certain it was a policeman knocking at her door to tell her she was a widow.

Her head was swimming when she swung her legs off the bed, and she realized she had fallen asleep. She glanced at the clock—3:03, so it had been just a brief doze after all—and went to the door, stopping on the way to run her fingers through her hair before the mirror above the bureau. Did wives do that when they knew they were about to receive word their husbands were dead? The terrible certainty came to her that she was unprepared to be a proper tragic figure.

The chair jammed under the doorknob reminded her of the need for caution. She put an eye to the peephole. No one was standing outside. Just as she took in that information, the knocking started again, and she realized it wasn't coming from the hallway.

As she followed the sound, it took on a kind of jaunty rhythm—not the conventional shave-and-a-haircut, more of a marimba beat. And she knew before she got to the door that connected with the next room who was on the other side.

"Yes?" The single word sounded prim. She was suddenly aware that she was wearing only a dressing gown. She clutched the collar ends together.

"Me, nursie. Open up." Abilene's voice was as clear as if nothing separated them. Which was nearly true. Two inches of air and a sixtieth of an inch of flimsy veneer on either side. All this time barricaded from the outside, and he'd been there all along. He could have punched through with his fist. She knew the power behind that fist. He'd held most of it back before and still drawn blood.

"I'm not dressed."

She regretted saying it. In the pause that followed she felt as if she were standing naked in an open doorway. She knew that was how he was picturing her.

"Well, throw something on. We're going out for a bite."

"I'm not hungry."

"Pardon me for calling a lady a liar, but I could eat the asshole out of a skunk, and I had a big breakfast. Them candies on your pillows wouldn't keep a Rhode Island flea alive."

"I had lunch. I ordered in."

"I ain't in Jersey. There ain't been a room-service waiter at your door all day."

"How did you get that room?"

"Tell you all about it over steaks. There's a chop house on La Cienega where good steers go when they die. They shot part of *Prizzi's Honor* there. I know all you farmgirls like your meat bloody."

"Medium rare," she said, surrendering.

She was famished.

FIFTEEN

A ce Aberdeen was observing the third anniversary of his decision to have his first name legally changed.

Ace was not a nickname. His father, who traced his lineage to a slave in Virginia, had inherited the family name Angus from that individual, who had taken the name of the Scotsman who had owned him and the plantation where he worked until Emancipation. In a move intended to ingratiate himself with his in-laws, the latest Angus had combined his first initial with those of his wife's father, Charles, and her brother, Everett, when it came time to christen his firstborn son.

People had considered Ace a cute name when he was small, and when he was in high school it had led acquaintances to think he had dash, at least until familiarity proved otherwise. But since his current standard of living depended significantly upon gambling, the name was a liability. It had become increasingly difficult to persuade fellow employees at the succession of firms where he'd worked to take part in football pools started by a man everyone called Ace, and poker games were hard to find. People were becoming more cynical. If it weren't for professional bookies, who didn't care what a man called himself as long as he settled his losses in decent order, he would have been forced to subsist on his paycheck, and the even more uncertain income brought in by his part-time fencing operation. This was

out of the question with an ex-wife in Kansas who was suffi-
ciently unliberated to accept alimony, and an eight-year-old boy
in Indiana named Angus who required support.

He'd settled on Darien. It was a name with poetry, slightly
studious, but not uncommon among black men. The Scots surname, coupled with the dubious Ace, prepared people for something else. By and large they were unaware of how many
Southerners were descended from Scottish colonists, or how
many of *them* lent their names to their slaves. People didn't like
to be surprised, to admit they were guilty of misconception, and
sooner or later they came to resent the person they'd been mis-
taken about. That was no way to begin a gambling relationship.
A Christian name like Darien kept them from jumping to con-
clusions.

Darien it was going to be, then. But it had been going to be
for three years, because whenever he had enough put aside for
the filing fee, the goddamn Saints (or Lions, Lakes, Steelers,
Nets, Ravens; enter name of team here) missed the spread and
he was back to case dough. The fee wasn't that much. It was
just that all his sure things seemed to go south on him just when
the rent was due or his alimony was late or his car insurance
was about to expire, and the longer he'd gone without changing
his name the less urgent it seemed against the prospects of moving into the street or going to jail or losing his only means of
transportation in a place where everything he needed was a
twenty-minute drive away, minimum. Lately he'd begun to think
God wanted Ace to stay Ace or He'd pick some other time to
fling shit at him.

He was still stinking up the place from the latest round, Tampa
fucking Bay tromping the Rams in a game that all the oddsmak-
ers had put in the win column for St. Louis a week before kick-
off. Jackson had played the second half like a kid in the Pee-Wee
League, and the Bucs had walked right over him and spiked
Darien Aberdeen right along with the game ball.

Ace rented his house in Leon Valley, a town whose address
he never used because it sounded to him like another name for
Steve Urkel, that annoying nerd kid that lived all over the TV

dial in reruns. Instead he'd taken a post-office box in the city. A. *Aberdeen, San Antonio* had resonance. Names, of people and places, were important to him. If it meant an hour there and back to pick up his mail, or by God another three years to scratch up court costs so the bank would accept his endorsement on checks made out to Darien Aberdeen, the results were worth the time. Time was one thing a man had plenty of in Texas, if he weren't an oilman or a killer on Death Row.

When the word *killer* occurred to him, he turned his head and spat, missing the sidewalk in front of the post office. He was as superstitious as any gambler, and he shared every other suburbanite's fear of the city, which, like most deposited its worst elements outside government buildings. The duffel bums and a couple of meth dealers he knew by sight if not by name were already working their way among the natives and tourists, smelling the coming of sunset. In a couple of hours they'd be shooting up and dealing in front of the monument to the heroes of the Alamo.

Today there was nothing in his box except bills and a glossy circular offering him the opportunity to acquire the world's greatest books for the low price of $39.95 a month for the rest of his life. He was still trying to get through last year's Stephen King, and there wasn't a third notice among the bills, so he chucked it all in the trash can outside the post office and went to the Riverwalk for an early supper.

Julio, his favorite waiter at the Mexican restaurant where he liked to read the sports sections in the L.A., Denver, and New York papers over a plateful of smothered burritos and two Dos Equis, led him to a table by the railing, where he could watch the tourists craning their necks on the flatboats, and ogle the fine tall Texas women in their little white shorts and blouses tied under their breasts. There was just enough breeze to blow away the humidity, and he was content to sit there with the papers stacked on the table and count belly buttons. He needed those tight tan midriffs and long brown legs to settle his thoughts, which for some reason had turned dark.

When Julio bustled out from the restaurant's shadowed interior to seat another lone customer, Ace looked up and damn near crossed himself. He wasn't Catholic, but he preferred to play the percentages. God was fucking with him again, sending Johns Davis to him only moments after he'd been thinking the word *killer*.

Well, Davis wasn't a killer, but someone had tried to kill him, and in Ace's book it amounted to the same thing. Death was contagious. People caught it like a cold, for no other reason than that they had stood too close to someone who was carrying it. It didn't help that it was Davis who'd taken his action on the Rams disaster. Ace snatched the top paper off the stack and spread it open in front of his face. It happened to be the financial section from the *Post*, all those rows of little numbers, with no odds in sight. Talk about gambling.

"Ace, it's me, for chrissake. You don't know Wall Street from Walgreen's. Put down the fucking paper."

He lowered it. "Jesus, Johns, it ain't been forty-eight hours. How'd you find me?"

"Your phone didn't answer. You eat here every time you're in town. I'm not collecting today. Unless you've got it."

"I don't, but I will. My credit's good."

"I don't care what your credit is. What do I look like, TRW? Your food's here."

He hadn't noticed Julio hovering over him with the steaming plate. He laid aside the newspaper and let the waiter set it and his beer down.

"Sir?" Julio looked at Davis.

"You serve Miller Lite?"

"Yes, sir."

"Okay. I'm not eating." He sat down opposite Ace. "I can't eat Mexican. You believe it, living here? I gas up like the Goodyear blimp. Go ahead and eat. I don't mind watching it. You heard what happened, I guess."

"I heard something." Ace took a bite of his beef burrito, then tried the bean and then the chicken. Today they tasted like the same grade of soggy cardboard. He'd never eaten in a bookie's presence before. Gamblers and the people who took their action didn't belong to the same class. One wasn't higher than another. They were just different.

"You hear anything else? Like who punched the ticket?"

"Hell, no. I saw all I know on the news. You think I'm an underworld character? Man, I *got* to change my name."

"You think *I* am? Which is why I came looking for you." Julio came with his beer. Davis waited until he left, then leaned forward on his elbows. "You still deal merchandise, right?"

"I sold some things."

"Guns?"

"A time or two. To friends. Other people, strangers, you never know when it's going to come back and bite you on the ass. These days you're better off selling dope, and I wouldn't touch that. Man in your work, I'd of thought you had all you need."

"What, dope? This beer and a Scotch later, that's it for my day."

"I mean guns."

"I had a gun, you think I'd let some shit choke me to death in front of the fucking Alamo? I place bets, Ace. I'm not in the Cosa fucking Nostra. I wouldn't know the handshake."

"You try Goliad?"

"Goliad's the first place I'd go, if I didn't know the Spaniard had controlling interest there."

"You think it's Rivera?" Ace lowered his voice, and they were already whispering.

"He says no. He wouldn't lie, right? So can you help me out or what?"

"I think I can help you out." Ace sat back.

After a moment Davis exhaled. "Okay, you're in for a grand and a half on the Tampa Bay game. Call it a grand and I'll credit you a dime next time out. That's pretty generous, considering I could score a Saturday Night banger on Commerce for a couple of dimes."

"If you could you would. But okay. You did all right on Tampa Bay, huh?"

"Couldn't've done it without Jackson."

"You know he was going to tank?"

"He didn't tank. No one can afford to pay a first-string NFL quarterback to tank. That went out when free agency came in."

"You knew something, though. I called all over Vegas and they wouldn't give me your odds."

"I haven't got Vegas's overhead."

Ace gave up. "Fall into my place around seven. I'll have something then."

Davis rose and put two singles on the table. "For the beer."

After he left, Ace cleaned his plate and ordered another Dos Equis. Everything had begun to taste better.

The gun was a 9-millimeter Ruger, with plastic grips and a brushed finish. It looked to Davis like a faucet. He knew next to nothing about firearms and Ace had to show him how to rack in a shell and take off the safety. He gave him a box of cartridges and demonstrated the loading procedure.

The bookie hefted the pistol, feeling awkward. "You got like a holster? I can't carry this thing in my pocket."

Ace rummaged through the junk drawer in his kitchen and snapped a couple of rubber bands around the handle. "Stick it in your pants in back. You got a nice little hollow there so it won't stick out. The rubber bands'll keep it from sliding down into your crack."

Davis did that, dropping the tail of his sportcoat over the handle, and tried walking around the room. "I feel like the fucking Tin Man."

"I hear you get used to it. I wouldn't know. I bought it in a lot from a collector that didn't want his guns going to his wife in the divorce. It's registered to a dealer in Dallas, so if you lose it, let me know so I can tell him to report it stolen. If you have to shoot anyone, get rid of it and call me."

"I hope to Christ I won't be calling you." He took another turn around the kitchen. "It's not so bad. I feel better just having it."

"Good luck, man."

"Fuck luck. I'm a bookmaker."

Davis couldn't get comfortable in the driver's seat, so he took the gun out and put it in the glove compartment. The car was a Cougar he was renting while the Jag was in the body shop. He hated the automatic running lights and the goddamn seat belt that fitted itself around his torso when he turned the ignition and that he had to duck under whenever he got in. The dome light came on whenever he parked and turned off the ignition, which made him a fine target. He'd taken care of that by switching the light off manually, but he'd be a lot happier when he had his car back. He hoped he'd live that long.

He'd been lost in these thoughts and had no idea how long the lights had been flashing in his rearview mirror when he heard the swoop of the siren. It scared the living shit out of him, but not as much as when he'd swung over to the curb and put it in park and remembered anyone could get hold of lights and a siren. He thought of the gun in the glove compartment. But if it *was* a cop, he could get shot reaching for it. And he was wondering irritably just what good a gun was at all when someone tapped on his window. He sighed and whirred it down. What the hell. It was probably better than the fucking garrote.

"Mr. Davis, I'm Lieutenant Childs, with the San Antonio Police. Would you mind telling me what you were doing at Ace Aberdeen's house? I've got a man there asking him the same question."

He looked from the gold-and-enamel shield in the man's hand to his face, young and black behind prim-looking spectacles that glittered in the bouncing red-and-blue lights. He remembered the face from police headquarters.

"Jesus, I'm glad to see you."

When the lights went on in the windshield of the unmarked car that separated his rental from Davis's, Macklin drifted over to the curb and killed his headlamps. He'd been aware since leaving San Antonio that his was one of two vehicles following the bookie, but had been uncertain until that moment whether Maggiore was doubling up on him. He knew then it was the police. The hunchback was superstitious about cops and would no more have one of his people impersonate one than a certain kind of person would sit in a wheelchair if his legs worked and he didn't want to tempt fate.

He watched as the young man in plainclothes stooped to accept something from the driver of the Cougar, and saw the light reflect dully off the brushed finish of the semiautomatic pistol as he carried it back to his car. The young man got in and pulled away, swerving around Davis, who drove off a moment later.

It hadn't been an arrest, then, just a disarming. If it weren't a Maggiore operation, he'd have suspected the police were cooperating. Instead they were just using Davis as bait. That was useful to know.

During the conversation up ahead, Macklin had reached down and poked the .38 farther under his seat so the handle wouldn't show in case the officer had noticed him pull over and came back to shine a flashlight inside the car. Only amateurs and idiots stashed guns in the glove compartment. That was the first place cops looked.

SIXTEEN

There was a forty-minute wait for seating at the chop house on La Cienega. Abilene left his name—the host, a twenty-something with zigzags shaved into his carroty temples, didn't raise a brow at the sound of it—and he and Laurie found a seat at the bar. There were rose-colored mirrors behind the bar and movie posters in frames on the walls. An ordinary-looking suit of clothes hanging in a glass case near the telephones had a printed card identifying it as one of the costumes Jack Nicholson had worn in *Prizzi's Honor*. A framed photograph of the actor with his arm around a man in a bad hairpiece bore Nicholson's signature in black marker. Laurie supposed the man in the hairpiece was the owner. She asked the bartender for a Kahlua and cream.

"Tequila, straight," Abilene said. "No fruit or shit."

"You want me to hold the lime?"

Abilene showed his teeth like Nicholson. " 'I want you to hold it between your knees.' "

The bartender's face went stiff and he turned away to pour the drinks. Laurie guessed he was too young to have seen *Five Easy Pieces*, even the last time it was shown on TV.

"You believe that?" Abilene said. "I mean, every time he looks up from the tap, Jack's staring right at him."

"Maybe he doesn't have cable." She wished the young man

would hurry up with her drink. Making conversation with Abilene was something she didn't want to do sober.

"What you think of Hollywood so far?" Before she could answer, he said, "Tell you what I thought the first week. It's phony, but I expected that. What I liked, it didn't know it. I mean, the town conned itself better than it did the tourists. It bought into its own backstory. 'Backstory,' that's a word you hear a lot when you hang around the studios. They think they can make anything stand up if they shovel in enough horseshit behind it. Thing is, most of the time they're right. That's how come a freak like Jim Carrey pulls down twenty million a picture and a great actor like Jimmy Caan has to do shit like *Mickey Blue Eyes*. You ever see *Thief*?"

"I think so. Carroll O'Connor was the crime boss?" She scooped up her glass and sipped. The bartender had used milk instead of half-and-half. She wondered if that was because Abilene had offended him.

"No, that was *Point Blank*, which was a pretentious piece of shit. Except for Lee Marvin, my man Lee, who couldn't help being great. It was Robert Prosky in *Thief*. Anyway, the studios will reissue a great flick like that in an anniversary edition, wet all over themselves telling how good Jimmy Caan is, sell them cassettes and DVDs, then turn around and cast him in a piece of shit for scale and all the doughnuts he can eat off the caterer's cart. They'll even mention *Mickey Blue Eyes* on the *Thief* box so the kiddies'll know who he is. They really believe it when they say both pictures are great, on account of what *Mickey* did the first weekend. They write puff and then they read it and say, 'Holy shit, this picture's even better than we thought.' It's kind of sweet."

Laurie took a long drink. She hadn't eaten all day and the coffee-flavored liqueur was filling her head like a balloon. "Do you think you could complete a sentence without using the word *shit*?"

"What's that?" He turned his head away from his glass.

"It's redundant. The word loses all its power. And it makes you sound stupid."

He turned back and watched himself drinking tequila in the mirror. "You're a cheap drunk, lady. One gulp and you're gone. That how Macklin got you in bed the first time?"

She unhooked one of her heels from the rung of the stool and put it on the floor. He grasped her wrist, shutting off her circulation.

"I need to use the ladies' room."

"I'll walk you over. The place is full of sleazebags."

Tiny, crowded tables took up most of the space on the way to the little corridor leading to the restrooms. He steered her expertly between them with his hand on her upper arm. He wasn't gripping it as hard as he could, but she knew his fingers would leave bruises.

There was no line, a lucky break. There was no window in the ladies' room either, which was not so lucky. She passed a pair of women freshening their makeup at the mirror—one wore a full-length evening gown and bolero jacket in black velvet, the other a purple leather miniskirt and red brassiere—and entered a vacant stall, where she sat on the toilet seat and thought.

She'd dressed for comfort, not for glamor: short-sleeved rayon shirt, loose, pleated slacks, flats with waffled soles, her walking shoes, packed with the Walk of Fame in mind. She'd left her purse in the room, clipped a hundred dollars in twenties, her driver's license, and American Express card together and put them in a pocket. No makeup case or even sunglasses, nothing to carry. It was as light as she'd traveled since she'd passed out of her tomboy phase. She felt like a spy, or some kind of fugitive from the law. Which, in a way, she was—a fugitive from the law, anyway—because Abilene had so clearly demonstrated that the police were not her salvation. It was as if she were the criminal. These were the thoughts that trampled through her head as she sat fully clothed on the toilet seat in one of the stalls.

Five minutes seemed to be the far frontier of Abilene's patience. The air stirred as the door opened from the corridor, followed by a sharp gasp from one of the women at the mirror. Cowboy heels clomped on tile.

"Pull up your panties, ladies. I'm a Texas Ranger. There's a woman in here kidnapped a little boy in Dallas for immoral purposes."

More intakes of breath, feet shuffling toward the exit. The door drifted shut on silence.

Abilene grunted. He was crouching to peer under the first in the line of stalls. Laurie was in the third, standing on the seat now, hunched over to keep her head from sticking above the partition. She reached out and carefully slid back the latch, holding the door shut with a thumb as she did so. She could hear her heart hammering.

She saw a glint off a silver-capped toe, heard again the grunt as he lowered himself to push-up position on the floor outside her stall. *Now.* She pounced, pushing off with her feet and throwing all her weight against the door.

He was just getting up. She pushed through the resistance when the door struck him, in the shoulder or head, tipping him off his hands and the balls of his feet. She hurdled him as he fell sprawling, lost her balance when she touched down, but caught herself on the edge of a sink and kept going, not looking back, tore open the door to the corridor and ran down it and across the lounge, bumping tables and knocking over glasses and caroming off a man who was putting on his coat. She used her shoulder as a battering ram to clear a way through a gaggle of customers in the entrance. Shoving open the door she tripped on the threshold and fell to one knee on the front step, skinning it and tearing her pants. A parking attendant in a red blazer threw away his cigarette and stepped in to help her, but she was on her feet before he could bend down, bounding down the steps to the sidewalk.

There was a line of cabs in front of the building, but the closest was the one at the end, where the driver was holding the door for a woman who was getting out of the back. Laurie shoved her out of the way and scrambled into the seat. For an instant their faces were two inches apart, but it would be minutes before she realized the angry expression belonged to Kathleen Turner.

"Go!" she shouted to the driver, but he was already behind

the wheel, pushing down the accelerator. Later she would wonder how many agitated females he had been called upon to sweep away from popular places in a hurry. She looked back through the rear window and saw what looked like the crown of a cream-colored Stetson bobbing above the heads of the crowd on the sidewalk, making its way toward the first cab in line.

"Please go faster."

The car lunged. The automobiles in Los Angeles, basted together as the place was by multiple lanes of concrete and asphalt, all seemed to be powered by engines not normally available to passenger vehicles. A pair of kind-looking eyes in a dark face looked at something in the rearview mirror, then met her gaze. They looked like Morgan Freeman's, tragic and tolerant.

"I can tie this guy up in knots," the driver said.

"Please."

The cab swung right into a side street from the inside lane, forcing the driver of a haulaway carrying yet more cars into the city to whoosh his air brakes to avoid collision, picked up speed in a narrow aisle between parked cars, spun left into a broad boulevard, then right again through a parking lot and out into a kind of alley that looked as if it hadn't been paved since before color television. Laurie had a good sense of direction, but lost her bearings quickly in the tangle of one-way streets, commercial drives, and palm-lined avenues that followed. After what must have been a hundred blocks, they slowed down, and she stopped looking through the rear window.

She leaned forward, gripping the back of the front seat. "My husband—"

She stopped. Nothing beyond those two words was safe to say.

They were stopped at a light. The driver twisted in his seat and rested a forearm with an anchor tattooed on it across the top. It made her think of Popeye, but there was nothing cartoonish about the expression that went with the sad eyes.

"I'm an old fart, I give advice," he said. "You can tell me to shut up and drive and it won't hurt my feelings none. Any husband worth running from is worth getting rid of."

"It's not what you think. But thanks."

The light changed. As if he could see it through the back of his head he turned back around and crossed the intersection.

Laurie sat back. She looked at the driver's face on his chauffeur's license attached to the back of the seat. He was younger in the photo, and wore a beard that he'd shaved off since, but the eyes were the same. She thought again of Morgan Freeman, and that made her think of something else.

"Your name's Martin?" she said.

"Yes, ma'am. I was named after Dr. King. Not Junior, his daddy. My mama used to sing in his choir in Atlanta, so she said. I never heard her sing a note."

"My name's Laurie. I was named after Lauren Bacall."

"I don't guess Miz Bacall would mind if she ever saw you."

"Do you like movies, Martin?"

"I always say yes to that question. In this town you got to, even if you don't. I don't know as you noticed, but that was Miz Kathleen Turner you almost knocked over getting in."

"I noticed. I wasn't that far gone. What about Jim Carrey?"

"I never drove him."

"I meant do you like his movies?"

"They're okay. I'm a Wayans man myself. But, yeah, he's all right. I guess I like him."

"What about James Caan?"

"I drove him once. He was with some people, so we didn't talk. He's made some good ones. *The Godfather*, that was terrific. My wife liked *For the Boys*."

"How does he compare to Jim Carrey?"

The brows in the mirror drew together. "I don't guess I can answer that. Who could? I mean, Carrey couldn't beat up a punk in an alley so's you'd believe it, but Caan couldn't twist his face around and make funny noises without you thinking he's having some kind of seizure. How you going to pick one over the other? Sometimes you feel like a banana split and sometimes you want pastrami. It don't mean one's any better than the other. They're just different."

"Exactly."

"So where to? Courthouse, airport, or home?"

She looked down. She was twisting her wedding ring around and around her finger. She stopped. "Airport."

"Yes, ma'am."

"On the way, if we pass someplace where they filmed something famous, or where the stars hang out, or a fireplug Rin-Tin-Tin once peed on, I'd consider it a favor if you kept it to yourself."

"Yes, ma'am."

"And please don't call me ma'am."

"Yes, Miz Bacall."

SEVENTEEN

Macklin spotted the surveillance vehicle right away.

San Antonio had experienced one of its brief, fierce autumn rains that turned its sandy soil to gritty mud, which adhered to tires and fenders like salt on flypaper. The panel truck bearing a logo identifying it as the property of a maids-for-hire firm was the only vehicle in Johns Davis's block that had been washed since the downpour. That spit-and-polish paramilitary training never went away.

He'd purchased a pair of cheap folding 4x binoculars at the local Walgreen's, which he moved from the truck to the handful of cars parked against the curb and in driveways within reasonable striking distance of the bookie's cedar-and-stone–faced house with the requisite clump of decorative mescal planted in the front yard. Depending upon the importance the local authorities placed on the Davis affair, the sparkling panel truck might have been a decoy. A late-model Plymouth with a recent wax job under a diffident sprinkling of mud seemed a likelihood, but he eliminated it when a tall man with his hair in a ponytail and a red bandanna tied around his head came out of one of the houses and got in behind the wheel and drove away. He'd been carrying two or three videotapes in plastic cases with the blue-and-yellow Blockbuster logo on the labels.

It was an upscale neighborhood, as Edison, the spotter, had

said. The residents took good care of their homes and drove new cars and pickups with all the options and some custom features. Macklin slid the binoculars along the street until he came to an automobile he liked the look of: a bottle-green 1960 Corvette Stingray with white inserts and chrome-reverse wheels, receiving a bath from a middle-aged man in an undershirt in the driveway of a brick split-level house six doors down from Davis's. The man was taking advantage of the last ray of daylight to scrub and hose off the destructive sand before covering the car with the tan tarpaulin he had rolled up on his front porch. Macklin focused in on a sticker that ran the length of the rear bumper, reading: PROUD TO SAY I'M N.R.A. He grinned.

He laid the binoculars on the passenger's seat of the rented Camaro, reached into the K-Mart sack on the floor, and retrieved an aluminum slingshot with a forearm brace and an industrial-strength rubber band. Although he'd seen the identical item in Walgreen's, and there formed the idea of using it, he'd gone to another store for that purchase, to avoid calling attention to himself at any one establishment. The police would put it all together in time, but there was no sense in making their job easier. Without opening his window, he fitted the brace to his forearm and sighted between the prongs, fixing the Corvette's sloping rear window a third of the way up from the bottom of his window, two inches right of center. In a few minutes it would be dark, and he couldn't be sure he'd be able to find the mark in whatever light remained.

Laying aside the slingshot, he scooped the .38 from under his seat and threaded the barrel inside the waistband of his slacks. He'd dressed loosely for freedom of movement, in shades of gray, which blended into the shadows better than black and wouldn't get him arrested as a suspicious person if he were spotted skulking about got up as a cat burglar, and high-topped black sneakers he'd bought at K-Mart and would discard later, along with everything else he was wearing. He'd known killers who were conscientious about discarding incriminating weapons and not leaving DNA behind, but who were waiting their turn on

Death Row because microscopic amounts of blood had shown up in their closets. And then there were footprints, which had been convicting people since Sherlock Holmes. Preparation was important, but it only counted for half. The rest was in the follow-through. If you paid proper attention to those two things, the act itself was automatic.

The Texas dusk slid in on its belly, gila-fashion, striped with yellow from the lighted windows and then the streetlamps as they winked on all of a piece. The Corvette owner wound his hose around a reel and covered the car, then went inside the house. For five minutes nothing stirred, Macklin included. Then he opened his window. He picked up the slingshot and fitted a steel ball-bearing the size of a marble into the pocket of the rubber band, rolling the ball first between thumb and forefinger to smear the prints. Again he fitted the brace to his forearm, took aim using the coordinates he'd noted, rested his arm on the window ledge, and drew back the band to the corner of his jaw. He took a deep breath, let out half of it, and released his grip on the band. The projectile whistled away into the darkness. After an improbably long silence, the shivery tinkle of collapsing glass drifted back toward him. There was another pause after that, a kind of gulp, and then the shrill pulsating wail of an electronic alarm, accompanied by the frenzied beep of the Corvette's horn and its headlights flashing.

The porchlight of the split-level house came on and the man in the undershirt charged outside. Light bounced in flat sheets off the mirrorlike surface of a huge revolver in his right hand. The bigger the bumper sticker, the bigger the gun, and Macklin had expected nothing less than a .44 magnum the size of a pump handle. He wasn't disappointed.

Things moved quickly after that. Light spilled out of the panel truck as three men in plainclothes boiled out, two of them drawing guns from belt holsters. The third carried a shotgun. They spread out in front of the split-level, shouting for the Corvette owner to drop his weapon.

Macklin got out and trotted across to Johns Davis's house.

A narrow strip of grass separated it from the house next door. He followed it around to the back, where three concrete steps led up to a screened-in back porch.

Edison's information had been thorough and, based upon the early evidence, accurate. The clapboard screen door was secured with a hook and eye. Macklin released the hook by drawing a jackknife blade up between the door and the frame and let himself inside, easing the door shut behind him against the tension of the spring. The back door was more of a challenge, but that, too, had been foreseen. Edison, or an experienced thief in his employ, had taken an impression of the deadbolt lock and had a key made. However, no one had had the opportunity to test the key. Keys used frequently tended to wear into patterns identical with the wear and tear on the locks, and new keys struck from fresh blanks often had to go back once or twice for additional grinding. This one was a tight fit. For a moment, Macklin thought this visit would have to be scrubbed and a different scenario planned for another time, as Davis would be more on his guard after the incident down the block. There was no room for play in the keyhole, so Macklin drew the key out and reinserted it. This time the tumblers gave. The bolt slid back.

Not much noise had been made, but there had been some. He hoped the commotion out front had drawn Davis away from the back. He pocketed the key, drew the .38, and crept inside, swiveling right and left to avoid ambush. When none occurred he inspected the darkness for the pinpoint glow of a keypad or the flicker of a motion detector. There was neither. Edison was worth whatever he was paid. Someone would miss him when the time came for Macklin to sweep up his tracks.

He was in a kitchen. Light leaking from the next room gleamed off countertops and appliances, a refrigerator cut in with a click and a hum. He tested the linoleum for creaks, then wasted no time getting across it and into a six-foot hallway paneled in blonde wood and carpeted with silent shag, the intruder's friend. There were pictures on the walls, copper-toned photographs of old-time Texas Rangers and a print made from a steelpoint engraving of a Civil

War naval battle in the Gulf of Mexico. The spotter had said Davis was as proud of Southwestern history as only a transplanted Texan could be.

The hallway opened into a large living room with more shag on the floor and overstuffed furniture covered in brown saddle leather with antiqued brass studs, emphatically a bachelor's room. Four torchiere lamps with distressed-iron shafts bounced light off a white ceiling, illuminating every corner. Football players skirmished in silence on a twenty-seven-inch TV screen in an Early American cupboard with shelves of books and videotapes in clear plastic cases.

The man standing at the picture window with his back to Macklin matched the description and the photographs he'd been given. Davis was thickset but not fat, with the square shoulders of a onetime athlete and a head of thick sandy hair, tinted from its natural gray. Underneath his light sweater and khaki slacks, Macklin knew, was an appendix scar, necessarily long for the year in which the surgery had taken place, and a pin in his right ankle where he'd shattered it in his only game with the junior varsity at Loyola University. He had six hundred fifty-eight thousand dollars distributed among ten U.S. banks and nearly two million in numbered accounts in Switzerland, the Cayman Islands, and the Principality of Andorra. He hated beets. At the moment he was holding the thick drapes away from the windowframe to watch what was going on in the street.

Macklin pressed his elbow against his ribs to steady his arm and took aim between Davis's shoulder blades. The drapes stirred, straightening themselves, and Davis turned around. He had something black in his right hand.

Macklin nearly fired on sight. He would have, a year ago, when his reflexes were on point. In the synapse of delay, he identified the item as a cordless telephone. He held off, with his finger resting on the trigger.

"I just bought it today," Davis said. "I can't use them in my work. Too many people have scanners, I might as well place bets over the P.A. system at the Astrodome. But the police won't let me have a gun, and I can't very well walk around stepping over a cord. I can't even push a vacuum cleaner without tripping myself up."

Macklin said nothing. Davis wasn't calm. His voice wobbled and the hand holding the receiver was shaking. His fear saved his life, or at least prolonged it. Macklin didn't trust coolness under the gun. What he didn't trust, he got rid of and saved his regrets for later.

"I dialed nine-one-one when that business outside started, then hung up. They'll trace the call, and when the police realize where it came from, they'll be through that door in two minutes. You might say they have a presence in the neighborhood." He tried to smile, but the muscles in his face wouldn't cooperate. "I can call them back and convince them it was a mistake. I used to be a con artist."

"I know."

"Yeah, I guess you would. You probably know some things about me I forgot. Well, I don't know anything about you. Not your name, or who sent you, but my guess is you've done this before, a lot. After that Schevchenko guy, they'd trade up, and if you don't mind my saying so, you're a little old for the work. That tells me you're good. Otherwise you'd be dead, right?" He cleared his throat, as if that was the reason he'd paused and not because he expected agreement. "I've got a pretty good idea who *didn't* send you. If I'm right, they won't let you leave San Antonio. Not alive."

Macklin made no response. He regretted making the one he had. You couldn't be human at work. It didn't make that much difference to the mark, he was dead, and that was how you thought of him from the time you were approached. When you reacted to language, when you acknowledged you were an intelligent thing instead of something that could not be stopped once it had started, you admitted to yourself you weren't a machine. You second-guessed yourself. You made mistakes.

"A man named Spanish Rivera," Davis said, "whose name isn't Rivera and who isn't Spanish, puts his stamp on whatever goes down in this part of Texas that doesn't get into the tourist pamphlets. If it's for money, he takes his cut off the top, and if it's something else, he makes sure it's worth risking a setup it took him forty years to—well, set up. If I'm right about what I'm going to say, I'm going to ask you to put down the gun. I'll call off the cops and we'll talk."

He'd decided to shoot him as soon as he stopped talking, if he ever stopped talking. But the shouting outside had quit. The Corvette owner had surrendered, and Macklin's window of opportunity had shut. The shot would be heard. Whatever further mistakes he made that night, they would all stem from the one he'd made when he spoke to a dead man. He'd been away too long.

Davis took his silence for encouragement. He didn't know how close he'd come.

"I kept going over and over this at first, wondering whose toes I stepped on. I couldn't think of anyone, because there wasn't anyone. Not bad enough anyway to kill me and wake up the cops and probably the feds to the fact the Alamo's not the only thing making money in this town. Well, they know, but for a long time they haven't had any reason to do anything about it. The graft gets paid, the bodies don't fuck up the traffic flow. That's why I was picked. I wasn't rocking the boat, and someone wanted it rocking, big time."

"Rivera didn't order the hit on me," he said. "He's the target. He's got the most to lose from a contract killing in this zip code. This is coming from out of town. I'm guessing *way* out, because the state's not big enough for two Riveras, like they say in the cowboy pictures. But not so far out that Rivera Number Two doesn't know how much money there is to be made here. One of the new breed, without honor or pretense of it. As if there was ever anything more to it than talk. This guy won't even bother with that. A hyena. Am I close?"

The bookie was babbling. The sense he made impressed Macklin more that way than if he'd laid it out straight, the way a good con artist would if he were selling wooden lightning rods or gasoline pills, making plenty of eye contact. This one kept looking at the gun. His sweater was too thin to conceal one of his own, even if he'd managed to score another after the police had taken away the first one, like a stern parent confiscating a child's water pistol. More than anything else, it was that image that moved Macklin to lay his .38 on an end table.

Davis took a deep breath and let it out. His hand shook as he called back 911.

EIGHTEEN

The clerk at the American counter ran Laurie's credit card and handed her a ticket and boarding passes for the 4:46 to Dayton, with a change in Denver and a stopover in Chicago. Laurie told the woman she wasn't checking anything through and when asked if her luggage had ever been out of her sight she said no. The clerk didn't seem to notice she wasn't carrying any luggage.

She felt more in control on her feet than she would have riding in one of the electric carts, so she walked the mile and a half to her gate. She passed through security without tripping the alarm and found a seat for the ninety-minute wait. She'd stopped at a newsstand to browse through magazines, but she couldn't concentrate on the articles, so she bought nothing. Once, glancing up from *People*, she'd seen a man in a Stetson hat approaching down the terminal and her heart had jumped. But he was years older than Abilene, with gray handlebars and a paunch, carrying a scuffed leather suitbag from a strap over one shoulder. She'd felt a rush of relief.

Now, she decided the diversity of the traffic at LAX was entertainment enough. Families in Mickey Mouse ears carrying stuffed Goofy dolls bought or won at Disneyland, hippified couples in retro tie-dyed T-shirts and bell-bottoms groping each other as if they were alone, red-eyed refugees from the gaming tables in Las Vegas, timid old men in garish caps being barked at by their wives, unsupervised children, Mexicans and Asians traveling in groups, and teenage boys with backward caps on their close-shorn heads and the crotches of their pants flapping between their knees tramped past in both directions or peeled off to claim whole sections of seating at the gate with their piles and piles of carry-ons. Laurie heard more foreign languages than she'd thought existed. Even the announcements over the P.A. system were broadcast in English and Spanish. She felt that the life she'd lived until now was embarrassingly provincial.

" 'Wretched refuse,' that's what it says on the Statue of Liberty," Abilene's voice said, close by. "Bet you never thought they'd wash this far west."

He'd slid noiselessly into the chair next to hers. The cowboy hat was absent. His long-skulled head with its band of untanned skin two inches above the eyebrows struck her as indecently naked, the thinning, wheat-colored widow's peak almost pubic. The skeejawed grin was in place.

She gripped the arms of her chair, but he made no move to hold her down.

"That's the thing about airports," he said in his lazy drawl. "No place to run. Can't catch your plane from the ladies' room."

She forced her heart rate to slow down. By degrees, as hundreds of pairs of feet whispered down the terminal and the clerk at the desk went on processing the passengers lined up to check in, she realized she was as much in control of the situation as he. They were in a secure area. He couldn't have gotten his wicked knife past the metal detector, and he couldn't threaten her with his fists in public. A big U.S. airport in the age of terrorist paranoia was the safest place on the planet.

"How did you find me?" She spoke calmly.

"You didn't go back to the hotel. I checked. You don't know anybody in L.A. Back home I never did shoot a pheasant on the fly when I knew where it was fixing to roost."

"You didn't know which flight."

"I figured Michigan or Ohio. One just left for Detroit. You weren't on it, and there ain't another to either place for two more hours. You should of picked someplace else, but most folks don't think when they're scared. They run home."

A distorted voice came on over the P.A. system announcing boarding of a flight to San Francisco. She used it as an excuse to be silent.

"Ohio's nippy this time of year," he said when it finished. "I bet you ain't even been to the beach out here. What you going to tell folks when they ask where's your tan?"

"I'm not leaving with you."

"Sure you are."

The grin was gone, discarded as easily as his hat, and Laurie realized how closely his face resembled a skull. The bony sockets of his eyes stood out under the skin and his face fell off sharply below the cheekbones, forming the keyhole shape found on poison labels and black leather jackets.

An airline employee, a flight crew member from the visored cap he wore with his uniform, stood nearby, waiting but not in line. He was holding a square fabric-covered case with the American Airlines double-*A* logo on the side. He had thick curly hair and a baby fat face and looked too young to be a pilot. Laurie raised her voice in his direction. "Sir?"

As the young man's head turned, Abilene leaned forward, and she thought he was getting up to leave. He pulled up the right leg of his jeans as if to adjust it, straightened, and turned his body into hers, sliding a hand under the arm of her chair. Something pricked her ribs.

Her breath caught. The point of the knife had passed through the fabric of her blouse as if it weren't there.

"Stuck it down in my boot." Abilene was whispering. "It set off the alarm, but a hard-on will do that. The lady with the wand stopped looking when she got to the metal cap on the toe. Bet you're glad I ain't an *A*-rab."

"Yes, miss?" The man in uniform smiled, appreciating her looks.

She shook her head with a tight smile. Any more motion than that and the blade would break her skin. He gave her a puzzled look and withdrew into his earlier boredom.

"Let's go," Abilene said.

She looked across at the family of well-fed Mexicans seated facing them, forted inside a half-circle of canvas bags. They were staring into the middle distance.

"You won't try anything here," Laurie said.

"Tell that to Jack Ruby."

"The place is crawling with security."

"They're to keep people out, not in." The point prodded her. A drop of moisture crawled down her side into the waistband of her slacks. It might have been sweat.

They stood up together. He withdrew the knife to clear the arm of the chair, then pressed it into the same spot. The move was so quick she hadn't time even to think about breaking away. The Mexicans looked at them, four broad brown faces moving up with them as they rose. Laurie felt a flash of hope. Then she realized their curiosity had only to do with the fact that she and Abilene were the only people there without luggage.

The journey to the ticket counters and the exit beyond seemed twice as long as the walk to the gate. They rode up escalators and walked past flower stands and souvenir kiosks, huddled close like lovers. Abilene was whistling softly between his teeth, some tune he had probably picked up from a country-music video, rendered shapeless by his tin ear. Twice, passing guards in uniform, big black capable-looking men with revolvers in flap holsters, she took in her breath to cry out, but the knife moved slightly and she exhaled without words. She was frightened more by sharp objects than guns. Could Abilene know she'd spent an hour in an emergency room with a gash in her scalp from a fall when she was little? He seemed to know everything else. She'd heard these people had dossiers on their victims: medical charts, family histories, friends and associations. She felt naked, as if in a nightmare in which everyone else was clothed.

A bunch of senior citizens—a tour group, probably, from their uniform flowered shirts and Mother Hubbards—clogged the security checkpoint, struggling to hoist their bags off the conveyor and setting off the metal detector with their pacemakers and gobs of jewelry and steel pins in their hips. A big-haired, withered apple of a woman wearing black wraparound cataract glasses stood to one side with arms spread while a short woman in uniform passed a handheld wand over her from head to toe, the device emitting beeps at almost regular intervals. The crowd-babble was excited and louder than usual to compensate for hearing deficiencies. When Laurie hesitated, looking for a way through, Abilene pressed in tight. The pressure of the knife was a constancy in her side.

She pushed back suddenly. The knife broke the skin and she felt the bleeding, but she gritted her teeth to keep from flinching away and followed through with all her weight, as she had when she broke out of the toilet stall at the restaurant. Abilene stumbled against the woman passenger and the security guard. Laurie ran through the arch of the metal detector from the wrong side, twisting sideways to avoid a collision with a white-haired man in trifocals who was preparing to come through opposite. He gasped something in Yiddish.

She picked up her pace, shoving a path through aging flesh and loudly printed fabric with both hands. Abilene shouted something in his nasal twang, the metal detector bonged. He'd followed her through the arch, still holding the knife.

"Halt! Security!"

She didn't know if the cry was directed at her or her pursuer. She was clear of the crowd now, running up the wide terminal. The P.A. blared something in a tone not usually employed to announce arrivals and departures, but her own heavy breathing and the slugging of her heart in her ears drowned out the words.

She didn't slow down until she reached the ticketing area. There she fell into a brisk stride, and without looking right or left passed through the automatic doors onto the sidewalk, where she joined the line waiting for cabs. Her heart hesitated a beat when a man in a police officer's uniform trotted toward her, but he went on past and entered the building. Shuffling forward in line, she kept her left arm pressed to her side to cover the stain of blood on her shirt.

NINETEEN

'm not sure as to the host's responsibility in this situation," Johns Davis said. "If you were any other visitor, I'd offer you a drink."

"I'm not thirsty."

Davis nodded, as if he'd expected that answer. Actually, he couldn't guess what the man in his living room would say or do next. He was calm in a way that invited Davis to supply the unease the setup demanded. There was nothing particularly fierce about the man. His tone was almost polite, and when Davis spoke, he seemed really to be listening, which was more than could be said even about the people he considered his friends. He'd been conditioned—by movies and popular fiction, he admitted—to expect flamboyance, or at least some show of understanding on the part of the man that he was something to be frightened of. This ordinary-looking fellow, with thinning temples and the tired aspect of someone who'd been too long in middle management, beyond hope of advancement and years to go until his pension, was more the stuff of Arthur Miller than Quentin Tarantino. Yet Davis knew, with the insight of a man who had felt a brush from the black wing, that this was death in its everyday clothes.

"I'm not thirsty either, but I need a drink. You can come out with me to the kitchen, if you think I might come back with something else."

"Or not come back at all."

Everything the man said was a conversational dead end.

Outside, a siren swung into the block. Davis jumped. His visitor didn't. The surveillance team had called for a unit to take away the Corvette owner. The car alarm had been going for so long it sounded like silence.

"Can I get that drink?" Davis asked.

"Not just yet."

Suddenly the car alarm stopped. Real silence boxed his ears. It was as if those three words had broken the mood of the whole block. Davis nodded, like his concurrence mattered.

"We may be interrupted," he said. "They'll want to know if anything went on here while they were busy outside. Maybe they'll just call, but they might send someone to the door. You can stand in the kitchen with the light off and keep the gun on me. Or do they just do that in the movies?"

"Sometimes the movies get it right."

He had a way of responding to questions without actually answering them.

The telephone rang, and Davis almost dropped the cordless receiver. He'd forgotten he was holding it. He looked at the man, who gave him nothing back. He found the TALK button with his thumb, hesitated, then pressed it.

"Yes?" He watched the man. The revolver the man had brought remained where he'd put it on the end table near him.

"Mr. Davis?"

He thought he recognized the voice, although he couldn't place it. It was polite, pleasantly deep, with the barely perceptible Southeastern twang he associated with black men whose families had lived in the North for several generations.

He said "Yes" again.

"This is Lieutenant Childs. I just thought I'd call and see if everything's all right."

He almost said "Yes" a third time, then thought his visitor might wonder what questions the caller was asking. "Everything's fine, Lieutenant. We had a little excitement outside just now."

"I heard about it," Childs said, and at that moment Davis knew he was calling from inside the panel truck in front of the house. "Just a domestic disturbance. Well, I thought I'd check. After the Alamo, you're our chief preservation project just now. Ha-ha."

"Ha-ha. Thank you, Lieutenant. You make me feel safe." He disconnected. "Prick. He's using me to flush someone out."

"It worked. Here I am." It sounded almost friendly.

"The age of electronic miracles, and they can't get nine-one-one to coordinate with the Criminal Investigation Division. He doesn't even know I called."

"He will."

"At the end of his shift." Davis knew he was contradicting himself, but he didn't want to panic the man into action. He changed the subject. "I'd really like to sit down."

"It's your house."

"Not alone. It makes me nervous. That is, more nervous than I already am. Can we both just sit?"

The man seemed to think about it. Then he walked around the end of the sofa and sat next to the armrest.

Physically, nothing changed. The gun was still inside reach. But Davis felt he'd won a stay of execution. If the dynamic changed again he thought that if he paid attention he could at least present a moving target. Any motion of the man's right arm would be the signal.

He started to sit in the matching armchair, but that placed the sculpture on the plain pine coffee table directly between them, impeding his view. It was an arrangement of gleaming stainless steel eighteen inches high, twisted into a sickle shape at the top, titled *Anasazi Moon*. He'd bought it at the opening of an exhibition at an art gallery in Austin, where he'd met the sculptor, a native-born Comanche, so it said in the brochure. He looked more like the Chicago South Side to Davis, despite the turquoise and braids, but the piece said *Texas* to him, bright and pitiless. He got up, moved the chair over six inches, and sat back down, without apology or explanation. The man gave no indication the action meant anything to him.

"I'm no mobster," Davis said. "Guess you know that. Rivera lets me operate here because I make him money, and don't chisel any more than I think is decent. I mean, a guy that isn't skimming a little off the top is probably skimming a lot off the bottom. Anyway it isn't enough to hang a tag on me and risk the wrong kind of attention."

He paused there, as if to see if he was on track. But he wasn't getting anything. Maybe the guy was a straight arrow, in which case Davis was being judged. It didn't matter. Instinct told him anything but the truth would kill him for sure. He went on. Never break or change your spiel—second rule. (First rule: Don't fall for your own con.)

"Killings are bad business. The press plays 'em up, the church and the PTA throw rallies, the police have to go out and look busy, which means busting up slots and tipping over horse parlors and sports books like mine and rounding up whores and johns, just when the conventions are in town, and *that* pisses off the chamber of commerce. You know Goliad?" No answer. It struck him Goliad was where the gun came from. "I'll assume you do; everyone knows Goliad. It's Rivera's cash cow, and not just because of the prostitution and the gun trade and the payoffs in the club rooms upstairs. The weekend legit receipts alone give the Alamo gift shop a run for its money when the tourists are in town. If the cops shut that down, the local economy goes blooey. Biggest hit since Santa Anna."

"Everything's the Alamo in this town. I've been there. I wasn't that impressed."

Well, fuck you, Davis thought. Aloud he said, "You got to understand it's all we have. If the Mexicans had torched the place when they pulled out—which believe me, they wish they had—San Antonio today would be a couple of taco stands and a place to take a shit on your way to Tampico. Think Detroit without cars."

A twitch, Davis thought; not quite that, but something, a flicker of light on the cornea maybe. He'd spent a lifetime learning to recognize tells. What had he said, Detroit? Detroit hitter, possibly. Schevchenko had been Detroit, but one botched attempt wouldn't sour them on the whole city. He continued before the man tumbled to the fact he'd let something slip. He wished he hadn't said Detroit.

"The point is—I've thought about this a lot; not much else to do when you're under the axe—this doesn't come from Rivera. Whoever set it up wants to kick a hole in the hive, devalue the local currency. Then when the old man's down, indicted up the ass, whatever, he'll roll in and take charge like—Grant took Richmond." He didn't want to say Santa Anna again, piss the guy off.

The guy didn't put anything into the silence. Davis couldn't tell if he was thinking or what. Except for that one little flicker before, he could play poker with the devil. He'd have excited Davis's professional interest if not for that death thing.

"You've been polite to listen," Davis said. "Here's where it gets interesting for you."

Now he had to be really sincere, not the fake kind. He wasn't selling phony software shares. Hell of it was, this time it wasn't a con.

"These are old-time tactics," he said, "I'm talking tommy gun-in-the-fiddle case. The organization's scared shitless of RICO; the last thing they need is to give the Justice Department a reason to come in like Waco and burn down the rest of the dons. So no way is this a sanctioned deal. Whoever's the hyena, if they find him out they'll slash open his scrotum and pull him inside-out through the hole. They'll suspect him, sure, when he makes his move to claim this territory, but they won't risk more heat without proof. If someone fingers him, they'll have to make an example. Otherwise they'll just finish what RICO started. Who else can finger him if not the shooter?"

Davis sat back. He was feeling light-headed, but his senses were sharp. He could tell the man was thinking now. The revolver lay on the table, inanimate, forgotten. Time to close the deal.

"Understand, I don't have any proof this is what's going on,"

Davis said. "I've made a good living playing the percentages. I won't accept evidence on sight, but I believe in the odds. Maybe you don't. Maybe this picture I'm painting doesn't look anything like the guy who recruited you. In which case you may get the chance to sit around some nursing home pissing your pants and waiting for the grandchildren to visit. Just in case I'm right, though, the clock starts ticking the second I'm dead. If I live, you live. Long enough, anyway, to take some steps."

Davis was exhausted then. His mouth felt furrowed and dry and he was hoarse, as if he'd been shouting to make himself heard over a noisy crowd. But he was only tired physically. It was the way he felt when he'd sweated out a game that had run closer than expected, then picked up a conversion in the last quarter, after which the elements of his inside information dropped into place, *plink-plunk-plink*. Fattening his wallet, sure, but confirming the lessons of his instincts and training, which was better. He couldn't tell what was going on in his visitor's mind, but for the first time he knew that something was. He'd stopped the progress of the machine. Bet the most important game of his life and covered the spread.

As the man leaned forward, Davis became attentive, ready to answer any lingering questions. He was tired and proud of himself and his brain told his reflexes nothing when the man stood and scooped up *Anasazi Moon* and swept around the end of the coffee table and brought the curved pointed apex of the steel sculpture up in an underhand motion that punctured Davis's spleen and hooked up under his breastbone and snagged his heart and tore it open like silk parting along a seam.

Macklin held on to the sculpture, leaning into it, as he watched the life drain from the bookmaker's eyes, his expression going from surprise to wonder to acceptance and a kind of pitying wisdom. In the days when he'd allowed his imagination to bleed into his work, he thought he'd pinpointed the moment when the Great Mystery revealed itself, and felt envious. Now he saw it as nothing more than the instant when the optic nerve stopped sending electrical impulses to the brain. The body was a mechanical device, without a soul or a divine spirit, no more valuable than the sum of its parts. He watched only to make sure the device was stopped. People were hard to kill. They had a way of coming back and lashing out long after you thought they'd ticked their last tick. Dead people had killed a thought-provoking number of men in his work.

The body shuddered finally, the sphincter let go, and as the muscles lost tension the entire sack deflated until the skeleton was all that prevented it from sliding to the floor.

He didn't withdraw the crescent-shaped end from the body. To do so would release a gout of blood that he wouldn't be able to explain if he were stopped later. He rested the circular wooden base against the fold of fat around Davis's middle and shook out the square of unstarched, absorbent cloth—not a handkerchief—he'd brought to remove latent fingerprints from the sculpture and everything else he'd touched since he'd entered the house. There wasn't much, thanks to old habit. He disliked gloves. Even the thin surgical kind deadened his sense of touch. He used it now to feel the carotid artery. It was still.

He picked up the .38 and slid it under the waistband of his slacks. Usually—always, before this—he left guns behind rather than risk being apprehended with it in his possession. Had he used it on Davis, he'd have abandoned this one as well, but now the worst that could happen would be a charge of carrying a concealed weapon and possession of an unregistered handgun, which were raps he could beat. In any case the risk was less than that of making a second trip to the Goliad Rod and Gun Club for a replacement. He still had use for the gun.

He let himself out the back with the cloth wound around his hand, waited on the porch until the scratching of the crickets told him no one was stirring in the backyard, then went out, not wasting much time with the screen door. Such sounds carried at night and no one listening could tell where they were coming from unless he was in the house. He used the sliver of moon and his own natural sense of direction to find his way around the surrounding blocks, coming up on his car after twenty minutes from the opposite side of the street. The men in the panel truck would be too busy watching Davis's house to pay much attention to someone approaching from the other direction. If they looked at all when he got in and drove away, they probably thought it was one of the neighbors going out for a case of beer. He cruised past the parked Corvette without turning to look at the ruined windshield.

The drive to Meadowwood Acres seemed to take half as long as it had the first time. At that hour, many of the houses were dark, but there was a light blazing in the double-wide trailer where young Edison assembled the information he gathered in his work as a spotter, put it into presentable form for whoever came to claim it, and burned or flushed his notes if he was half as smart as Macklin thought he was. Macklin didn't know the man's habits—a spotter who spotted spotters would have to be very good, and in any case he hadn't time to set it up or spot this job himself. That's how it was with cleanup. You just had to allow for the necessity and be prepared to count on a combination of speed and luck. Emphasis on speed, which at least had the virtue of being under one's own control. Many a well-planned and successful operation had ended in a capital conviction based on a botched follow-up.

He was grateful he'd adopted his old device of not eating within twenty-four hours of the job. Apart from stimulating the circulation to his brain, his hunger kept him from becoming too comfortable. He never played the radio during these vigils, to avoid distraction as well as the possibility of someone overhearing it. The gnawing in his stomach—sharper than he remembered, but then he was out of practice—prevented him from dozing off, and increased his focus. His night vision was better. He could tell the difference between the jerky gait of a squirrel making its way across the yard and the shadow of a mesquite bush stirring in the breeze.

Shortly after one o'clock, the lights went out in the trailer, but instinct told him Edison wasn't retiring. Spotters and killers kept different hours from everyone else.

A two-year-old Ford Ranger pickup with extended cab was parked in the driveway, at an angle that suggested carelessness, but was actually the practice of a man for whom caution was a habit. The angle placed the vehicle between the front door and the street, allowing the owner to exit the house and enter the pickup without exposing himself to fire. It was too bad for him, and an irritating inconvenience for Macklin, that that caution had not prevented him from letting slip that he knew who Macklin was.

The parking gambit was effective. When, two minutes after the trailer went dark, Edison unlocked the cab using his keyless remote and hopped up onto the seat, Macklin had no clear shot from the rented Camaro. That's why he had left it and was crouched in the driveway on the other side of the truck. When the lock clunked open, he swung wide the passenger's door and shot Edison in the face when he turned his head.

TWENTY

Carlo Maggiore liked everything about Los Angeles, even the traffic and the smog.

Although everyone, even the doorman, knew him as Charles Major, which he'd gone to the trouble and expense of making legal, he never thought of himself by that name. He'd say, when he nicked himself shaving, "Nice move, Carlo," and when he attended the Oscars in a $5,000 silk tuxedo with Sandra Bullock's body double on his arm, sliding in under the paparazzi radar, who didn't recognize either of them, he wondered what Salvatore Maggiore of Siracusa, Sicily, and later the South Bronx, would think of his little hunchback boy if he saw him now.

If, that is, the drunken old pipefitter would even recognize him. After recovering from a nearly fatal shooting, already feeling institutionalized by hospital life, he'd gone ahead and scheduled surgery to correct his hump, which although only partially successful had enabled him, with good tailoring, to create some semblance of balance in the line of his shoulders. Now he might conceivably be taken for a man with a slight stoop caused by a bad back. This was a far enough cry from his childhood nickname, Charlie the Frog, that still showed up in his FBI file, to encourage him to complete the metamorphosis by moving as far from Detroit as was physically possible without abandoning the

North American continent. When an opening occurred in the administration of the union to which all the catering personnel belonged who prepared and transported meals for all the major Hollywood studios, he had plugged it with one of his own people. That had given him unlimited access to the pension fund, which had emboldened him to liquefy his Detroit assets and relocate. Now he was leasing a Frank Lloyd Wright knockoff in Bel-Air, with a stainless-steel Sub-Zero refrigerator big enough to hold all the stiffs he'd helped bury back in his formative years and a redwood deck with a view of submentally developed movie stars ripping their motorcycles and RVs through the Hollywood Hills.

He liked it all, *especially* the movie stars, a dozen of whom accounted for two-thirds of the income he'd made supplying one thousand junkies in southeastern Michigan with low-grade heroin and crack cocaine. A twenty-two-year-old high-school dropout with his own production company and a ten-million-dollar price per picture thought nothing of dropping a grand to load up his arm one time with quality Asian shit, then coming back to do it again the next day. Even better, when one of these young fucks ran his Porsche into a plastic palm tree on Sunset or popped off a .357 mag at a party in Laurel Canyon and was arraigned, the dumb shits in the media focused on him, ignoring his connection. Just for an extra buffer, Maggiore stocked his sales force with other stars, some of them as well known as their customers or better, so that if the investigation proceeded any further it would stop with them. And they were grateful for the extra income, since movie stars were the most insecure race on earth, whose futures depended on the first weekend of their next feature, and the longer they dodged that bullet the shakier they got. Maggiore had gotten some of the best blow jobs of his life from internationally-known beauties whose fortieth birthdays were bearing down on them like a fast freight. After that it was character parts and whatever they could pluck out on the side to maintain their fifteen bedrooms and monkey-gland injections.

It was so easy to lose oneself in a town full of famous

faces. Back home, where celebrities were rare and generally colorless—tenth-carbon Henry Fords, washed-up former sitcom stars playing road shows at the Fisher Theater, presidential hopefuls on their quadrennial voyage of rediscovery in the Heartland—Combination men with much less authority than Maggiore wound up with their pictures in the paper with a frequency all out of proportion to their actual importance. He himself had had his picture taken descending the steps of the Frank Murphy Hall of Justice with his lawyers so often that if he'd had kids and those kids had kept a scrapbook on their old man, *their* kids would think he was a politician or worse. But in L.A., one conservatively dressed Midwestern mobster wasn't worth the expenditure of film, particularly when some solidly wed megastar like Tom Hanks or Paul Newman might happen by on the arm of a surgically enhanced soap queen at any moment and catch the shutterbug in the middle of changing rolls. Maggiore made it a point not to be seen in public with anyone better-known than he was, which left him with a wide field of obscure beautiful women from which to choose while allowing him to blend into the landscape. Notoriety was a lightning rod: Ask Tony Jack Giacalone, a second-string spear carrier if ever there was one, with his three hundred custom-made suits and fourteen counts of racketeering, conspiracy, and extortion that followed him right into the ground in suburban Southfield, where, let's face it, a man can only wear one suit. But that was how things were in a connected town. In an open city like Los Angeles, there was plenty for everyone, made guys and tabloid hacks alike.

He knew it couldn't last, though. That's why when he opened the buff-leather case he kept in the floor safe in his home office next to the bedroom, a bolo tie with a turquoise stone in a heavy hand-worked silver setting lay among the diamond pinky rings, gold Rolexes, and ruby studs in their compartments lined with blue felt. Worn with flared lapels and patch pockets, it would help him remain invisible in urban Texas the way his lightweight flannels and woven Italian leather loafers did here on the Coast. Talk at parties in Beverly Hills and Hollywood always centered around three things: the Industry, recreational drugs, and D.C., and lately there had been rumors about a congressional investigation locally, which as soon as it was established that it would not involve narcotics, surrendered its interest in favor of what Spielberg had in development. Maggiore knew that if it was *not* drugs, it could only be one thing. Certainly not the daily and widespread violations of contract law that went on in every studio, and had since the last of the original moguls finished coughing up his lungs in Cedars of Lebanon. The money skimmed there went into too many campaign war chests to risk rocking that particular leaky boat.

No, with the mob already tottering on ankles fractured by the unconstitutional RICO laws, all the *capi* selling one another out to avoid dying in the prison wards of hospitals, it was the safest target for a junior congressman to take aim at and bag himself headlines in the glamor capital. He could grill expensively dressed Sicilians on TV about their investments in projects starring Matt Damon and Julia Roberts, invoking the magic names without implicating them or the generous contributors who paid their elephantine salaries, and cop golden airtime on CNN, MSNBC, and *Entertainment Tonight*. Who knows, he might even get a grand jury to indict one or two of the poor dago fuckers before their kidneys shut down.

Maggiore wasn't afraid of public servants. If pressed to be truthful, he would say he even liked them as a class, and thought everybody should own one. It was the pilot fish that swam in their wake he feared: The puffed-up TV reporters who blocked your path with their people and equipment on the sidewalk and pressed their rhinoplasties against the windows of your car when you tried to pull away, the reptilian district attorneys who couldn't be bought unless you promised to whack the governor and everyone else who stood before them in the line of succession, issuing subpoenas and seizing your books and computers and convening press conferences to call you names you'd have blushed to spell in the presence of a child. They and their accomplices built you up into a celebrity in order to suck your famous neck in a ten-second sound bite. They were the best goddamn press agents in the world and if Maggiore thought there was a Gangster Heaven he'd exterminate them all, take his conviction and his death sentence, and wash down his dead blessed mother's homemade linguini with wine from God's private stock for all eternity. But since that wasn't an option, he was going to San Antonio.

Tonight he was attending a fund-raising affair—he couldn't remember for what, some broken-down actor running for the Senate or one of those dumbshit animal-rights organizations, or maybe AIDS, God forbid the fags should die out and force Jennifer Lopez to go to a straight designer for her Oscar undress— and since he was bound to be tapped for not less than ten thousand he chose a gaudy pair of diamond-horseshoe cuff links and the ruby studs. He dressed carefully before the full-length mirrors that covered the sliding doors of his closet, pausing as he often did before putting on his shirt to examine the pink semicircular scars on his left pectoral, one stacked on top of the other and a little to the right, leaving a depression where the nipple used to be. Either one of the two .38-caliber bullets would have been fatal if he hadn't been born with his heart on the right side, a little secret he'd managed to maintain on the theory that someday it might save his life. The surgeon who'd patched him up had explained it had something to do with his being a twin, and that his congenital hump had been mostly made up of the undeveloped fetus of his sibling. In which case, he supposed, he owed his life to a brother he'd never suspected he had. Well, why not? He'd been carrying the little son of a bitch his whole life.

He finished dressing and spent some time reseating his tuxedo jacket until the padding lay naturally across his unafflicted shoulder. He was picking up Téa Leoni's ass in thirty minutes and if he caught her looking away from him, avoiding the freak, it would spoil the evening. Perfection was more than a necessity in Hollywood. It was an obsession, with specific goals fixed along mathematically precise lines: size twos had to be zeros, for instance, lest they photograph more like Marilyn Monroe than a victim of the Holocaust. The stars raised hundreds of thousands of dollars—never their own—to treat Asian infants born without palates and those darling Ethiopian children with skeletal features and swollen bellies, but the threat of one of *their* offspring developing an incisor one degree off ninety sentenced the miserable little bastards to twelve years in orthodontia. The actors' eyes welled up over the bravery of plucky hunchbacks, but as for going to bed with one of them he had to be an executive producer, minimum.

When the telephone rang, he assumed it was his driver informing him his car was waiting. He'd arranged for unlimited use of the limousine service employed by Warner Brothers in return for settling a caterer's strike last year. He lifted the receiver off the imitation Louis XIV table an assistant director had diverted to him from the set of the DiCaprio remake of *The Man in the Iron Mask* and listened. He never initiated the conversation on incoming calls. He flattered himself that in the little pause before the caller spoke, he could hear if anyone was picking up on a wiretap. He had his home and office swept twice monthly and never, *never* discussed other than legitimate business over the telephone, but he liked to know when he was under surveillance.

The pause this time was too brief for him to detect any odd clicks or dropouts. The caller was aware of his idiosyncracy. "Charles, this is Len Brightman. You need to spare me a few minutes."

Leonard Brightman was senior partner in the oldest firm of entertainment lawyers in Los Angeles, which in keeping with the general flux of things locally meant it went back less than two generations. His father, Josef Brechtmann, had emigrated from Berlin in 1940 to escape the Nazis and organized his firm along lines borrowed from Hitler. When the old studio system fell before white-collar invasion from the East, the firm had added personnel versed in corporation law. More recently, the need for criminal attorneys on the part of a growing number of its clients had necessitated it branch out in that direction as well. The imperative nature of Brightman's wording—*You need*, rather than *I need you*—told Maggiore the summons did not involve entertainment or business.

"Okay," he said. "How's tomorrow morning at nine? I got a thing tonight."

"You've got more than one."

Shit. He knew that dry tone, which in anyone but Brightman would be shrill panic. "I'll drop by on the way. You know where." He hung up.

Eighteen minutes later, he shook the old lawyer's hand in the basement room where the firm kept the backup files to the information stored in its computers. It was built like a vault, with poured-concrete walls two feet thick, zinc-lined and impossible to wire, although Brightman made it a point to inspect the built-in steel cabinets and plain table and two chairs personally before each meeting with Maggiore, just in case the technology had gotten ahead of him. Under RICO, federal agencies bugged arenas formerly protected by the Bill of Rights, including lawyers' offices and Catholic confessionals. In a way, this jump-wire around the Constitution was a compliment to Maggiore and his colleagues, as it admitted that they had defeated the United States according to its own rules. Instead of celebrating, he and Brightman chose to take measures which twenty years earlier they would both have considered paranoid.

The senior partner, a fit man of sixty-one despite the low-grade skin cancer that made him shed patches of flesh in scales that appeared even in his thinning white hair, dressed in a combination of southern-California fashion and Harvard Ivy League, exquisitely tailored houndstooth tweed over a knitted polo shirt buttoned to the throat without benefit of a necktie. When they were seated opposite each other he folded his flaking hands on the table and said, "Your man Skeets called me from County. He breached security at LAX. Weapon involved. Specifically, a knife with a six-inch blade."

Maggiore nodded, as if his people hijacked planes daily. Under the table he was gripping his thighs hard enough to fuck up the seams in his formal trousers. "What in the goddamn hell was he doing there?"

"He didn't say. He was in custody, so the conversation wasn't private. He didn't use any names."

"He's smarter than that. But then I figured he was smarter than to try to smuggle his Arkansas toothpick through an airport."

"Apparently he did more than try. They caught him coming *out* of the secured area."

"How the fuck did they do that?"

"Details were lacking."

"Can you bail him?"

"It's more complicated than that. It's always complicated when federal authorities are involved. Airports are U.S. jurisdiction."

"Yeah, yeah." Maggiore willed his hands to relax. "Talk to Bob Wydra in Sacramento. He's with the FBI office there. You shouldn't have to tell him why he should take an interest."

"Good. I don't want to know. I'm an officer of the court." He said it without twitching. Maggiore admired that.

"Send someone up. Don't call. Draw up a writ or whatever. It needs to be legal."

"I'll put Salerno on it. He's a partner."

"Just so long as he doesn't serve it. Use a busboy for that. Some associate. Guy shows up in Armani, it gets back to Justice, and my face pops up over Dan Rather's shoulder at six o'clock Eastern Time."

"I know just the person, a woman. We've got her doing pro bono until she racks up some courtroom hours." Brightman touched an eyebrow. A flake floated down to the tabletop. "This isn't going to be a habit. Two things I won't defend are counterfeiting and terrorism. Washington never lets go of those."

"I don't form habits, Counselor. I make my buck off them." He rose and shook the lawyer's hand again. He felt like crushing it, but it was Abilene he was thinking of. It was a simple enough job: Button yourself to the Macklin cunt and don't turn loose until you hear about Johns Davis on the news. It shouldn't have to involve the feds.

TWENTY-ONE

Forgive me for asking, dear. Are you by any chance part Indian?"

Laurie looked up from her writing. The only other person in the dining room was the old woman who had been introduced to Laurie by the owner of the bed-and-breakfast as her mother-in-law. She was a small-boned woman with a slight hump, flesh-colored hearing aids in both ears, and bright black eyes like a sparrow's. Her white hair was brushed back neatly and she wore a brocaded jacket over a tailored dress and pearls around her neck that were a fraction too large to be genuine. She was looking at Laurie with a cringing kind of smile, as if she expected to be batted down for speaking out of turn.

Laurie smiled back. "No, I'm American."

"That's what I meant. They're the only true Americans, you know. Perhaps you thought I meant Indian from India. You have such lovely cheekbones, that's why I asked."

"I'm not, as far as I know. I was told my ancestors were German."

"Too bad. Not that you're German; I'm part Austrian myself. Having an Indian in the house would be a nice change. We get almost everyone else. Not many black people, though. It's the decor, I think. I told Alicia the place looked too much like a Southern plantation."

The room had Victorian touches: sepia-tinted photographs in mahogany oval frames, cabbage roses on the wallpaper, quite a lot of chintz. Laurie's bedroom upstairs was more of the same. She'd had to remove a dozen mohair and tapestry pillows to make room for herself on the bed. She preferred a more stream-lined look, but going back to the hotel was out of the question and she'd called six other places listed in the L.A. directory before finding a vacancy here. The owner, a tall horsey brunette named Alicia, had told her she was lucky, they'd had a last-minute cancellation. Otherwise she'd have had to go to another hotel, and she thought Abilene, or someone else if he was in custody, would check all the area hotels first. She'd registered as Lauren Rothmiller, using her mother's surname and a Christian name no one ever called her. (She was Laurie on her birth certificate.) She'd paid cash.

At the time, she'd just wanted a place to sleep. The airport had exhausted her, physically and emotionally, and without rest and a chance to collect her thoughts she was afraid she'd dash off in a direction that would put her right back in danger, like a panic-stricken horse running back into a burning stable. Now, having slept six hours, showered, and put on a T-shirt and a pair of jeans she'd bought at a nearby K-Mart, she felt more in con-trol.

She was writing Peter a postcard to tell him she was all right. The strong tea she was drinking had hardened her resolve, formed under the shower's bracing spray, not to flee Los Angeles after all. This Major-Maggiore person would know where she came from, she couldn't go there, and she hadn't the means or the desire to go someplace new and start all over again under a different name like someone in the Witness Protection Program. She couldn't trust the police. That left only one person.

Peter was one of them. Peter loved her. He hadn't lied about that. It was the one thing he'd told her that he had nothing to gain from—except her—and the reason he'd lied about every-thing else, to keep her from finding out whom she'd married. At this point she was more sure of his love for her than of hers for him, but he was her one ally. He'd gone back to his old life to save hers. That he was interested in her welfare was the one thing she could count on, after the evidence of the past few days had destroyed her faith in all the others. Peter loved her. And he was one of them.

"My grandparents wouldn't have been so happy to see an Indian."

This time, Laurie pretended she hadn't heard the old woman. She was concentrating on her writing. She wanted to word the message so Peter would think she still cared, but not to let anything slip that would give anyone else a clue to her whereabouts. Hotel clerks could be bribed. That's why when she'd gone through the rack in the foyer she'd ignored the picture postcards that featured the bed-and-breakfast, selecting a funny one instead, showing a group of teenagers with spiked hair and metal studs in their faces, captioned, WILDLIFE OF SOUTHERN CALIFORNIA.

"When I was a little girl, my grandmother told me their train was attacked by renegades from the reservation. My grandfather scared them off by firing his shotgun out the window. That's it, over the fireplace."

Laurie looked up despite herself. A double-barreled shotgun rested on pegs above the bric-a-brac on the mantel. It had a pair of large curled hammers like the ones she'd seen in western movies.

"Alicia didn't want to put it up, but I shamed her into it. I told her she owed it to her late husband, my poor Herbert. It's his heritage."

"A gun like that ought to be in a museum." Right away she regretted having said anything. Encouraging conversation was the last thing she wanted to do. She was trying to think of a way to suggest a meeting place with Peter that wouldn't tip off anyone else.

"Museums already have security." The old lady's face became sly. She leaned closer to Laurie's table, and in a harsh whisper fully as loud as her normal speaking voice, confided: "It's loaded, but don't tell my daughter-in-law. I've kept it that way since the riots. I clean it when Alicia's out. My grandmother taught me how to take care of it, just the way my grandfather taught her. Anybody wants to break in and rape an eighty-two-year-old woman, he's going to get himself a faceful of buckshot for his trouble." She snickered. It was an oddly nasty sound.

"You shouldn't keep it a secret. What if it goes off when she's dusting?"

"Tush. You could hit it with a mallet and it wouldn't go off, unless you cock one of the hammers." She raised her voice suddenly. "You should see the Hollywood Wax Museum while you're here. Get your picture taken with Rhett Butler."

The owner had entered the room. She shot her mother-in-law a suspicious look, changed it into a tight-lipped smile for Laurie, and went over to the sideboard to shake the orange-juice pitcher. It made a substantial sloshing sound. She put it down, used a paper napkin to wipe invisible crumbs off the marble serving surface into a wastebasket, and left.

The old woman seemed to have exhausted her store of conversation. She spooned All-Bran into her mouth and made crunching sounds long after even a bad set of dentures should have turned the crisp flakes into mulch.

Laurie worried the end of her Bic between her teeth and stared at the writing: *If you get this before Friday, come to . . .* That's as far as she'd gotten. Then she thought of the seafood restaurant in Santa Barbara, where they'd had a disappointing lunch just hours before he'd left her. There was nothing particularly memorable about that. She couldn't be sure he would pick up on the vague reference she would have to make. What had they talked about? Peter had suggested the restaurant belonged to the—*Combination* was the word he'd used. *The Organization, I guess they call it here.* That took it out of the running. Abilene had said something about Peter having been seen. That might have been the place. No sense repeating that mistake.

What else had happened on that trip? Peter had swerved to avoid hitting a seagull. They'd talked about where they would live. California and Florida were considered. Laurie had suggested they just travel. Peter had asked if they should be Gypsies.

Then she remembered the little shop in Montecito and the

painting she had bought of a man wearing a bandanna because she thought he looked like a Gypsy. Without hesitating, she resumed writing. She signed the card with her initial, then read what she'd written:

> Peter,
>
> I got away and am staying somewhere else. If you get this before Friday, come to the place where we found the Gypsy. I'll wait for you there until dark.
>
> L.

She hadn't been able to bring herself to begin with *Dear Peter* and end with *Love, Laurie.* Not because those things weren't true, but because she didn't know. Separated from him, having learned what she had, she thought it was too easy to assume that those things that had held her to him no longer existed, or hadn't been there to begin with. But she'd come too far and discovered too much to trust him now with those two words that deeded over the rest of her life.

When she rose from the table, the old woman looked up at her with her bright avian eyes. "Forgive me for asking, dear. Are you by any chance part Indian?"

Laurie paused. There was no irony on the pleated face, only a docile blankness she'd seen before, in the features of patients suffering from senile dementia. If *suffering* was accurate. Most of them had seemed quite contented.

"I am, as a matter of fact," Laurie said. "Cherokee. Why do you ask?"

The old woman's lips parted. She glanced toward the shotgun above the mantel, then back to Laurie. She smiled. "No reason. You have such lovely cheekbones."

Laurie went out to find a public mailbox with a noon pickup. She felt a little ashamed of herself for teasing the old woman. Then she realized the poor soul probably wouldn't even remember the exchange. That was when she stopped feeling sorry and became envious instead.

TWENTY-TWO

Macklin pulled the Camaro into a numbered slot at National and deposited the keys and rental papers in the dropbox by the door of the little building. It was a warm night, the streets were brightly lit, and there was a bready smell in the air of the day's departed heat. He turned out of the lot and walked briskly along the sidewalk like someone with a destination in mind but who wasn't in a mad hurry to get there.

Which was only half a lie. After he'd made sure of Edison, he'd wiped off the .38 and dropped it behind the nearest mesquite bush, where the police would find it within half an hour of making the call. Nothing about the gun would link it to the man who'd used it, but until he could get to a shower and a change of clothes, Macklin was a walking evidence kit in two murders. That was the hell of having to be dragged back into the work. He'd been happy to have gotten out just as DNA testing was coming in. It was such a delirious success it made the cops giddy, dumping decades-old homicide cases back onto the table like Halloween candy and gorging themselves on dried blood and old semen and bits of hair and epiderm, closing files right and left that had lain open since Jimmy Carter. Just smearing your prints wasn't good enough anymore. The process alone left more evidence than it removed. *Get in, get it done, and get out fast.* Try that while wearing a radiation suit and gauntlets and an oxygen mask.

The first order of business was to put distance between himself and San Antonio. He couldn't risk the airport. The odds were better than even that Johns Davis's watchdogs had decided to check on him in person after that bit of street theater Macklin had treated them to. When they found his body they'd dispatch men to all the gates and the train stations. Roadblocks would go up, but they'd take time. He had a narrow window if he went by car, but not the one he'd rented. They'd have a lookout order on all the rentals outstanding, on the very good theory that the Organization would go out of town for another killer after the first had failed. By tomorrow the police would have been through all the recent airline passenger manifests, cross-matched them with FBI felony murder files, and found out that Macklin, Peter, no middle, no aliases, known associate of Michael "Mike the Bone" Boniface, deceased, and Carlo Maggiore, should-be-deceased, was visiting south central Texas.

He slowed his pace. He'd broken into long strides without thinking, fresh proof that his internal metronome was out of whack. It was a wonder to him how quickly the habits of a lifetime fled once a man began to think of himself as a citizen.

Macklin maintained the rhythm when a city cruiser drifted by, both officers in the front seat turning their heads to look at the lone man walking the streets after two-thirty. He didn't think they'd connect him here with Davis, a suburban job, too far away to walk. But if they questioned him and decided to take him in as a suspicious person and they got a report on Edison, they'd be sure to run a carbon test on his hands and clothing. When he tested positive for gunpowder residue they would book him on suspicion of murder. Then their computer would talk to other computers in Detroit, Atlanta, Cincinnati, and some other places he'd forgotten, and the printout would start. When they convicted you of murder in the Lone Star State, they stamped a freshness date on your forehead, and when it expired they stuck a needle in your arm. He wouldn't like that. He even avoided getting a flu shot.

The cruiser slowed almost to a stop. He braced himself from old instinct, and to prepare for the little war that went on with his intelligence: *You don't kill cops, you don't fight cops, you don't run from cops.* Any one of those things was a gift for the prosecutor. But you didn't refuse to defend yourself either.

Then the car's brake lights went off. It picked up speed, and at the end of the block its flashers and siren went on, a volume of sound he could feel like a blast from a furnace, and the cruiser shot away as if propelled by an enormous rubber band.

Saved by an emergency. But the officers would remember the man they'd seen out walking, and would have a record of the time, based on when the emergency call had come in.

He picked up his own pace then, made a few turns. Anyone watching would have thought he knew where he was going and belonged there. At length he entered the parking lot of a four-story apartment building, not new or upscale enough to justify any security beyond a mercury vapor light glowing blue at the top of a twenty-foot tower, as if muggers and carjackers were like moles and feared light. He walked among the rows of cars, window-shopping, until he came to a four-year-old LeBaron. It had been washed recently and its tires were practically new. That indicated it was properly maintained and probably wouldn't break down. Meanwhile the age and model—it was a *Chrysler*, after all—kept it off the Top Ten list for targeting by thieves, which meant no LoJack and probably no alarm, although alarms were easily disabled and no one paid attention to them anyway.

There was little specialization in the killing business. It was blue-collar work and if you were in it for the long haul you needed to develop a number of satellite skills, like a struggling actor taking singing and dancing lessons and learning to ride a horse, in case the part was for a musical or a western. Macklin was a good burglar of the residential variety (subcategorized *working class*; when motion- and heat-detectors and closed-circuit cameras were involved, he partnered up with an expert) and a fair car thief. He didn't drill locks or dismantle steering columns, but if the car fell far enough below the anti-theft radar he could hold his own with the average talented high-school dropout.

The car had button locks, a big help. He fished a twisted length of sixteen-gauge wire out of the pocket of his Windbreaker, straightened it, and bent one end into a crook. A Slim Jim was more efficient, but harder to explain if you were caught with it on your way to work. He inserted it into the door on the driver's side between the window and the rubber gasket, worked it around until the crook encountered resistance, then jerked it upward. The button popped up with a satisfying clunk.

He balled up the wire and chucked it into an overflowing Dumpster, where if they wanted to the cops could root around among the used diapers and rotten lettuce, if they thought they had an orchid's chance in the Arctic of lifting a print off it. No alarm sounded when he opened the driver's door. He bent under the dash, stripped two wires with his jackknife in the glow of a pencil flashlight attached to a keychain with a couple of dummy keys on it for looks, and crossed the wires. The engine turned over twice and caught. He twisted the wires together and pulled the car out into the street thirty seconds later.

The gauge read a little over a quarter-tank. He'd stop to fill it before he left the city limits. Waiting at a light—for reasons of caution he was the most law-abiding creature on the planet, if you didn't count the killing thing—he reached over and popped open the glove compartment to see what had turned up in the Detroit lottery. There was a two-year-old Texas road map inside, a break. That meant one less stop. He missed the days when every service station offered free maps. The times were ganging up on fugitives.

If he caught another break and the owner of the car didn't miss it before sunup, he could be as far as El Paso before it showed up on the Public Safety officers' call sheet. He never counted on breaks. He'd stop off around Fort Stockton and hit an employee parking lot for another low-profile vehicle. Post offices were good. They were too busy looking out for their own shooters inside the building to worry about what was happening outside.

Once he'd crossed into New Mexico, his options would open. Allowing for food, toilets, and coffee, plus another detour or two for fresh wheels or maybe just to trade license plates, he figured to be in Los Angeles by Friday.

TWENTY-THREE

The pretty chiquita at the desk wouldn't bribe. When Abilene suggested it, she laid a set of fake nails on her telephone and asked him, in that in-your-face accent they all got from Ricky Martin videos, if he'd rather talk to security. Abilene shrugged and left, as if some lard-ass with a Motorola scared the lead right out of his pencil. It was almost noon. He took a seat in the lobby and waited for the shift to change.

Actually, a round or two with a hotel dick would have been welcome. He'd spent a night at County, getting his asshole checked for drugs or weapons and his record inspected for terrorist activity, and the thought of busting open somebody with a badge gave him a pleasant moment. But he'd been warned to behave himself.

The lawyer Mr. Major had sent, a flat-chested woman in one of those ugly suits like a grocery sack, floppy bow tie and all, had done most of the talking when they met in conference, then left him to go talk to the undersheriff. She'd been gone hardly long enough for a proper blow job before she came back to escort Abilene downstairs to sign for his personal effects. Abilene, it seemed, had forgotten all about the knife in his boot when he'd passed through airport security, then when he realized his oversight, took it out and went back to report it like the concerned citizen he was. When he tripped the alarm and the guards saw the knife, he didn't have the chance to explain himself, lying as he was on his face with someone's knee in his back.

Which was the only true part. Nobody would buy the rest, and nobody had, he was sure of that. His record would note that he'd been arrested for carrying a concealed weapon, but there would be no charges filed, and nothing from the feds. His knife had been confiscated and he'd been kicked as not worth the arresting officers' time in court. All in all he'd gotten off easier than what the guards in the airport were in for.

He knew Mr. Major had friends all over, but that was impressive. That was federal.

Mr. Major had picked him up in front of the building in a white stretch limo like the movie stars used when they wanted everyone to know they were movie stars. He was as mad as a bitch. Abilene didn't say much beyond explaining what had happened with Macklin's wife at the airport. He didn't try to defend himself. Mr. Major told him he'd burned up one of his best contacts springing him and it was up to Abilene to prove he was worth it. He could get the Macklin woman back or he could make a run for Mexico, it was Abilene's choice. He might even reach Tijuana before someone cut him to pieces with a machete and the *rurales* put it down to an attack by Zapatistas. Then he'd dropped him off at a fucking bus stop. A Mexican woman sat on the bench with her jugs in her lap, Wal-Mart bags at her feet and Gyp gang-bangers all around. He wondered if Mr. Major had picked the spot to make his point.

The passenger window had whirred down behind him. He'd had to turn and lean down to hear what Mr. Major was saying.

". . . and if you don't fuck up, I'll give you Macklin when it's over. Call it a Mulligan."

He said nothing to that. He didn't know how he felt about it. Yes, he did. He was a hurter, not a killer. The distinction meant something to him. It was like asking a master carpenter to chop wood. Only there wasn't any asking about it.

Abilene knew he'd do it. He'd shit the bed and he had to clean up. It was just a matter of bearing down that last inch.

He'd taken a cab back to the airport to claim his Jeep, then gone to his place in West Hollywood to scrub off the smell of jail disinfectant and sleep. It was better to let the Macklin woman wait, start thinking he was off her case and get careless. She was still in town, he was sure of that. She'd made her run, now she'd wait for Macklin to get her out. Abilene had done a good job convincing her she was no challenge on her own. One way or the other she was tied to that hotel room, the last place she'd seen Macklin. So was he. He'd gone back to wet work for her sake and he wasn't going to just give her up.

Abilene had slept eleven hours, and when he woke up in the dark, hungry as hell and with a hard-on from here to Yorba Linda, he'd shoveled down two platters of enchiladas in an all-night greaser place in East L.A. and picked up a hooker on Whittier and broke her nose and three or four ribs in a motel room under a cloverleaf where the traffic drowned out all the wailing. It cost him five hundred to keep her from blubbering to her pimp and avoid having his cojones sliced off and fed to him by a dozen zooters some night when he was too drunk to pay attention to his surroundings, but it took the edge off. He'd stopped himself just short of ducking her head in a tub full of scalding water. You had to leave something for later.

Later being now.

At a minute past noon, the spick girl left the desk and the beach bum Abilene had bribed to give him the room adjoining the Macklins' came on. There was nobody standing on the suckers' side. Abilene got up and went over, wearing the whopper-jawed grin Paul Newman, his man Paul, had used on Patricia Neal in *Hud*. He'd bagged her with it, his own stepmother.

A hundred told him there was a message for one of the Macklins and gave him a look. A bargain, after the whore in East L.A. He snorted at the pierced and painted punks in the photograph and turned the card over. It had been posted in the city yesterday afternoon.

. . . If you get this before Friday, come to the place where we found the Gypsy. I'll wait for you there until dark.

He gave the card back to the clerk and handed him another fifty not to say he'd shown it to anyone. That was a gift. Admitting he'd done it would mean his job. But you never knew when you might need someone's help again.

Friday was half gone and Macklin hadn't picked up his mail. He was probably still in Texas. There had been nothing on the news about any gangland-style murders in San Antonio. Abilene rode up in the elevator and let himself into his room. The bed was still turned down from the night before, and possibly from the night before that. He wondered if they just kept doing it over and didn't question where he was sleeping. He opened his suitcase and took out the little zip-up case he traveled with, with nail files and clippers in it so the steel picks wouldn't arouse the suspicion of a nosy maid at a glance. He used two of them to unlock the second door that separated the adjoining rooms and stood on the other side for a minute, looking around.

The Macklins' bed had been made, but drawers hung out of the bureau and clothes were scattered all around, draped over chairs and slung from lamps. Hurry had been involved, but Abilene had lived with two women and had traveled with several, and it was his observation that no man could trash a hotel room like a woman, not even a rock star. At home they busted your nuts for missing the hamper with your shirt, but when no one was expecting them to clean up after themselves, they reverted to prairie hogs. It was almost enough to make you understand why so many men turned fag.

He walked around, lifting slips and hose and unidentifiable garments and letting them drop. He checked the drawers in the nightstands and the writing desk. The notepads and stationery hadn't been used, even to scribble a telephone number or the time of a restaurant reservation. The bathroom was unenlightening. The maids had replaced the towels and squirted around that sweet disinfectant that smelled like cheap shoes. When he stepped out, his eyes met the black gaze of a Gypsy.

The painting was propped against the wall above the bureau, turned at a slight angle so that the man in the blue bandanna seemed to be peeping into the bathroom. The leer on his face completed the illusion. Abilene hadn't seen it because one of those tackle boxes women carried their makeup in blocked the view from the other direction.

He snatched up the painting and turned it over. Brown paper covered the back of the frame, with a printed gold sticker attached to the lower right corner:

LOS OJOS ANTIQUES & GIFTS
94200 Pacific Coast Highway
Montecito, CA 93101

TWENTY-FOUR

Henry Antigua was a native Texan, old Spanish on his father's side, whose ancestry went back in the region for two hundred years before the Mexican War. There was a viceroy there, and one or two of those *commandantes* who were always giving Zorro trouble—or was that California? Not that even the slightest hint of autocracy clung to the manner in which he ran the detective bureau. Lieutenant Christie Childs thought Antigua's bloodline may have had something to do with why there was nothing overtly Texan about the man or his office. He had nothing to prove.

The walls were painted a very pale powder-blue, almost white, and apart from the requisite police academy class photograph and his Ph.D. certificates in twin brass frames (he had doctorates in criminology and law from the University of Texas at Austin), they were undecorated. Rows of law books with buff-colored, thumb-smeared spines filled two barrister cases, and pictures of his blonde wife and towheaded, brown-faced children smiled up at him from under a sheet of laminate stuck to his desk blotter. He combed his graying hair forward over his thinning widow's peak and wore glasses in heavy black frames, without which his rather bland face looked naked. Today he had on a gray suit and a red conventional necktie—no bolo—on a shirt the same pale blue as his walls. His long slender fingers, inherited from the

Court of King Philip-the-Something-or-Other, wore only a plain wedding band and a class ring.

He stood and reached across his desk to grasp Childs's hand, clamping the lieutenant's wrist with his other hand at the same time in a politician's grip. But Antigua was no politician. He exerted torque to steer Childs toward the comfortable leather chair that faced the desk. That was an improvement—one of many at that station—over the torture chair his predecessor had used to keep his visitors ill at ease.

The man who had been chief of detectives before Antigua was a martinet, and from his first day in the office the new man had worked to wean the Criminal Investigation Division away from militarism. Old Glory and the Lone Star flag no longer intimidated people from behind the desk, having been removed to less conspicuous corners, and Antigua discouraged officers from saluting him on uniform occasions. These things didn't sit well with some senior detectives, who referred to him as "Auntie," but Childs knew him to be a tough administrator who stood up for his subordinates and refused to interfere with their work except when it involved department policy. Shortly after taking charge, he had quietly dismissed two ranking detectives within months of their pension qualification, and when challenged by union representatives to defend the action, presented them with evidence that the men had been in the pay of a Mexican druglord to escort his shipments for three years. Not a word of scandal reached the ears of the media. Even more impressively, Antigua had declined the FBI's offer to assist in the investigation, and made it stick. In another time, he'd have led the fight to break with Spain.

The chief sat down and laid his palms flat on his desk, framing a color snapshot of the Antigua family cavorting on the beach at Galveston.

"No small talk," he said. "I'm calling a press conference at two o'clock to address the Davis case. I need you to give me what you can by noon, with suggestions on what to hold back. I could make that decision, but I'm not in the trenches."

Childs nodded. He'd been expecting that. "I'd sure like one

more day. If the killer's going to start worrying that he didn't finish the job and come back to clean up, this would just about be the time."

"That's a desperation measure. You talked to the M.E. The killer made sure, then blew town. By now he's already back in Vegas or wherever."

"Probably not Vegas. Things've changed there, unfortunately. I was a lot happier knowing most of those spaghetti-benders were all in one place."

"Thank you. I was considering asking you to take part in the press conference, but I can see your sensitivity skills need tweaking." He didn't smile. They both knew diplomats made shitty detectives. "The boys and girls of the fourth estate will nail our cocks to the cross if we hold off another day. Frankly, I'm surprised they haven't sniffed it out before this."

"I'm not."

Antigua ignored the compliment. "Turn anything yet at the airport?"

"Which one? Back in Milwaukee I only had to worry about Mitchell. We're working on the manifests, but it's slow. Only first initials of Christian names, and these days no one bothers to check spelling. Man named Harrigan changes planes at Dallas–Fort Worth, when he lands in Houston he's Hansen. It's not quite that bad, not most of the time, but if they transpose a couple of letters or hit the wrong key at the start and we're not even in the right part of the alphabet, the cross-match is just a waste of time. In the end we're probably better off waiting for the ticket information from point of departure. But that can take a week. Unless we got lucky and he used the name Pittsburgh Phil or Nitti the Enforcer."

This time the chief smiled, a polite indulgence. "What about this Edison kill, anything?"

"M.O.'s different. Davis was stabbed, Edison was shot, and it looks kind of hurry-up, nothing tricky like that business with the Corvette." Childs managed to keep his expression blank. The morning after Johns Davis was found skewered to death in his living room, a search warrant had turned up a steel ball-bearing lying among the glass fragments on the NRA freak's backseat. Later that day a gift-wrapped package had appeared on Childs's desk, containing a kid's plastic slingshot. He knew it had been put there by one of the cowboys in Fraud or Vice.

Antigua looked troubled. Childs thought, *Here it comes.* But it didn't. The chief was thinking about something else.

"I'm worried about the murder weapon on Davis," he said. "It looks spontaneous. Back on Felony Homicide we'd have booted it over to Domestic Violence on that feature alone."

Relieved, Childs shook his head. "No spouse or significant other. Then there was that diversionary tactic, which screams premeditation. You can try all day and still not convince me some kids chose that night to raise hell. It isn't the barrio. I admit it's unusual. Maybe there was a fuckup and he had to recover. The good ones are trained to use the means at hand when the plan goes flooey. Anything else, a pregnant girlfriend or a sore loser among Davis's clients, is too much coincidence. I wouldn't buy a massive coronary if the M.E. dug out the fatty deposits and stuck them under my nose."

"Death by statue. Let's hold that back. The media's going to be pissed enough we sat on the rest."

"Okay by me. M.O. aside, the kills are connected. Edison was a jobber for Spanish Rivera, strictly small-time, but he'd have been in on the sweep for questioning, and he might have had something to say. Murder weapon, S and W thirty-eight, ditched at the scene, no prints. If it traces, I'll fly to Vegas myself and try my streak at the tables. None of this went on the blotter, not even the victim's name. Pending notification of next of kin. The press will buy that; they don't like to think they're ogres."

Antigua said nothing. They both knew what the press was.

Childs said, "So Edison was a professional job, and this time it went off without a hitch. It wasn't retaliation for Davis. Timeline's too tight. But we don't get two of those in one night without they tie in. Not here in the Cradle of the Texas Republic. We're looking for the same asshole in both cases."

"You talked to Rivera." Not a question. Policy was to notify the chief whenever a VIP—Very Important Perpetrator—was rousted.

"Courtesy call, at his restaurant. I recommend the flan."

"So nothing."

"Worse."

, The chief waited politely.

Childs lifted his glasses and resettled them. He hated theorizing in front of brass, even friendly brass. When the boat you built sprang a leak you went to the bottom alone. But he was good at holding his breath.

"I've talked to these made guys before," he said. "Nothing changes except the table settings. They've got it down to a few phrases they use over and over, and they've done it so much they aren't even listening to themselves anymore. He didn't use any of them. He wasn't surprised. That'd be a tip-off, after one attempt was already made on Davis. He wasn't happy either. He acted like a broker who just got bad news from Wall Street. He was expecting it, but it was still bad. I don't think he set this one up."

"Rivera's lied to more cops than you and I know. It's no stretch to assume he's gotten good at it."

"You're probably right." Childs let out his breath. The chief had spotted the leaks before he pushed off. Then he went ahead and pushed off anyway. "I've just got a bad feeling this is more than just a housecleaning."

"Someone's muscling in?"

"Muscling in, yeah. Someone's being taken for a ride."

They shared a bitter chuckle. TV networks were bouncing reruns of *Mister Ed* off satellites and kids were buying lasers in corner drugstores, and two DNA-savvy detectives were sitting around still talking like Jimmy Cagney. Gutter talk was past due for a makeover.

Childs cleared his throat. "If this were Detroit or Chicago, the cops would let these boys whack each other, no sweat. This is an unconnected town, and we like to keep it that way. Rivera knows that, or he'd let his whores hang their titties over the balcony at Goliad. His madam's Mrs. Brady. Well, Mrs. Brady on cable—she says 'cunt' a lot. Whoever pushed the button on Davis and Edison is out to burn down Rivera."

"Why not just hit him?"

"These people have people to answer to. Call it the Commission or whatever, no one hits a *capo* without clearing it with someone. You might as well put out the hit on yourself. But a rookie's another animal, a pigeon. Wing one and ten more fly in to shit on your car. Why not whack him and let the police do the rest? Then when the heat dies down, step in and rebuild."

Antigua turned one of his hands over and looked at the palm. "I should be mad. Wonder why I'm not."

"We've been using them all these years. Luciano helped whip the Nazis and we deported him. Giancana fought commies and we let him get killed. We ought to have expected them to return the compliment."

"Maybe. What else?"

"This has to come from out of town. Rivera's lieutenant retired to Arizona last year and no one replaced him. At this point the local organization could run itself: no growth, but no losses either. It's what the folks in Corporate call a prime takeover target." Childs paused. "So what now? Feds?"

"We won't bother Washington with this." That had the snap of finality. Antigua's issues with the Justice Department were his own. "We'll use their facilities, like the good taxpayers we are, but we'll keep this local. Get a warrant for Rivera and bring him in. I'll coordinate a sweep and put Vice on Goliad and the parlors downtown. If your hunch is right, that's just what the bastards want, but we can't sit still. Police police." It was the chief's favorite phrase, a noun and a verb. He'd used it in press conference and it showed up on the turnout sheet some mornings. "When it's finished, we'll see who's new in town and start a scrapbook. Meanwhile, get me the shooter."

"If someone else doesn't get him first. Whoever paid him has to be looking over both shoulders. He's either a genius or a nut."

"Let's hope genius." Antigua's smile was chilly. "Geniuses outsmart themselves sooner or later, but you can't predict what a nut's going to do. They don't know themselves."

"Okay, boss."

The chief stood to shake his hand. He hung on. "A little advice. Go easy on that 'Cradle of the Texas Republic' business. You never know when you might need these redneck sons of bitches."

Childs grinned. But Antigua's face was grave.

"Get me the shooter," he repeated.

TWENTY-FIVE

Great thing about a knife, when you needed a new one you didn't have to meet some guy behind his car in a fucking alley, or go to some pee-smelling house in Tarzana and squint at serial numbers in an attic tricked out like the gun room in the J. Edgar Hoover Building. You just parked at the nearest K-Mart and went to Sporting Goods.

A glass case on the wall behind the counter contained an assortment of hunting knives on pegs, ranging from an outsize jackknife with a ceramic blade to a big bowie with a black composition handle and fourteen inches of razor-edged steel, suitable for use on Cape buffalo and small trees. Abilene figured a man had to have a pretty small dick to want to strap on a sticker that hung to his ankles.

The store was close to deserted in the middle of a weekday, just like every other K-Mart in the world, a situation that had been going on for as long as he bothered to remember. If he didn't know better, he'd think the chain was mobbed up. Except the Organization would have finished looting it and put it out of its misery long ago. There wasn't a clerk in sight, and after waiting three minutes he started around the counter for a closer look.

"Can I help you?"

Carrot-topped kid with four-alarm acne, swimming around in

one of those dopey blue-green smocks. MICHAEL on his cute little nametag. He'd been hiding in the aisle between bicycle tires and sleeping bags. Now he was standing on the customer's side of the counter looking at Abilene with one foot behind it.

Abilene said, "Let's find out. I want a look at that Buck knife there in the case."

The kid reached up under his smock to dig a ring of about a thousand keys out of his baggy pants pocket. He said, "Excuse me," and when Abilene didn't move, he walked around him, barely missing a beat. He unlocked the case, swung open the glass and reached for the bowie.

"No, the Buck," Abilene said.

"Let's see." The kid stood staring at the display.

"Third from the top, Hawkeye."

He took down the big folding knife with the wooden-and-brass handle and handed it to Abilene, who bounced it on his palm, testing the heft, then pressed the thumb-latch and grasped the blade by its dimple and snapped it open. It worked stiffly, not like his old one that he could open with a one-handed flick, letting the weight of the handle do the work. A little oil and a lot of opening and closing would take care of that. He tested the edge with the ball of his thumb. It needed honing. He wondered how long it had been in the case. Since last deer-hunting season, anyway, and probably longer. No one in L.A. hunted. They couldn't cut into tofu without fainting.

Abilene was about to ask the kid a question when the telephone rang behind the counter. The kid picked up the receiver. "K-Mart Sporting Goods. This is Michael." He listened, said, "I'll check," then laid the receiver on the counter and walked around Abilene, excusing himself.

He was gone five minutes. When he returned he said "Excuse me" again, and lifted the receiver. "No, we don't have that. I can put in an order. Sorry. Thanks." He hung up. "Is there something else you'd like to see?" he asked Abilene.

"Yeah, you got—"

The telephone rang again. The kid picked up. "K-Mart Sporting Goods. This is Michael."

Abilene took hold of the receiver cord, made a loop, inserted the knife blade with the edge turned upward, and sliced the cord in two with a backward jerk. The cord resisted slightly. The blade needed sharpening for sure.

It took the kid a second to realize he'd been disconnected and another second to figure out how. His pimples got fiery-red against his sudden pallor.

Abilene said, "You got a whetstone? I'll need some three-in-one oil, too. You should take better care of your inventory. Why you think Wal-Mart's kicking your ass?"

Michael wasn't as slow as he looked. After a moment of staring at Abilene's pale eyes he cradled the dead receiver and took a blister card off a peg on the wall next to the knife case and laid it on the counter. Under the transparent plastic was a whetstone in an imitation chamois leather case. The kid cleared his throat. "You'll find three-in-one oil in Hardware."

"Thanks, Mike."

"Michael."

"Fuck's the difference?" He waited for his purchases to be scanned in, then paid for them and took the bag and walked over to Hardware. Taking his time. He had six hours till sundown and Montecito was an easy three-hour drive.

Macklin made his last change in San Bernardino—frost-green Catera, last year's model, the Ford Pinto of Cadillacs—and drove straight through to L.A. He parked it in a Safeway lot and walked four blocks to the hotel. The doorman, in a white summerweight uniform with yards of gold braid, broad Hershey-brown face battered like the part-time stuntman he probably was, wished him a good afternoon on his way through the revolving doors. Macklin's rumpled clothes and two days' growth of beard didn't appear to concern him. It was the look that multimillionaire producers wore to parties at Spago's.

Any one of the loiterers in the lobby might have been spotting for Maggiore, but Macklin didn't care. His shirt clung to his back like cellophane, he had a bee sting between his shoulder blades and thirteen hundred miles of desert grit clogging his tear ducts. To hell with sneaking around.

He used one of the beige courtesy telephones to call the room. It rang four times, then a canned voice came on offering to record a message. He hung up.

The clerk behind the desk was the polite young Hispanic who had checked him in, a few days and a couple of hundred years before. "One message, Mr. Macklin." He reached into one of the varnished maple pigeonholes on the back wall—a holdover from the Hollywood of Nathanael West—and handed him a picture postcard.

Macklin glanced at the glossy photo, then read the writing on the back. He recognized Laurie's script: . . . *the place where we found the Gypsy* puzzled him for a moment. Then he remembered. He went back out, pausing briefly by the bullet-shaped trash can near the door to tear the postcard into small pieces and throw them away.

Laurie kept reaching for the shift lever between the seats and grabbing empty air. She missed her six-year-old Corsica back home. The new Buick she'd rented operated almost entirely from a stick on the column and the interior was like a helicopter cockpit. It reminded her of a medevac run she'd gone on when her turn came up her first year as a student nurse. The sensation of climbing up out of the Valley was identical to that experience. She felt disconnected from the earth.

She turned off the air conditioner and powered down the window, thinking the damp salt air might help keep her alert. She wondered if the mental condition of the old woman in the bed-and-breakfast was contagious. *Keep it real, keep it real.* The phrase had never meant anything to her before.

She put on the radio, but the selection of rock oldies, telephone call-in shows, Spanish-language stations, news, hip-hop, and musty old jazz had nothing for her and after scanning AM and FM the length of the dial she turned it off. Now she could hear the hum of her tires on the pavement. She couldn't before, and she decided the floating episode was over.

The drive seemed to take longer than it had before, but clocks had had no significance then. She and Peter had been on Pacific Honeymoon Time, a zone in which there were no Maggiores, no Abilenes, and most important of all, no secrets. She'd been fascinated by the ocean, by the searching and swooping patterns of the seagulls, and by the sea lions flopping about on the rocks like something in a cartoon. It was all destruction. The Pacific threw its shoulder against the rocks again and again in its tireless effort to eradicate the continent that kept it from its meeting with the Atlantic, the gulls were hunting for fish, there was blood and scales on the comical whiskers of the sea lions. None of it had mattered, because of the calm male presence separating her from the mayhem. Now she deliberately avoided looking in that direction.

She'd seen too many movies—most of them shot along that same stretch of highway—in which careening cars burst through guardrails and walloped down cliffs and erupted in flame. Hitchcock and the rest had made such things too easy to picture. But she wasn't living in one of those films. In those films you were reasonably certain the hero and heroine would survive, and even when you weren't, when it was *Psycho* or *Chinatown* or *Basic Instinct*, you knew that when the credits crawled all you had to worry about was finding your car in the parking lot and getting away in the general crush of the exodus. Chances are the man you left with wasn't a murderer.

In Montecito she drove right past the little shop and had to turn around on the gravel apron of a scenic overlook and go back. A rutted drive led down at a thirty-degree angle to a bungalow sort of structure, a small shotgun-style house with pitted aluminum siding and a shingle roof, left over from a time when vacation cottages outnumbered permanent homes along the highway. A swayback porch ran the length of the building, cluttered with cast-iron cookstoves, decommissioned road signs, split-bottom rockers, and a vintage Coke machine, discreetly chained to the columns supporting the porch to discourage scavengers. An oblong sign painted to resemble a human eye hung from chains stapled to the overhang, with LOS OJOS ANTIQUES & GIFTS hand-lettered inside the iris.

A dilapidated pickup truck peppered with rust was parked in the same spot it had occupied on Laurie's first visit, next to a pair of late-model cars probably belonging to customers. She pulled into an empty space and went inside.

Picture windows on the ocean side had been designed to flood the interior with light. That was before great carved slabs of oaken and walnut furniture had been moved in, skillets and lanterns and cartoon-character lunchboxes strung from the ceiling, and a counter erected to hold up a computerized cash register. What light managed to filter in through neglected layers of salt-wash crept between dark massive German Expressionist shapes and crawled with dust-motes. The shop smelled of dry rot and cheap furniture polish.

Behind the counter, a woman in her late sixties, with bleached-out hair flying wild about her head, sat in a captain's chair mounted on a swivel. She looked up from her fat, dog-eared paperback to greet Laurie and tell her to be sure and ask if she needed help. She was the same woman who had waited on her before, wearing what looked like the same faded pink sweats and high-topped tennis shoes and reading the same Danielle Steel romance, but she gave no sign of recognizing Laurie.

"Actually, I'm looking for a man."

The woman gave a short bawdy laugh. "You're in the wrong place, dear. Unless he's old enough to be an antique."

"It's my husband. Medium build, six feet, in his mid-forties. I'm meeting him here. We were in before."

"Don't remember, sorry. I get a lot of drop-ins."

"We bought a picture, a painting. It was a Gypsy. A man in a blue bandanna, anyway. He looked like a Gypsy."

"I remember the picture. I spend a lot more time with the merchandise than I do with people. I don't think your husband's been in, but like I said, a lot of drop-ins. You're welcome to browse while you wait. I'm open till six."

She felt the sudden sinking certainty that Peter wouldn't be coming. She'd known it was a long shot—he was still running Maggiore's errand, or had decided to give her up as a bad risk—but she hadn't let herself entertain the thought that she would be leaving the shop without him. And under it all she felt a kind of chilly relief. She hadn't known what she would say to him, or how she would react if he tried lying to her about what he was, or—more horrifying—told her the truth. But then there was Abilene. On her way out of the bed-and-breakfast she'd heard something on the radio in the owner's office about a security breach at the airport, but nothing had been said about the police having a suspect in custody.

A mantel clock in need of a cleaning bonged four times, its mechanism grinding and wheezing between the chimes. Her wristwatch told her the clock was eight minutes slow. She had almost two hours, and another hour before the sun went down. She decided to take her time browsing. The shop was full of homely things, books and butter churns and old outboards and eggbeaters with hand cranks, ordinary domestic objects that had survived their time. It seemed no place for the Abilenes of the world.

He cruised past the shop without slowing or looking in that direction. Three-quarters of the population of Los Angeles was convinced there was such a thing as sixth sense and that they had it, which was horseshit or no one would have signed off on *Man in the Moon.* But there was no sense asking for it, staring at the place and little nursie feeling it at the base of her neck and looking out the window just as his Jeep rolled past. He parked at a scenic lookout to figure his approach, got out to stretch his legs, and damn if he didn't have a sweet view of the shop off there to the left and down a couple of hundred yards. All Abilene had to do was lean on the redwood railing like a rube and wait.

Back in town he'd been stuck in traffic for twenty minutes, waiting as it turned out for AAA to show up and change some pussy's flat tire, and he'd used the time to put an edge on the

Buck knife's blade with the whetstone and some spit. Now he got the can of three-in-one out of the Jeep and dribbled a little on the hinge and walked back to the railing, working the blade open and shut to loosen it and watching the ocean and the front of the shop like Rudy Rubbernecker from Des Moines.

TWENTY-SIX

etective Sill was doing the good news/better news thing. He'd irritated the hell out of Childs the first several times he'd done it, but then Childs had discovered how good Sill really was, and if a little personal drama made the detective's day easier to get through, it seemed a small enough price to pay to keep him from burning out and going into private security. And the lieutenant wondered if this little bit of tolerance was a sign he'd begun to go Texan. He saw himself in a year or so, trying on his first pair of shitkickers in Shepler's.

"L.T.?" Sill said.

Childs opened his eyes, then adjusted his glasses. "Sorry. I need a new prescription. What you got?"

The big detective looked at the computer printout he'd carried into the lieutenant's office. "I got cross-matches from Washington on five passengers. Two Dallas–Fort Worth, one Houston, two San Antonio. Starts out good and gets better. I already said that, sorry. You want dates and times?"

"Later. Start with felony convictions."

"One in Dallas–F.W., robbery armed, three busts, one stuck, twenty-six months in Ossining, that's Sing-Sing?"

"I heard of it. I go to the movies."

"Second Dallas, one bust, one conviction, assault with intent to commit great bodily harm less than murder, a year and a day in Q. That's—"

"San Quentin. Mob affiliation?"

"All I got's summaries of rap sheets. Fella landed in Houston, five arrests, three stuck: B and E, armed home invasion, possession of burglar tools. Six months Elmira, New York, two years Ossining, sixty-two *months* total, McAlester and Ossining, on burglar tools and parole violation. Should of stood back East."

"I like the change of scenery. New place, new job. I'd like it more if the charge was CCW. What else?"

Sill read on, poker-faced. But he had that Ben Johnson glint in his eye. "First San Antonio, one bust, one conviction, *nine* counts A/B, one resisting, one officer assault with intent. Stabbed him in the neck."

"Whoa!"

"Not quite. Served less than two years. Released last month on a compassionate medical. Testicular cancer, final stage. They rolled him off the plane on a gurney. He's got relatives here."

"Okay, give me the winner."

The detective's tone was even, featureless. Childs would have tossed in his hand if Sill made a raise using that voice. "Last San Antonio. First, really, day ahead of the A/B. I was saving him." He looked at the sheet another moment, then said, "Shit," and handed it to the lieutenant.

Childs looked at the last entry, circled in blue pen. "Shit," he said.

TWENTY-SEVEN

Dear, I have to close. I'm sorry."

The white-haired woman in sweats managed to keep irritation out of her voice. Laurie had been hearing her sighing and clicking her tongue off her teeth for twenty minutes. Six o'clock had come and gone, and Laurie was pretending interest in a cheap woven basket full of campaign buttons, rummaging among the Nixon Nows, Mondale-Ferraros, Come Home Americas, and a psychedelic assortment of pink and yellow and vomit-green numbers promoting someone named Abolafia. She'd been around the shop four times and had outlasted a half-dozen customers who had wandered in, taken their time browsing, made purchases or thanked the old lady (apparently for not throwing them out), and left. Now, one of those spectacular sunsets peculiar to the poisonous atmosphere of southern California was gathering its colors on the other side of the brine-streaked windows.

The first several times the little copper bell mounted above the door had tinkled to admit customers, she had looked up, but the succession of strange faces had dulled her expectations and finally eliminated them. She knew Peter wasn't coming. But she would see the day out, if for no other reason than she had no place to go.

Feeling suddenly guilty, she picked up a black Bakelite ashtray with SCHWABB'S embossed on it in white letters and carried it over to the counter. She didn't turn it over to look at the price and flinched when the woman entered forty dollars into the computer.

"Can that be right?"

The woman looked at the sticker again, as if the number might have changed since she'd looked at it the first time. "Yes, the store closed down, oh, years ago. Lana Turner was discovered there, you know. For all anyone knows, she could have used this very ashtray. Will that be cash or credit? We recognize all the major cards. Except American Express, of course."

Laurie hesitated, then separated two twenties from the fold she'd been carrying in her pocket and put them on the counter. She was dangerously low on cash, but couldn't bring herself to cancel the purchase. Neither she nor Peter smoked.

"And three-twenty for the governor." This time the woman sounded annoyed.

Laurie added a five-dollar bill. "That's a myth, about Lana Turner."

"Oh?" The woman made change.

"She had an agent. A producer at MGM discovered her picture in a stack on his desk. He gave her a bit in *A Star Is Born*."

"Really? Judy Garland?" The woman wrapped the ashtray in a sheet of newsprint and taped it.

"No, the first one. Janet Gaynor."

The woman put the package in a small paper sack and stapled the receipt to the top.

"So it's just an ashtray," Laurie said.

"Well, it's *your* ashtray now, dear. Thank you and come again."

The wind had come up from the west, heavy with the sea. She hurried to the car, hugging her shoulders, the sack with its ridiculous contents flapping in her hand. She would probably leave it in the car when she returned it, let someone for whom Hollywood still meant movies and glamor discover it. It was no wonder the Abilenes of the world recognized her for a victim. She couldn't even stand up to a woman who read Danielle Steel.

She threw the sack onto the passenger's seat and reached into the backseat for the cheap thin sweater she'd bought at K-Mart, then remembered what it was covering. She left it where it was, started the engine, and waited, shivering, for the heat to kick in before turning on the blower.

The woman came out of the shop wearing a man's zip-front jogging jacket with an enormous woven-leather bag slung from one shoulder, and unlocked the rusted pickup. She looked across the top of the cab, saw Laurie's car, and frowned. Then she unslung the shoulder bag, tossed it inside, and walked around the bed, hands deep in her jacket pockets, hair flying about her head. Her face wore a steely smile.

Laurie opened the window. The woman leaned down to look in. Her gaze swept the interior of the car. Laurie was glad she'd left the sweater where it was.

"It's none of my business, dear. You aren't doing either one of you a favor by waiting around for him. You have to train a man for marriage."

"Thank you." She was getting tired of women of a certain age calling her *dear*. What gave them the right, apart from managing not to contract cancer or walk in front of a bus before they were invited to join AARP? She ought to be calling *them* dear. She'd spent most of the week with Abilene.

"I never married, myself. But you hear a thing all your life— and I've been around a bit longer than you—you start to think it must make sense."

"Like the Lana Turner story," Laurie said.

"What?"

"Thank you." She closed the window.

The woman drew her chin into her neck. Then a flush appeared under the patches of rouge on her cheeks. She straightened with a jerk, spun around, and strode back to the truck, pumping her fists as if she were climbing a hill. The motor started with a roar and a rattling of tappets. The pickup swept around in a wide arc, popped its clutch, and jounced up the incline to the highway, spraying Laurie's trunk with sand and bits of gravel. It spun its wheels entering the pavement and headed north, accelerating with a whine between gears.

Laurie felt a stab of shame. Then she remembered the forty-dollar ashtray—three-twenty for the governor—and the feeling went away.

Abilene, who had started to make some headway against the stiffness in the mechanism of the Buck knife, straightened when he saw Laurie Macklin leaving the shop. At first he wasn't sure it was her. The tailored student nurse with the middle-aged husband had disappeared, replaced by a lanky teenage type in a T-shirt and jeans, the cotton tight across her titties. But she walked the same and when she turned away from the stiff ocean wind, he recognized the face he'd tapped a few days before. She didn't look like a teenager then.

He'd thought she was pulling out, and took a step toward the Jeep, but that was as far as he could tear himself away from that balcony view of the antiques store and its rutted little parking lot. He was afraid if he took his eyes off the Macklin woman for a second, she'd dematerialize. He'd only half believed she was inside, didn't recognize the car, and now that he knew he'd played it right . . . Then there was that shitty old Dodge pickup, which meant there was someone still inside, the owner or the manager. A witness.

And finally there was the postcard in the hotel back in town. *I'll wait for you there until dark.* She wasn't going anywhere, not yet. That big-ass sun would be going down for another hour. She'd made the trip, she'd waited this long. When women put the time in they saw it through, no matter what. Just like the old lady back in Blytheville. Standing around saying, "Please, Ritchie, don't. He's just a kid, he don't know,"—all the time the son of a bitch that pissed him out the end of his dick went on slugging him, filling his throat with bloody snot and trying to kick his spine up through his skull when he curled up on the floor covering up. All for looking too much like his mother. Or maybe too much like the old man. Well, Abilene could understand that. Some mornings, wiping the steam off the mirror and seeing that fucker looking back at him, the same long jaw and shallow blue eyes, he felt like caving in his own face. And then the day the old man strangled him to death the old lady was in Little Rock, shopping for oven mitts. Giving herself an alibi. They stuck by cock no matter what. They didn't care what it was attached to, or anybody else, not themselves, not their own flesh and blood. He worked the blade of the big Buck knife open and shut, open and shut.

He knew a flash of doubt when she got into the car and a minute later smoke started coming out of the exhaust pipe, thick and blue in the brisk air until the wind shredded it, but he stayed leaning on the railing and the car didn't move. A woman dressed like a man, with a mane of white hair, came out of the store and put something in the pickup and walked around it and bent down next to the car. After a little she shot up stiff and stomped back to the truck. Abilene grinned, wondering what the Macklin woman had said to her. He pretty much hated everybody except Mr. Major, but he most enjoyed hating people who plowed everybody's field except their own. They were the ones who came out of nowhere to testify just when you thought you were going to walk because some dumb cop failed to show probable cause for a search.

The old cunt scratched some serious gravel getting out of there, and Abilene folded his knife and put it in his pocket. He didn't want his hands cramping up on him. He decided to give the white-haired woman ten minutes not to come back for something she forgot, and watched the sun setting behind Laurie Macklin's Buick.

There was nothing peaceful about the Pacific, Laurie thought. Balboa must have caught it on a good day when he named it, or else he'd fortified himself with Madeira during that climb up the mountain and the world was pitching and rolling so hard the ocean had looked calm by comparison. As the surface went from blue to violet, long white bars of what looked like molten iron hurtled into shore as if they were tumbling off a stack and exploded when they hit, flying up like sparks. Sitting in the car with the blower going, warming her ankles and feet, she could feel the reverberation through her tires, and imagined all of North America had given way a quarter-inch to the east.

"Balboa discovered the Pacific Ocean climbing up a mountain," she remembered her grandfather saying, more than once. The image had always made him laugh.

She felt hot suddenly. She switched off the engine, but it was as if she'd turned up the volume on the crashing surf. She opened the door and got out. She wanted to walk up to the edge of the highway with her back to the ocean. Maybe she'd see Peter coming her way around the curve to the south. But then she had no idea what kind of car he'd be driving.

A haulaway semi swept around the curve, taking up part of the other lane, changing gears and accelerating as it climbed the grade. For a moment the bellowing diesel and the groaning transmission wiped out the ocean noise. The vibration made the soles of her feet tingle. Then came the slipstream, pulling at her so that she had to spread her feet to keep from being sucked under the wheels. She felt the heat of the engine, her nostrils filled with the brown smell of the exhaust. The red-and-silver cab and then the yellow articulated trailer flashed past carrying its rainbow of shiny new cars, feeding the insatiable maw of the mother of all vehicular states. She waited until the truck had gone and her clothing stopped rippling, then turned away from the road and started back down to the car, hugging herself. The ocean hammered on, obsessed with its errand of demolition.

Tires crunched gravel behind her. She swung around. Peter. Then she saw the black Jeep Cherokee bouncing on its springs, brake lights redder than the sun, a roostertail of brown dust cresting from under its tires, lifted by the shoreward wind, the door popping open before the frame finished rocking, a glistening black lizard-skin toe headed for the ground.

She turned and ran for the car. The rutted earth slowed her down. She was afraid of turning an ankle and falling. She leaped the last six feet, grabbing for the door handle. Something swung around her neck, a hickory limb in a flannel sleeve. Her feet actually flew out in front of her. Before they could touch down she was moving backward. She felt as if the wind were pushing her away from the direction she wanted to go. She was reliving an old nightmare.

"Wrong way, little nursie," Abilene drawled close to her ear. "You might fall in and drown."

Something pushed against her ribs and she knew what it was before she felt its sting.

One of her heels caught in a rut. She twisted her foot sideways. Abilene pulled, stopped. His grip tightened.

"You don't want to fight. I ain't your husband. There's loads of shit I can do to you short of finishing you off."

"Where are you taking me?" Her voice croaked in her ears.

"My crib. West Hollywood. Smells like a Mexican shithouse, but it's home. You can yell your head off and they'll just think it's Ramirez beating his wife again."

"I need my sweater. I'm cold."

"Jeep's warmed up. We're headed south. In a mile or two you'll want to go topless."

"I want my sweater!" She writhed. The blade broke her flesh. He pulled it away to keep her from goring herself. Then he uncoiled his arm and shoved her hard. She stumbled and had to twist to the right to keep from putting her face through the window. She struck the doorpost with her shoulder.

"Get the fucking sweater! Jesus Christ! Button it up to your ears. You get hot, you can take off your goddamn panties."

She tore open the door and sprawled across the backseat. When Abilene stepped forward, prodded by some reflex, she swung the antique shotgun around, bumped the headrest on the driver's seat with the barrels, and jumped them over. The sweater was still hanging off the muzzles when she raked back both hammers with her palm and tripped the triggers. Bits of pink fiber continued flying around long after the ocean had swallowed the roar.

TWENTY-EIGHT

She lay twisted on the seat long after the concussion of sound had subsided, wanting to scream but unable to fill her lungs with the breath necessary. She had been six years old the last time that had happened. She'd fallen while playing on her grandfather's parked tractor, striking her head on the flywheel and opening a gash in her scalp that bled and bled, the blood stinging her eyes and blinding her. She'd staggered up the lane, gasping and trying to cry, nothing coming out, until her grandmother looked up from her flowerbed and dropped her watering can and ran to scoop her up and throw her into the car and drive her to the emergency room. Laurie still had the scar, its raised whiteness visible when she spread her hair, and although she had no memory of the pain she remembered the desperation of her silence.

And then she broke free in a loud, gulping sob, just as she had at the hospital when the doctor was stitching up her cut. He'd been reluctant to use a local anesthetic on so young a patient, and the pricking of the needle had burst the bubble. A neighbor who'd been visiting a friend at the hospital had told her grandparents later he'd heard Laurie shouting as far as the parking lot.

But in front of Los Ojos Antiques & Gifts there was no one

to hear, just the chugging of the surf and the wind carrying its mixture of water and saline in thick salty gusts.

The cry had restored locomotion to her limbs. She pushed herself into a sitting position, groped at the ground with a foot, and stood, dragging the shotgun out of the car for no reason other than that it was harder to release her grip than to carry its weight. She looked down, half comprehending, at the body spread in a Maltese cross on the ground, the upended Stetson lying two feet beyond the head as if frozen in the act of flying off, a cartoon attitude of surprise. Abilene's fingers were still curled around the handle of his big folding knife. His slantwise grin was in place, unconnected to the emptiness in his eyes. His flannel shirt was plastered and dark from the third button down to where he'd tucked it under his belt, and almost flat to the ground, as if he'd been stepped on by an enormous foot where he lay. Two barrels full of ten-gauge shot had simply obliterated the middle third of his body.

"Laurie?"

It was the exact same tone her grandmother had used when she'd seen her staggering up the lane, her face a mask of blood. Laurie spun around. She hadn't heard the car approaching, angling in past the front of the Jeep, or the door opening. The man coming her way was a giant. Then she realized the extra ten feet was his own shadow, cast by the horizontal rays of the sun against the slope behind him and seeming to sprout from the top of his head.

She swung the shotgun level and in the same movement palmed back the hammers and jerked the triggers.

When the hammers snapped on the spent shells, the man, who had lunged to take hold of the gun, closed one hand around the barrels. He'd started to twist the gun out of her grip, then in his realization and relief simply pushed it aside.

"You used up your load," he said.

"Peter?"

She really was uncertain. The sun lay full on his face and she recognized the deep lines, the eyes of indeterminate color, the receding temples. But the face was not Peter's. Then when she said his name, the features seemed to blur and shimmer and rearrange themselves, assuming the tired gentle cast she knew. It was as if he'd removed a mask of some kind.

Or put one on.

Then his arms were around her and she resisted, not because she wanted to resist but because she wanted to surrender, and then it was too much effort because the shock was wearing off. She dropped the shotgun and flattened her palms to his back and laid her face against his chest, smelling his musk. He hadn't showered, she could tell, probably had not changed clothes in days, and she preferred the humanness of stale masculine sweat to the cold clean ventilated breath of the heartless Pacific.

Something went through her then, a hot bolt. She shoved away, breaking his grip, and clawed at his face with both hands.

"Bastard!" She was shrieking. "Fucking murderer! How many? What's the score? Killer. Fucking killer! How many? You going to kill me, killer? I know you're a killer, so you have to. Isn't that how it works?"

She'd drawn blood. It ran down from his cheeks like tears. He took hold of her wrists, exerted leverage, and twisted them down and away from his face, turning her elbows out. She felt a stinging in both forearms and then immediate numbness. His face behind the tracks of blood was the one she'd seen before she'd spoken his name.

"We have to get rid of the body," he said.

There was nothing suitable in the Jeep or the two cars, so he jimmied open a window in the shop and crawled inside, navigating by the fading light until he found a canvas dropcloth stiff with old paint and a coil of yellow nylon rope in a storeroom.

Laurie had regressed into silence. She was still in shock, but she'd recovered enough reason to stay out of the way. He was grateful for her nurse's training. She even obeyed when he told her to find some rocks. While she was combing the beach behind the building, he pocketed Abilene's knife and rolled the body into the dropcloth. He used a flashlight he found in the Jeep's glove compartment to locate bits of entrail and a roadmap to scoop them up and deposited them and the map inside the bundle. Finally he kicked dirt over the spray of blood on the ground and scrubbed it around with both feet. By daylight it would be just another wet patch among many that close to the ocean. He hoped. The first good rain would wash away most of what remained. There were always microscopic traces, but if he did the rest of his job properly it would be a long time before anyone thought to run a test, if ever. He would get rid of his stained shoes.

When Laurie returned, lugging a double armload of rocks, the largest of which was about the size of a grapefruit, he tucked them in with Abilene, jammed his Stetson and Laurie's ruined sweater into a convenient space, folded down the ends of the dropcloth like a burrito, and tied up the bundle, tightly enough to hold but with sufficient play so the ropes wouldn't burst with the first pull of the undertow. Fortunately, there was no danger of bloating and floating. The shotgun had carried away everything that would hold the gas.

He looked up from his handiwork, aware that Laurie was watching him. It was too dark now to see her expression, but he knew what she was thinking. There had been no wasted movements, no pauses while he figured out what had to be done next. She'd probably concluded this was how he cleaned up after himself all the time. Actually there had been only two burials at sea before. One, if you didn't count Lake Huron.

He put a hand under one of the cross-ties palm up, gave it a tug to make sure it held, then reversed his grip, inserted his other hand, and began dragging. His back was stiff from fifteen hundred miles of almost continuous driving, and he had to stop inside a dozen yards to stretch his trunk and work the rubber out of his arms. He shouldn't have used so many rocks. But he knew he'd used just enough. He'd lost count of how many things had happened during the past several days to remind him he was middle-aged. He bent back to his work.

He'd dragged the bundle another five or six feet when suddenly it stopped resisting. He looked back—and saw Laurie's silhouette against the slightly lighter sky, her shoulders bent over the other end. She'd picked it up and was carrying it behind him.

There was just enough light bouncing off the water to allow them to pick their way down the rocky slope to where the waves smacked the shore. Finally they came to a shelf of granite just wide enough to stand with the bundle hammocked between them, parallel to the water's edge. The surface was slimy. He shouted at her to make sure of her footing.

"It has to clear the rocks." His voice cracked. He'd come all the way from Texas without using it and now he had to compete with Neptune. "On three." He began to swing.

"Wait!"

He stopped, exhausted past exasperation. She was having second thoughts.

"Throw on three, or one, two, three, throw?" she shouted.

He exhaled, relieved. "On three."

They swung in tandem, rocking the bundle toward shore, then out toward the Philippines and Japan, gathering momentum. Once, twice.

"Three!"

They grunted together as they let go. The bundle (*Roy Skeets. It's Leroy, actually, but you don't have to bother with that. Folks generally call me Abilene*) arced up and out beyond the bulge of the California coast and fell. It turned over once, just before it splashed, without a sound against the thrashing of the waves. A flap of white ocean peeled back to receive it, then closed like the petal of a carnivorous plant.

Peter used his flashlight to find the drag marks and scuffed them out with his feet. Then he picked up the shotgun and went back the way he'd come. He wasn't carrying it when he returned. She thought it a shame to have to throw a piece of frontier history into the ocean. The old woman in the bed-and-breakfast was going to be upset when she found it was missing. Then she'd forget. Then she'd find out again it was missing. She'd probably blame her daughter-in-law. Laurie was thinking ahead and away, willing herself out of her body.

But Peter was talking again, saying he was going to take Abilene's Jeep north and abandon it and that she was to follow him in the rental. After she picked him up, they would return here and she would follow him again until he found a place to leave the car he'd driven. She'd asked what was wrong with it.

"It's stolen."

She said, "Oh, right," as if she should have thought of that.

Following him north, she realized he hadn't asked if she was up to driving. It seemed funny she would think of that. She'd just finished helping him dispose of a body. A body she— But she stopped thinking in that direction. She had to think ahead and away. She wondered if it was possible for a person to live her entire life in forward motion. It certainly seemed worth a try. She supposed she was in a state of shock. Another dangerous thought. Like realizing you were dreaming, and then waking up because you realized it. She concentrated on the back of the Jeep, memorizing the plate. She didn't want to become separated and wind up following the wrong vehicle.

They drove a couple of miles past Santa Barbara and a mile or so inland, where Peter parked in a commercial drive and threw away the keys. In a day or so the Jeep would probably be towed to some impound lot and forgotten until someone decided to run a trace on the absent owner.

Peter tapped on her window. She lowered it.

"I'd better drive."

She unlocked the door and climbed into the passenger's seat. Nothing was said during the drive back to Montecito. She looked ahead through the windshield. The last time she'd ridden that stretch with Peter at the wheel, she'd spent it looking at him.

As they passed the scenic overlook nearing the antique shop he slowed down, and she knew then why he'd insisted on driving. He was making sure no one—the police, for instance—had discovered the lone car parked off the edge of the highway. She couldn't be trusted to be in control if it came to a chase.

Macklin pulled into McGrath State Beach by Ventura and left the car in one of the diagonal spaces, pausing to pull his shirtcuff over the heel of one hand and wipe the steering wheel and shift lever and the smart stick on the column. Cops never bothered to dust stolen vehicles unless they were pretty sure they hooked up with something heavier, but you never knew when some bored plainclothesman might catch the squeal and get a bright idea.

This time when he approached the Buick, Laurie climbed over without waiting to be asked. She didn't say a word for twenty-five miles. Then:

"Is there anything you've told me since the day we met that wasn't a lie?"

He went another mile. "The only time I lied was when I said there was a problem with the store-chain transfer. Abilene was in the hallway. There wasn't time for the truth."

"Were you afraid of him?"

"Abilene? He was a bug. Step on one."

"You told me you were in the retail camera business."

"I was."

"Didn't you make enough killing people? I thought there was money in that."

"You can't put it down on Form 1040."

A pair of headlights came around a curve on high beam. He looked away and didn't flash. He couldn't afford a possible case of road rage with traces of blood on the soles of his shoes and nitrate all over Laurie.

"I came back," he said.

A pause. She started to say something, stopped. She swallowed and said, "Did you do what they wanted?"

"Yes."

"Was it—like Abilene?"

"Not quite. He was a crook. Nobody very important. But not like Abilene."

He was suddenly drowsy. Adrenaline was like that. You could travel on the fumes for a long time, and then when they were gone it was all at once. He had to bug his eyes to keep them open.

"That's why you have to understand I came back," he said, speaking faster now. "Maggiore's a treacherous prick, but he doesn't kill legits if he can afford not to. He'd have let you go as soon as he heard. I didn't come back because I had to."

"Do you like it?" It came so fast he couldn't believe she'd been listening. The dash lights glowed blue-green off her profile. She was staring through the windshield.

" 'It'?"

"You know."

"No. I'm not a psycho."

"Is that why you retired? You're retired?"

"That's another truth I told. It's one reason. The other one is I'm not young anymore."

"Is that why you started? You were young and stupid?"

"If I were stupid I wouldn't have gotten old."

"Then why?" Her voice cracked.

"Why did you decide to become a nurse?"

"I wanted to help people."

"That's what you told the registrar. He didn't believe it either."

"She." She let out her breath. "I thought I'd be good at it."

He let up on the pedal on curves, obeying the signs. "I didn't just want a clean start." It was a murmur.

"What?"

He raised his voice. "I didn't just want a clean start. I wanted everything that happened before you not to have happened. That's why I didn't say anything. If I didn't say anything maybe it was something that happened to someone else."

"That's childish."

"It had to be. I wasn't much more than a child when it started."

After another half-mile she said, "What now?"

"Finish up."

"You said it was finished."

"Not as far as Maggiore's concerned."

She surprised him. It was easy to forget how quickly she picked up on things at her age. "You said—"

"I said he doesn't kill legits. I'll drop you off at the hotel. Unless you want to fly back home tonight. After that, whatever you decide. I won't contest it."

She started to say something. She cleared her throat, started again. "I think I will."

"Will what?"

"Fly back home tonight. Alone."

He accelerated coming out of the last curve. "All right."

"Oh God."

She broke then. It was like with adrenaline. You never knew when. They were driving past state-owned beach, no houses. He lowered her window and let her scream out into the night. Said nothing.

Which was a mistake. As long as he'd been talking he'd kept himself entertained.

"Peter!"

He was drifting off the road. He hit the brakes, skidded on gravel, wrestled the wheel left, bumped up onto the asphalt, and had to correct right to keep from slewing into the opposite lane, where a line of cars blared their horns in a warped chain as they passed. He took his foot off the accelerator and coasted to a stop on the apron.

Laurie opened her door. Her face was drawn and streaked under the dome light. She looked thinner than he remembered. But she'd stopped screaming.

She said, "I'd better drive."

He nodded and got out to trade places.

TWENTY-NINE

His name's Macklin. He's wanted for questioning in two murders in Texas and is a suspect in about a dozen others, starting when Reagan was a pup."

The Los Angeles Homicide sergeant, Martin Milner type with a youthful freckled face—approaching fifty, Childs guessed—nodded. "Must be in his dotage. You don't go *to* Texas to squiff someone. You lure him over the state line with cheese and do it in Louisiana."

"I can't get my fill of execution jokes. I got a couple about L.A. cops I bet you haven't heard." He watched some palm trees slide past, wondered like a couple of hundred thousand other tourists if they were real or made out of Legos. "Is this a new unit? Can't go above forty for the first three thousand miles?"

The sergeant accelerated without comment.

When Macklin's last known address came up on the FBI printout, Childs had called the P.D. in Southfield, Michigan; then while they were checking went ahead and touched base with Detroit Metropolitan Airport. Point of departure on his San Antonio ticket was LAX, which meant that was where he'd been staying, unless he had the world's worst travel agent. Southfield called back first, said the house was locked up, and neighbors interviewed said he was on his honeymoon, they didn't know where. They knew damn little else except they thought he was divorced from his first wife and had a kid and was some kind of retired business executive. *Best kind of neighbor, Officer. Quiet, no loud arguments or parties, maintains the place. Keeps to himself.* The Ted Bundy Fugue.

Then a lot of information all at once. Marriage license, ink still wet, corn-fed Ohio girl, German surname long enough to strangle Erich von Stroheim with, about the age of Macklin's first arrest on suspicion. Student nurse, handy to have around for patching bulletholes. Northwest flight 512 to L.A., nonstop. Fax of Macklin's last mug sent to taxi companies in Los Angeles.

Dead end there. The perp's face is as memorable as pocket fuzz.

Then Ohio State University weighs in with the better half's senior picture, and unless she's let herself go to pot in two years they're going to remember her even in the city of a million rhinoplasties and boob jobs. Dispatcher with Champion Cabs shows it around, driver remembers picking her up at LAX, she's with some guy. Records has the hotel where he dropped them. Desk clerk with a Kato Kaelin accent answers, checks, says yes, Mr. and Mrs. Macklin are registered. Childs takes the call in-flight, Southwest 2249 to Los Angeles. Detective Sill looks up from his copy of *Cowboys & Indians*, grins back.

Now they were greasing up Sunset, Sill in the backseat of the unmarked, taking in the sights. If Sacramento drags its feet on extradition he's sure to drop by the spot where the Cocoanut Grove burned down, pay his respects to Buck Jones's ghost. That was all right with Childs. For the first time since he left Milwaukee he felt like he was living in the right century, and it wasn't just the change of scenery. In San Antonio he was afraid if he stopped fighting he'd be chasing John Wesley Hardin for all eternity.

The sergeant tried again. California cops were still Californians, couldn't stand not being liked, unless it was Zsa Zsa or a black motorist. "So this guy Macklin's a heavyweight?"

"Cruiser class. Came up in the old Boniface outfit in Detroit. I think he did some covert work for the FBI. I can't swear to it. There are blanks in his file where there ought to be some garden-variety mayhem. Thirty-eight revolver's his weapon of choice, but he's flexible: knife, garrote, bare hands in a pinch. That's all field information. He did a bit for officer assault, most of it in the infirmary at Jackson, Michigan, recovering from GSW. No other convictions."

"And I thought all the good lawyers were out here."

"The best lawyer in the world's only as good as his client. Macklin's smart. Not smart enough to work a regular job, though. Hope you're wearing a vest."

"Duh."

Holy shit. They really talked like that.

Four other unmarked units awaited them at the hotel, two under the canopy and two double-parked on the street, plus a blue-and-white around the corner with the uniforms sitting in the front seat waiting for a call to back up. One of the plainclothesmen, tricked out in a navy suit and striped tie that screamed East Coast, greeted the sergeant at the door, where he was standing next to a luggage cart that anyone who didn't know he'd been there for the last hour would assume contained his bags. Childs wondered if the department had a wardrobe room or if the man had had to go to a costume shop.

"Anything?" asked the sergeant.

The man shook his head. "If he was in there when I came on, he's in there now."

"What about the other doors?"

The man shook his head again and opened his coat to pat the Motorola on his belt.

"You didn't check at the desk?"

"You told me not to."

"That's why I'm asking now."

"I didn't." The man's face went flat.

The sergeant and Childs and Sill went inside. The lobby was decorated in ivory and white, with veined pillars and black-and-white blow-ups in frames of movie stars, either dead or still discussing keylights with C. B. DeMille at the Motion Picture Actors Home. The bellmen wore Philip Morris jackets and matching pants, Dorothy's ruby slippers twinkled in a glass case with an alarm-company logo pasted in one corner. The place was as bad as San Antonio. It had just picked a different year to get stalled in.

It was checkout time. All the clerks were busy with customers and a line had formed between the velvet ropes. The sergeant stopped at the end and put his hands in his pockets.

Jesus Christ. Childs pushed his way to the front and showed a short dark woman in a green blazer his gold shield. She told him "one moment" in an accent and went on clattering her keyboard. A fat man in a Hawaiian shirt stood next to Childs smelling of Brut.

"*Excusa, señorita. Lo siento, pero esta función policía.*" The sergeant appeared at Childs's other elbow and opened a folder containing his ID and a shield with a sunburst engraved on it. Outside, the sun was cloaked in saffron smog.

The woman looked up, showed three thousand dollars' worth of crownwork in a square smile. The hotel was just a stop on the way for the next Jennifer Lopez. "What can I do for you, sir?"

"You've got a couple staying here, Mr. and Mrs. Peter Macklin?"

The woman apologized to Hawaiian Shirt, cleared her screen.

The sergeant smiled at Childs and lowered his voice. "It helps to be bilingual."

"She speaks English."

The sergeant returned his attention to the woman.

"I'm sorry, sir. Mr. and Mrs. Macklin checked out this morning."

"When?" Childs asked.

"I'm showing ten o'clock."

He did the time-zone math. "You said at ten-thirty they were registered."

"I'm sorry, sir. You must have spoken to someone else."

"The fuck's that got to do with what time they checked out?"

The smile went out like a bulb. "Would you like to speak to the manager?"

"What language should I use, esperanto?"

She shifted her focus back to the man in the Hawaiian shirt. Childs showed his faxed photos to the doorman, an acre of black in a white uniform trimmed in gold.

"The woman, yeah, I got her a cab. Very pretty. A little tired looking. She had two bags. She was alone, though."

"Hear where she was going?"

"I think she said the airport."

"Bullshit."

The doorman returned the faxes, touched two fingers to his visor. "Have a nice day, sir."

Childs figured you had to belong to the uniform class to flip somebody the bird without actually doing it.

Sill touched his arm. His biceps twitched. "Look at the room, Lieutenant?"

A pillbox showed them up. An Asian housekeeper was stuffing items of clothing into a plastic bag. The sergeant spoke to her. Childs was surprised he didn't use Japanese.

"People always leaving things behind," she said. "Jack Daniel's once, whole case, almost. I sold my neighbor."

"Traveling light," the sergeant told Childs. "Had to have something in the suitcases or answer too many questions. Box up the rest?"

"Think you can get a good price?"

Sill said, "Look at this."

Childs studied the painting the detective had picked up from the bureau. A hippie with a handkerchief tied around his head. Maybe a pirate. He turned it over. There was a rip in the brown paper where a sticker or something had been removed. He asked the housekeeper if she'd emptied the wastebaskets. She shook her head and pointed to a square plastic container on the floor. Childs removed the liner and turned it inside out. It was empty. So was the one in the bathroom. He stared at the water in the scrubbed toilet.

The sergeant joined him. "Figure he flushed himself?"

"Fuck you," Childs said. "How do you say that in Spanish?"

THIRTY

What Maggiore liked about the chauffeurs in Los Angeles, they all had martial-arts training and knew the drill when it came to evasive driving. Some of them—the ones he used—had carry permits. Everyone in the picture business was under some kind of threat, or thought he was, or *said* he was in order to jump-start the first-weekend box office on his pathetic Christian Slater hand-me-down, and hired muscle. If they preferred polished characters in uniforms and blue serge cut to make room for the artillery, so much the better for Maggiore. The pool of mouth-breathers he'd had to choose from in Detroit had always made him self-conscious, particularly when he told reporters he was a misunderstood businessman, but out here in the multitasking capital of the U.S. of A., employing a wheelman who doubled as personal protection was like driving around with a two-thousand-dollar mountain bike strapped to the roof of your Beamer. Everyone was a gangster in L.A.

Riding in the gray leather interior of the stretch Lincoln he'd drawn in that day's limo lottery, he admired the tapered haircut on the back of his driver's neck, seventy-five bucks at Lupo's of Hollywood, and knew what it must feel like when a director or producer rode away from the Oscars with the little gold fucker on the seat beside him. He was on his way back from a men-only party aboard a yacht moored at Long Beach, thrown by an Arab emir to celebrate the whopping overseas gross on a picture he'd financed that had only performed modestly on the domestic market. There had been Havanas and Jeroboams and Venezuelan cocaine and grand-a-pop whores. Maggiore, sloshed and cokey, reeking of Moroccan perfume and his own semen, had wobbled into the saloon and paused before a seventy-inch TV screen hooked up to a dish. It was an HD job, and the reporters looked life-size and real as they swarmed around a spick who looked like an accountant but whom a legend on the screen identified as the chief of detectives of the San Antonio Police Department.

The sound was off, but when a mug shot appeared of Johns Davis from an old Chicago arrest for bunco, Maggiore had found the remote and bumped up the volume. A local anchor, looking very grave for his fifteen seconds of network fame, announced that although police were not releasing details, the bookmaker's homicide was being investigated as mob-related. When file footage came on of Spanish Rivera, surrounded by bodyguards and attorneys and striding past excited reporters in the lobby of some court building, Maggiore punched the mute button and went off to thank his host for a pleasant evening.

He was elated, but a little sad. He would miss living in California full-time. He preferred its climate and its tourists, who came and went in such a steady stream the year around that they were almost invisible, and there was no nightlife in Texas, unless you were a Chicano and liked to unwind by smashing beer bottles on the sidewalk. But absentee management was not an option. It encouraged even legitimate subordinates to steal, and when all you had to work with was crooks to begin with, you were on the scene most of the time or else you might as well sign everything over and go on the dole. He might manage three months in Bel-Air—say, January through April, when all the best parties took place—but the hard money was in San Antonio, after the cops finished mulching up Rivera. Maggiore could get in ten years there, at least, before the feds decided it was time to take notice. Then, who knew?—maybe L.A. would open up again. Reform fever was cyclical.

Checking up earlier, he'd been concerned to learn no one using the identity his people had prepared for Macklin had boarded any plane for Texas during the past week. Maggiore had begun to wonder if he'd been blown off, maybe the son of a bitch had concluded his wife wasn't such a catch after all, when just for the hell of it he called the airport again, this time asking for Macklin by name. The bell rang then. Tricky asshole was going in naked, which meant none of the other arrangements Maggiore's people had made—hotel, car, line of credit—were in play either, so there was no way to check up on him.

Nothing new there. He should have seen it coming. Button men were loose cannons by definition, wouldn't be intimidated because, let's face it, they were the reason men in Maggiore's position managed to intimidate anyone at all. And Macklin had been the loosest of all. He was the one who had put two slugs where Maggiore's heart would have been if he'd been born the same as everyone else. Macklin had taken a couple of magnum rounds himself soon after, and he hadn't been expected to live, either. So they had that in common.

But now that he'd come through on Davis it was time to put him down and no fucking-up this time. Maggiore had people to answer to just like everyone else. A bunch of creaky old dons had been convicted finally, and now the ones left standing shit their pants when they heard a cop say "Freeze!" on TV. Texas was going to be too hot to put a toe in for a long time; the feds and the Rangers and the San Antonio P.D. would see to that. That meant loss of revenue, and according to the dons *that* was the sin that burned and burned without consuming. But if Rivera took the fall and authority was satisfied, the dons would let it go, even if they knew within the last tenth of a percent who was responsible. They needed that last tenth of a percent, just like the courts, before they would risk cranking up the heat again with a punitive action. But once they had it, they would burn him down and shit on the ashes. They were Sicilians after all, no matter how many Swedes and micks their mommies and daddies had fucked to make them. They couldn't afford to look soft in front of the pack. Macklin represented that last tenth of a percent. Every time his heart beat, Maggiore moved closer to the pit.

That was why he'd made the choice he had after Schevchenko went down. The hitter had to be a throwaway, but he had to be good. Macklin was the best he knew, and the man he hated and feared above all the rest. After his own recovery, Maggiore had bowed to the dons, forgoing revenge in the interest of détente with the police and a healthy bottom line. Then had come that black cloud on the Hollywood horizon from D.C., followed by the idea to relocate to San Antonio, topped off by a chance sighting by one of his people of Macklin honeymooning in Maggiore's own wheelhouse. When things worked out like that, you had to believe God or the devil was in your corner.

Abilene was the X factor. He hoped the crackbrained cowboy had the stones to do Macklin. Losing Macklin's wife was a confidence-shaker. The thing itself didn't matter now, Macklin had believed they still had her and had gone ahead and carried out the assignment, but you had to wonder about a guy who couldn't sit on a little hick girl from Kansas or wherever. Well, Abilene would be eager to please now. Enthusiasm counted for something.

The car slowed to a stop. He looked up to see what was wrong and realized they were in his carport. He hadn't noticed when they'd left the boulevard and glided up the composition driveway to his house on the hill. He was more wasted than he'd thought.

"Need any help, Mr. Major?"

He looked at the driver holding open his door, searched his tanned face for that serving-class contempt he knew so goddamn well. They were always expecting him to slurp his soup or lose his temper and stab someone to death with the wrong fork. This time, though, all he saw was professional interest.

"I'm fine," he snapped, then blew it when he overcorrected

getting out of the car and almost threw himself onto his face. Just for that he tipped the driver fifty. He usually went a C-note. The car swung around and started back down without laying rubber, which irritated him all the more, displays of restraint and good breeding being just one more of the many ways you can spit in someone's face. He'd taken in too much blow and champagne for sure. He'd had a reputation as a mean lush before he'd learned to nurse his drinks. There had been a girl whose hospital bills he'd had to pay, and an emergency-room doctor whose student loans he'd settled in return for not filing a report with the police.

The alarm squealed when he unlocked the front door. He blew the eleven-digit alarm code the first time, had to wait a second, then entered it again. The squealing stopped, but the damage had been done. He felt the first split in the seam of the pleasant foggy cloak between his nerves and tomorrow's red-alert hangover. He had to do something to combat the blood in his alcohol system if he was going to get any sleep. Abilene would probably be calling in tomorrow.

He went into the barn of a living room, shedding jacket, tie, and cummerbund on the way, stooping a little from exhaustion. Standing at the bar pouring himself a tall gin he caught a glimpse of his reflection in the glass balcony doors and straightened. For a second there old Charlie the Frog had returned. The hunchback was always lurking just under the surface, waiting to shuffle out and be laughed at.

He carried his glass over to his thirty-six-hundred-dollar recliner and used the remote built into a hatch in the right arm to turn on the TV. The screen was ten inches smaller than the emir's and it wasn't high-definition, but then, shit, he didn't have to stick up his ass and kiss the floor to Mecca every day. He laid his thumb on the up-arrow button and left it there while the images skidded past, like a drowning swimmer's life. Five hundred fucking channels and they all seemed to be soccer and *Independence Day*. He was going to dream all night about Martians zapping Nicaraguans in baggy shorts.

Shit. He'd had a hard-on against that picture ever since he'd dumped a bushel investing in *Battlefield Earth*, thinking he couldn't go wrong with Travolta *and* science fiction. After *Independence Day*, even turkeys like *Starship Troopers* made money. It was the one time he fell under Lansky's curse. Old Midas-Touch Meyer, who never lost a penny on any dishonest enterprise, took a bath back in the fifties when he bought a company that made TV sets and tried peddling them to bars the same way he'd done with slot machines and hootch. The sets turned out to be lemons, and the competition from established companies like Philco and Admiral was too stiff. Lansky cut his losses and went back to dope and horse parlors. That made sense to Maggiore. Legitimate business was just a scary proposition.

He hit the power button and closed his eyes. Something whooshed and he thought it was just another goddamn special effect, he'd hit the wrong button. It wasn't *Independence Day*, though. Someone was coming at him from the middle of the picture tube, carrying something that gleamed in the lamplight. Then the clouds broke and he knew it was the reflection of someone striding in from the balcony behind his chair, but his reflexes were gone. An upside-down face, haggard-looking and unshaven, came down from the ceiling and he smelled stale sweat.

"Thing about throats," Macklin said, "they're always in the same place." He jerked the big blade across Maggiore's Adam's apple.

Macklin waited until the fountain of arterial blood subsided, then checked for a pulse he knew wouldn't be there. He used a clean cotton cloth on the Buck knife's handle and let it roll out of the material onto the carpet. On his way out of the room he avoided stepping in the big stain. He didn't want to have to get rid of another pair of shoes.

Carlo Maggiore had risen as high as he had despite being Carlo Maggiore. Everything he'd done right he'd learned by watching Mike Boniface, his mentor and the only one of the old dons for whom Macklin had felt anything like loyalty. Mike had believed in safes and telephones. He'd always said, "Have 'em both, but don't use 'em for anything that counts." A quick search of the office connected to the master bedroom, done in dark oak and blue leather, with real books on the walls, turned up a floor safe in the kneehole of the desk. Macklin ignored it—he wasn't any kind of pete man, had trouble enough with combination locks when he knew the numbers—and removed all the drawers from both sides of the desk, laying them side by side on the floor. One of them contained a 9-millimeter automatic, but it didn't interest him any more than the contents of the others and he left it where it was.

The deep drawer designed to hold files on the bottom right side was ten inches shorter than the others, a dummy. He got down on the floor, reached into the recess where the drawer had been, and groped until he found a handpull. The panel came off with a tug and he laid it aside and dragged out bricks of currency until the compartment was empty. He didn't count bills, just glanced at the numbers on the paper bands and did the math in his head. A little less than three hundred thousand dollars. It wasn't as much as he'd hoped—Boniface had kept as much as half a million on hand, for a getaway stake—but with what he had in Swiss accounts it was enough to interest a top lawyer in the case San Antonio would build against him. Maybe. Nothing was certain short of killing, and you couldn't kill everyone.

He took off his Windbreaker, laid the bricks inside it, zipped it up, and tied the open ends into a knot. He wiped his prints off the removable panel and the drawers, but didn't replace them. Let the cops think robbery was the motive. Then he picked up his bundle by the knot and left.

A funnel-shaped lamp was burning above the front door. He found the switch, flipped it down with his hand wrapped in the cloth, waited a beat, then flipped it up and down quickly. He held the door open a crack and watched as a pair of headlights blinked on, then off, fifty yards down the driveway, but he didn't come out until the car slid under the port and he recognized the driver in the light from the house. Then he went out and climbed in on the passenger's side.

Laurie watched him sling the bundle into the backseat. "Are you all right?"

"Yes."

She turned on her lights. "No more secrets."

"No more secrets."

She drove away at legal speed.

LOREN D. ESTLEMAN

Since the appearance of his first novel in 1976, Loren D. Estleman has published forty-eight novels in the fields of mystery, historical western, and mainstream. His Amos Walker detective series has earned four Notable Book of the Year mentions from the *New York Times Book Review*, and he has been the recipient of fifteen national writing awards, including four Golden Spurs from the Western Writers of America, three Shamuses from the Private Eye Writers of America, two American Mystery Awards from *Mystery Scene Magazine*, and two Western Heritage Awards. He has been nominated for the Edgar Allan Poe Award, the National Book Award, and the Pulitzer Prize. In 1997, the Michigan Library Association presented him with the Michigan Author Award for outstanding body of work. Estleman is the current president of the Western Writers of America. He lives in Michigan with his wife, who writes under the name Deborah Morgan.